I0630811

SMILE NO MORE

A RUFO THE CLOWN NOVEL

JAMES A. MOORE

Prologue

The natives were restless. He could feel it in the air, hear it in the impatient shuffle of programs and the murmured voices of families gathered together to see a special show.

He checked his tie again, feeling the first flutter of nervous excitement come to him. It was infectious, that thrill of waiting for the good times when they were only moments away.

His tie was perfect. He had to accept that it was time and there was no longer any reason for delays. His shoes tapped smartly on first concrete and then hardwood floors as he made his way toward the stage. He rolled the top hat from one hand to the other and finally placed it on his head at a jaunty angle. Style counted, no matter what anyone had to say about the matter.

The music started, a full orchestra worth of musicians, all of whom had played the same notes too many times to count. He hoped they could keep their professionalism in place. Oh, there was a backup sound system for emergencies, but that wasn't quite the same as the real thing.

The curtain parted before him, and the first few patrons of the show noticed, sending a subtle ripple through the audience. The excitement grew stronger until it was nearly a physical wave, and he felt his lips part in a smile that he no longer even tried to hold back.

Adrenaline kicked him in the chest and rocketed his pulse into the stratosphere. No matter how many times he was on the stage, that part never changed.

"Layydieees and Gennnntlemeennnah, Girls and Boys! If I could have your attention please!" His voice boomed through the auditorium, carried to the farthest points by the acoustics of the building. He waited a moment, let them adjust to him, to where he stood, dwarfed by the massive curtain that still stood closed behind him. "Welcome one and all to the Alexander Halston Carnival of the Fantastic!"

For one moment the orchestra faltered, weakened, but then they caught on and started playing again. A change of venue: they'd been through worse before.

The audience applauded, but weakly. The name was wrong. The show they were here to see was called the Carnivale de Fantastique and no one named Alexander Halston had anything at all to do with that.

Just the same, he bowed to their applause as surely as if they had given a standing ovation.

"My name is Rufo the Clown, and I'm your master of ceremonies tonight." He paused, just for a moment, as he looked at a tyke in the first row. The boy smiled at him and he fired off a quick wink. "You are, I promise you, in for one hell of a show!"

Chapter One: Looking for Millie (Part One)

When I was a kid, I wanted to be just like Harry Houdini, the greatest escape artist there ever was. I even wanted to meet him, but he'd been over twenty years in the grave before I was born, so that wasn't going to happen.

I practiced, you know. I studied everything I could learn about Houdini and all of his secrets and then I practiced whenever I could. My parents scoffed at me; well, my father did. My mom just shook her head indulgently and warned me not to talk too much about my dreams in front of my dad. Seems she knew even then that he didn't like it when people got too ambitious around him. Life on the farm was good enough for him, and it had to be good enough for everyone else. Later, when the farm went broke, life was good enough in the factory for him and it was for everyone else. You get the idea.

My number one supporter was my sister. For some crazy reason, Millie believed in me, even when I lied. She was half my age, maybe ten when I left home, and through everything that happened, she managed to have faith that her big brother would never do her wrong.

I told her I'd be home for the holidays, but I never made it. I swore I'd buy her a pony…another lie, and still she trusted me and believed. I never wanted to lie to Millie. That was the last thing I wanted to do. Sometimes you have no choice. Sometimes the world makes a liar out of you and there's nothing you can do to stop it.

That doesn't make you feel even a little better about the lies though, not if you have a conscience, like I did back then. These days? Well, let's just say that whether or not I have a conscience is up for debate and leave it at that, shall we?

Life changes you, whether you want it to or not. The only escape from that particular fact is death and, believe me, death is no guarantee.

Have you ever seen a ghost? I don't mean the floating sheets and graveyard type, or even one of the floating trumpet gimmicks the so-called mediums like to use. I mean the sort that can really haunt you.

I was in a Starbuck's of all places—in a little upscale community where I would have never fit in as a kid—eating a breakfast with my overpriced latte and reading the Times when I saw Millie's ghost. I hadn't thought about Millie in years. I maybe even went out of my way not to think about her, because too many decades had passed without contact and she was better off without me in her life.

Mostly I tune out the people around me when I'm in a place like that. If I look at them or notice them, it starts me wondering about who exactly I'm looking at. We all have secrets, right? Well, some of us have darker secrets than others and there's a part of me that always wants to know what a person is thinking and hiding. And sometimes that same part of me feels like punishing them for whatever they might be hiding. I'll admit it: I have a few issues when it comes to unpunished crimes. I'm not exactly a vigilante, and I'll never be a cop, but now and then I feel a need to get a little payback, even if it's second hand. So, not really my thing to notice the people around me when I'm trying to relax.

I heard laughter and turned my attention to the door where a woman and her kid were just walking out. The girl carried a small sack of pastries and her mother balanced two carrying trays full of drinks to wash them down. It wasn't a school day, so all I can do is guess they had a group they were meeting with. The woman had on too much makeup and enough perfume to blind anyone with allergies. Her glory days were gone and she was desperate to keep them. She hadn't gone into the latter stages of her curse of faded youth, where she got bitter and started drinking too much, but she was definitely heading in that direction. Her daughter was a different story. She was too young for makeup and didn't need any. She had her ears pierced but everything else about her was, well, enough to make people notice that she was a kid. The girl was dressed in a light sweater and a skirt that was knee high or so. Scandalous back in the day, but conservative in this age of immodesty.

I don't know what the mother said to her kid, but I looked up just as the girl was opening the door with a smile on her face. I heard her laugh. The way she sounded, the tilt of her head, the way her fingers idled through her hair: for just one instant, she could have been Millie.

A kid, ten years old, tops, too young to be my little sister, but enough like her to bring back all the feelings I'd tried to forget. I shivered, absolutely absorbed in memories of my little sister, and haunted by her as surely as if her ghost had whispered in my ear.

Here's the thing, that kid at the coffee shop? If I saw her on the street right now, I probably wouldn't recognize her. Another face in the crowd, you know?

She didn't look all that much like Millie; she just set off all the memories with her laugh, her smile. Just enough like my sister to haunt me.

I went a long, long time without letting myself think about my family. I left behind a loving mother, a father who was a good provider, if stricter than I'd have liked and a little too comfortable with a bottle of wine. I left behind the family dog and my little sister. For all I knew they were all dead and gone, but catching a glimpse of a stranger was enough to start me on my search.

I wanted to see her again. I wanted to know what sort of life she'd made for herself after her lying brother disappeared from her world. The decision didn't happen just like that. I didn't drop my breakfast and run off into the cold hard world or anything. I just couldn't get the idea out of my head. I couldn't escape the guilt of doing Millie wrong, you see. I could look back at my life and never regret forsaking my parents, but not my little sister.

After mulling the idea over for close to a month it was decided. I had to find her. If she was dead, I had to know it, and if she was alive, I wanted to see my little sister again and maybe let her know that I never meant to lie to her. Maybe even explain what had happened to me that made me a liar. If it's possible to really explain that sort of thing.

Was it an obsession? No, not really. Believe me, I know all about getting fixated on a person or a notion. I've done it before. I can definitely tell the difference. No, I think it was more about redemption. I've hurt a lot of people in my time, and I don't imagine I'll stop anytime soon, but I hated that somewhere along the way, through circumstances that I caused and that simply befell me, I'd let down the only person I think I ever really loved.

I guess for a lot of people there're too many obstacles in the way. There are families, obligations to employers, to loved ones. I didn't have any of those burdens. You could say I'm something of a free spirit.

The work I do, well, it leaves me a lot of free time. I'm not exactly in demand, not that I ever really was. No family, except Millie, no girlfriends to leave behind, or even a goldfish. I set aside the few cases I was thinking about looking into and I got my affairs in order. As for the work I did back in the day, the stuff that led me to where I am now, well, most of the good outfits are long since gone and the few that are around wouldn't know what to do with me.

There was only one place where I could really start, wasn't there?

I had to go home.

That thought was almost enough to scare me, and believe me when I say this: I do not scare easily.

————

It was a living. Julio Regaldo told himself that as he walked along the street and looked at the people around him, hauling the latest batch of boxes into his van. No one bothered him, but he could feel their eyes on him, like cockroaches with an attitude.

They could be called people, technically. Mostly he thought of them as wastes of breathing air. The homeless, the desolate and the wretched, plus those who fed on them; the predators who found whatever they needed by taking it from people in worse condition than they were. A bad side effect of working for a delivery company that had their offices in the low rent district.

He unlocked the back of the battered metal van and started sorting boxes by the road where they'd be delivered. Next to him, Lou Harper kept an eye out to make sure no one got too close.

Ten minutes later he was riding away, breathing a sigh of relief, because even with the burly security guard who made sure he didn't get mugged on his way out with a large shipment of other people's shit to deliver, he didn't like going down to central processing to handle a package delivery. Most days he worked from the satellite office and that was a sweet deal, but now and then some asshole called out sick and who do you think got stuck taking his route? That's right, Julio, who was always willing to go the extra mile to make sure he got noticed and got one of the sweet deals out in the 'burbs. You had to pay your dues, and whether or not his old man had worked for the company, he had to pay them, too.

Julio lit a cigarette and drove, knowing full well that he could get into deep shit if he was caught smoking in the company van and not caring in the least. The window was open and he had another ten miles to drive.

He let his mind drift a little, happy that he was back in his comfort zone and well away from the sleazy bastards in Cabbage Town. Atlanta wasn't exactly the safest place to be in the first place, between traffic and the losers on the street always looking for a fix or a quick meal the easy way, but it could be a good place, too.

It wasn't that he was a coward, really, not as far as Julio was concerned. It was just that he wanted to have a safer life. He'd left Detroit because of the shit going down on the streets and he didn't want to have to deal with it all over again now that he was down in the south.

He made a mental note to kick the crap out of his cousin Raul next month at the family reunion. Raul was the one that told him Atlanta was just getting a bad rap on the news.

No, he knew he was to blame. He'd listened to Raul in the past and it always ended badly.

"Fuck it all, man. Just do the job and get back home, that's what I'm saying."

He had a date with Terry to think about. Cute little thing from New York, not the city but the state, as she always said, and he was looking forward to it. Girl was pure class, and had looks like a model.

The first delivery was coming up on Peachtree Street, and Julio pulled the van over into the alleyway between the building and its closest neighbor, narrowly avoiding a dumpster in his way, grateful, again, that he'd gotten away from the central hub in one piece.

He killed the engine, climbed into the back of the van and sorted until he found the right package. Seeing the name put a smile on his face. He'd delivered a few other things to the recipient and she always tipped good and liked to flirt, too. He wasn't looking and he knew she was just yanking his chain, but it was nice to get a little attention from a pretty girl now and then, especially one that was famous.

Just one delivery at the theatre. If that was any indication, the rest of the day would be easy.

He opened the back door of the van and stepped out, making sure his uniform looked presentable. It wasn't cool to look unprofessional, not with what he was paid and sure as hell not when there might be a few tips coming in. He always made sure he looked professional and well groomed for that reason.

The alleyway almost made it a waste of time. The buildings were clean enough, but the ground was covered in sludge from the most recent rain and he had to step carefully to avoid getting it on his shoes. The heavy shadows in the area didn't make it any easier to step in the cleaner spots, either.

Julio hadn't taken fifteen paces before the man came up from behind him. In front of the place, he would have been fine with it—you expected heavy foot traffic in the city. But like most of the places around downtown, all the deliveries were done in the back of the building and there weren't too many people who had a reason for hanging around in the narrow alleyway.

He nodded at the guy and tried to look confident. Back when he was a kid, he'd gotten mugged twice. Both times by single guys who looked innocent enough until they hit him. The man moving his way made him nervous because he moved the same way, like he owned the street and everyone should be grateful he was letting them share his air.

He was reaching for the buzzer on the back door when the stranger moved.

"Don't push that button, Rube." The man smiled. He could barely make out a face in the twilight of the alley, but he could see the flash of teeth that split the darkness. "You don't want to do that."

"But, I have to make a delivery." It was all he could think of to say while the man was looking at him.

Light blue eyes considered him, and the smile on the face grew a little wider.

"I'm going to take care of that for you, my friend. I'm going to make your day a little easier."

Julio looked at the man and straightened up a bit. He didn't want to. The last thing he wanted was to make the man angry. He knew that deep in his heart, because that gnawing feeling of dread wasn't getting any better. The guy sounded cool enough, almost happy, but Julio could feel sweat starting to stipple his brow and it wasn't nearly warm enough for him to be sweating.

"I can't do that, man. I could lose my job."

"I won't tell if you don't." The man's voice was soft, but brooked no argument.

"Seriously, I can't let you do that. I need the job, man. It's all I've got."

"Well, I wouldn't go that far. I mean, you have your life, right?" The stranger stepped closer. He wasn't much taller than Julio himself, but he seemed like a giant at that moment. The faint light in the alley let him see the face of the stranger better than maybe he wanted to. He could see the makeup on the man's face, and slight spots where it looked like the makeup was covering scars. Somebody had cut the dude in a bad way once, and whoever had done it had been stupid enough to leave him alive.

Icy blue eyes looked down from Julio's face to his shirt and then back up as the lips peeled back again, showing broad white teeth that looked like they could maybe bite through steel.

Julio tried to step back, ready to run if he had to.

"Julio… Listen carefully. I don't want to hurt you. I just really need to deliver that package for you."

Julio tried to swallow but his mouth was too dry. In the end, it was pride that did him in. He had learned a lot since he was a kid and got the shit knocked out of him a few times. He'd taken courses in Judo and he'd taught himself to be brave. Cowards just got picked on more and more, but if you stood up for yourself, you sometimes got lucky.

"Look, I'm trying to be nice here, but you're starting to piss me off. You go do your own shit. Get a job as a courier. I got a delivery to make." He deliberately thickened up his very faint Latino accent and made himself sneer at the stranger.

The smile on the face grew wider and the voice became patronizing. "Julio, are you trying to get macho with me?"

"Hey, fuck you!"

The knife came out of the shadows and slashed deeply into Julio's throat. The blood didn't spill from the gash in his neck, it erupted. Julio dropped his package and staggered backward, more surprised than anything else. Both of his hands moved to his throat and tried to catch the crimson waterfall that spilled from between his fingers. He knew he was cut and badly, but there was almost no pain.

No, wait, there it was, a red-hot blast of agony across his neck and throat that overshadowed the warmth running down his shirt.

Even as he fell backward, the man reached out and snatched the cap from the top of his head.

Julio looked up at the man, and choked on his own blood. He coughed and felt the spray of warmth push past his fingers again, even as more of it spilled past his lips.

The stranger slid the cap in place and picked up both the package Julio had dropped and the electronic clipboard for signatures.

"I said I didn't want to hurt you, Julio. Not that I wouldn't." He shrugged and then grabbed Julio by his feet. A moment later the stranger was dragging him into the back of his own van and slamming the door.

He heard the man walk to the driver's side and heard the rustling sounds of his jacket being taken from the back of the seat.

"Little snug, Julio, but good enough for government work." The man was whistling as he walked away.

Julio wanted to make a comment, but his muscles weren't working anymore. He drifted into sleep first and death a few moments later.

Is there anything more magical than a circus?

The Carnivale de Fantastique qualified as a circus in every sense of the word, except the most traditional. Oh, to be sure there were acrobats and clowns, there were jugglers and dancers, and on occasion there were even a few animals, but none of that had anything to do with the sort of circus that set up in tents and put out thousands of poorly printed flyers in the hopes that people would attend.

No, quite to the contrary, the Carnivale was one of the new generations of circuses, a monumental vision designed, developed and funded by major forces in the entertainment industry. The advertising budget alone would have financially crippled almost any traditional circus in existence, or let a good number of the performers retire comfortably. There were program books, t-shirts, and a dozen different other chunks of merchandise that had to be reordered from the manufacturers after damned near every weekend worth of performances. The money generated by the overpriced DVDs of the different shows The Carnivale de Fantastique had performed was enough to guarantee the backers of the show their money back with a tidy profit, and that money was nothing compared to what the show hauled in annually from touring.

The premise behind the shows, and the source of the name, came from an urban legend that had grown over the last fifty years. Alexander Halston's Carnival of the Fantastic, to be precise. There were stories of a circus troupe that had vanished one day, never to be seen again. There was even, according to whom you talked to, some evidence that the circus had even existed. Somewhere along the way, the tale had been examined in almost every way possible. Tales of murder, talk of a mass disappearance worthy of the colony at Roanoke, and even stories of alien abductions had all come and gone over the years.

The founders of the Carnivale de Fantastique were enchanted by the stories, and so they recreated them. The least successful version of the story they told was the one that involved aliens, but most of the variations on the theme of a circus that disappeared had been met with amazing approval. This year's entry, the Carnival of Wonders, was a rousing success so far.

Critically speaking, the Carnivale was considered art in the truest form. The reviews were almost always positive and the few that were not usually came from the sort of naysayers who hated everything they encountered. While not every performer reached a level of stardom, there were many from the current show and earlier ones as well who had become celebrities in their own right. Hell, some of the performers who'd left the oversized troupe maintained their stardom well after they'd retired and moved on to different fields of interest. There were even plans, though not solidified as yet, to take the show across the waters and hit both Britain and Europe.

The Carnivale was reinvented every year—the premise was always the same, but the stories were almost completely unique—often with entirely new casts, because the stress of performing within the neuveau circus was both physical and emotional. Sets were designed that put all but the finest displays on Broadway to shame, and the current season had required costumes that broke the one hundred thousand dollar mark, each one custom tailored to the individual performer, because the show had to be flawless.

There were two shows a night, every night, for at least three weeks, in ten major cities. That was the schedule and the producers intended to stick with it, regardless of the physical wear and tear on dancers and acrobats alike. Every part in the performance came complete with a second set of wardrobes and at least one backup performer. A sprained ankle or a broken bone would not be enough to stop the show and the cast knew it, just as they knew that each and every one of them could be replaced with a minimum of muss and fuss. Everyone was salaried and everyone also got a cut of the profits, provided they stayed through the season. Most of the serious money got divided between the performers who managed to survive until the end of the tour. That was the way the Carnivale had always been handled and despite a few attempted lawsuits by disgruntled ex-employees who had dropped out or been canned, that was likely the way it would always be handled. The performers had to sign a contract that said as much and to date no one had found a loophole on the seven-page document.

That suited Elizabeth Montenegro just fine. As one of the leads in the show, she was guaranteed to make a ridiculous amount of money, and the performances, while demanding, were not likely to cause her any permanent injury as long as she remembered to stretch before and after every show. She'd had a harder workout when she was one of the minor characters in *Cats* when it ran on Broadway.

The worst of it was the down time, because as much as she might wish that someone else had to pack her outfits and prepare for the next town, the Carnivale didn't work that way. When the shows were done in one town, she had to inventory everything and pack it herself. She might get help actually transporting it, but her costumes and all of their accessories were her responsibility.

She was elbow deep in the costume for the final scene of the play, the "Ice Princess" costume, with all of the glittering arcs of sequined metal and foil streamers. It wasn't a delicate costume, none of them were, but it still had to be handled carefully.

Elizabeth carefully wrapped the cape, sliding foam rubber inserts in between the long streamers and the two sweeping shoulder pads that made her look like something from another planet. The audience always ooed and ahhed when it was all said and done, but she still thought the costume was atrocious.

The last of her packing materials were in place and she was just sliding the cape into its carrying case when the knock came at the door to her dressing room.

Elizabeth sighed and frowned. She didn't want to be disturbed and little ticked her off as quickly as interruptions during her down time. "Who is it?" She tried to keep the bitchiness out of her voice, but only half-succeeded.

"Special delivery, Ms. Montenegro." She stood up quickly. The last six months had garnered her a total of two stalkers and as a result, no one was informed about which dressing room was hers unless they had a legitimate delivery. There were only two packages she was expecting, one from her mother and one from her dealer.

"Can you tell me who the package is from, please?" she spoke calmly, but did a nervous dance on her side of the door. She needed a quick fix before they left town. Just something to keep her calm when she got on the plane, because she hated flying.

"It says it's from 'Nana Montenegro,' ma'am."

That was exactly what she wanted to hear. Her hands quickly unlocked the door and pulled it open. The man on the other side was no one she'd seen before, but Julio normally sent the packages by legitimate couriers so that wasn't exactly a surprise for her. He stood a little less than six feet in height and was as lean as he was tall. His hair was slicked back and half buried under a cap that advertised the local delivery service, and his face was handsome enough, not that she was looking, with a friendly smile, a broad nose and the coldest blue eyes she had ever seen.

He handed her the package without hesitation and presented a clipboard with a signature sheet and a pen attached.

Elizabeth scribbled her signature down on the paper and smiled briefly at him as she slid the small box into her jeans pocket. "Thank you."

"My pleasure." His voice was a purr.

She stared at him for a moment. He was…unsettling. Despite his pleasant demeanor, there was something about him that gave her the creeps. Still, there were matters of decorum to consider. She reached into the back pocket of her jeans and pulled out the two folded dollar bills she kept there for just such situations.

"Here you are. Have a nice day." The bills were proffered and she stood facing him. No way in hell was she going to turn her back on him.

The deliveryman looked at the bills for a moment and his lips stretched out in a smile. "That's very sweet of you." He took the bills and held them up for her to see. They trembled lightly between his index finger and middle finger for just a moment, and then simply vanished.

She smiled, pleased by the cheap parlor trick.

"Neat. You have to practice that a lot?"

"These days it almost comes naturally." His hand turned around, so that the palm was to her, and then turned again so that she could see the fine, dark hairs on the back of his hand. He turned his hand a second time and there was a shining flash of metal held between his fingers.

Elizabeth barely had time to be surprised before the blade pressed against her face. "Now, let's you and me step into your dressing room and have a little talk, hmmm?"

She felt the cold metal slide softly across her cheek and down to her neck and shivered from top to bottom. "Unnn?"

"No talking. Not yet." The pressure increased, and she took a step back into her room. The man followed, giving her no chance to escape.

After he'd entered the room, he closed the door and locked it.

"Please, don't hurt me." Her voice cracked and her knees were trembling.

"Shhhh. Don't speak until spoken to. Don't make a noise." His smile grew broader. "If you play nicely we can both forget all about this in a little while, and I won't have to carve your pretty little face off of your skull."

She almost nodded her head and then realized it would be a bad idea.

"We're going to have a talk, Elizabeth. I'm going to ask you questions, and you are going to answer them truthfully." His voice stayed soft and low, but despite his smile, she could feel the hatred coming from him like heat from an oven. He kept pressing her backward and she kept going, horrified by the idea of what the blade against her neck could do.

"What do you want to know?"

The cold blue eyes that stared at her glittered.

"Well now, we have a lot to discuss. Let's get started, before anyone interrupts us."

Life On The Road: Part One

I was what, maybe sixteen when I left home. There were a lot of reasons, but mostly it was because there was no work in town that didn't involve being in a factory or mill for most of the day. We'd been away from the farm for three years or so and I'd seen what the factory did to my father. It ground him down and sapped away his strength a little at a time. Sometimes I thought it was leaving the farm that did him in, really, but other times I knew better. It was the backbreaking work and the knowledge that it wouldn't get any better. It would never get any better.

He wasn't an old man. Neither of my parents were old. I think my old man was nineteen when he got married, but he was looking closer to sixty by the time I packed a few sets of clothing and took off. And the reason for it was obvious to me. He was working himself to death in order to pay the bills and keep a roof over our collective heads. Not even to get ahead of the game, just to make ends meet.

He came home six days a week, seven sometimes, if there was extra work to be had, smelling of molten metal, that had fused its odor to his clothes and his skin alike. There were days when, as soon as he was done with his shower, he'd sit in his favorite chair with a handheld mirror and pick the black spots from his skin, particles of hot metal that had burned themselves onto him. You can see why a day or two of that would put a man in a bad mood, right?

Well, it left my father worse than bitter. It left him defeated. After a while I think he was just going through the motions. He'd always been a proud man, and losing the farm had been a bad blow, but believe me, he changed when he went to work at the foundry.

Now and then when I talk about him I think I'm too harsh. He wasn't a bad sort. He just wasn't really built for fun. My father's idea of a good time was a Sunday visit to the church, followed by a picnic in the back 40, and then a few hours of chores before dinnertime. I guess I'd have been the same way if I'd been through the Second World War and depression before that. Most of his generation seemed to be that way, at least to my eyes. That probably changed later.

He didn't beat us, he didn't do any of the things I've heard tales about over the years. He was just stern. Sometimes that's enough to make you dislike someone. I loved my father, but it's fair to say we never had the chance to be friends. I guess that can only come later in life, and I wasn't around when that time could have or should have come around.

So after we left the farm, I only stayed around long enough to know I couldn't bear the idea of being like my father. Even that revelation took a while. I told myself I was leaving to help the family, to make sure that they could pay the bills on time, and to make damned sure my little sister didn't end up living on the streets.

I left a note for Millie. Don't ask for the exact words, because you won't get them. They were for her and her alone.

After I hid the note beneath Millie's pillow, I slipped out of the house and moved away like a thief in the night.

I'd planned on heading for New York, to try my luck as an escape artist. I thought if it worked for Houdini, I could go the same route.

Fate had other plans.

Chapter Two: Looking for Millie (Part Two)

I could have driven, or taken a plane. I could have even walked it in a pinch. Instead, I took a Greyhound Bus headed for the old stomping grounds and almost had a stroke when I heard how much people pay for the privilege.

I didn't pay it. I almost never pay.

Ever been on a bus for a long-distance trip? It ain't living in the lap of luxury. I've been in worse places, but some truths are universal: put enough losers in a confined space and at least one of them will go it without deodorant. My old buddy Burt Calhoun told me that simple fact, and he was right.

Home. It's an interesting word, isn't it? Four little letters that are almost as filled with complexity as the word 'Love.' If home is where the heart is, then I have had several places I could have called home and all of them have been taken away from me at one time or another. But the one that mattered the most right then was not the farm where I grew up, but the last ramshackle house where I saw my family before I ran away. Where I gave Millie a good night kiss and promised I'd come back when I could and bring her a pony, a life worth living. For me home was first and foremost where I saw my little sister, right up until the time I never saw her again.

She was all I thought about on that bus trip. Well, that and the loser without the deodorant. He's a story for another time, though. Not really important to the tale aside from the fact that he distracted me and later, when everything else was taken care of, I decided to make him my latest hobby.

Checking out the old home front seemed like a nice idea, anyway. The old neighborhood was gone. Not changed, but completely eradicated. Some of the street names were the same, and the geography of the roads was similar, but the tenement buildings and run-down houses I'd known had been destroyed and replaced by bigger houses that had been around long enough to get threadbare, shiny new condominiums and a few shopping centers. There wasn't even enough left to get nostalgic about.

I think I stared at that damned street for close to an hour. I know at least one of the people in the house that stood where my home used to be peeked out the window a few times and frowned at me, her mouth pulled into an ugly expression as she contemplated whether or not I might be dangerous. Believe me, she didn't know the half of it.

I didn't feel like enlightening her, either, so I finally decided to leave. There wasn't much she could have told me, nothing she could have found in her attic that would have helped me find Millie, anyway.

You know what the problem with going away for fifty years is? The trail you want to follow is half a century old. How many feet had walked down the sidewalks, how many cars had cruised down Sullivan Street since last Millie had been there? I don't think I could count that high on a bet.

So I had nothing except a name, and I needed to find out what had happened to my sister. Not an impossible challenge, but I have to tell you, it sure as hell seemed that way.

Millicent Ariella Phelps. My little Millie. Where the hell do you look when you've only got a name? The first place I tried was the phonebook, because, maybe, she was still living under the same name. I found exactly what I expected to find, nothing.

I've gotten older, but not much wiser. I spent a lot of years indisposed for lack of a better word and though I understand some of the tricks of modern technology, I haven't yet figured out computers.

So, lost without any idea what I was going to do to find my sister, I started walking and trying to remember a bit more of the past I'd worked so hard to set aside.

I was fourteen when we left the farm. My father was calmer than I expected when it came to losing the place his family had owned for three generations. He wasn't happy about it, but he didn't lose his temper and go around beating on anyone. That wasn't his style. Instead, he did what he had always done and got busy with working himself half to death. Was it pride that made him so obsessive? I don't know. All I know is that he never stopped when he became set on doing something.

Maybe I got a little of that from my old man. Maybe that was why I decided to keep looking for Millie. I had nothing to go on but a name and a last known address from when she was ten. I didn't have the money to hire an army of private investigators, and I surely wasn't about to use a computer to find out anything.

Still, I had to try. I walked along the old streets that should have been familiar and barely held a hint of the past any longer. They were cleaner now, there were kids running around and laughing, crying, being kids. Every last one of them made me remember Millie a little more. I still can't decide if that was a good thing.

Millie was sweet. Millie was bright and precocious and adorable. I can look back on my life before everything changed and I realize that most of my pleasant memories involved times when Millie was with me.

I remember the first time I managed to escape from a rope trap it was Millie who helped tie me up. I had to ask her again and again to make the ropes tighter, because she was afraid of hurting me. When she finally got it right, I spent thirty minutes wriggling my way out of the bonds and she never left my side. She simply crouched next to me and watched, now and then giving me words of encouragement. Half an hour doing nothing but watching me sweat and writhe along the hay and dirt of the barn. That must have been like half a lifetime to her. No six-year-old should have that sort of attention span without the help of Howdy Doody or maybe the Mouseketeers.

When I was finally free, she told me I would be the greatest escape artist ever someday. She said it with such conviction that I could almost make myself believe it. Maybe she was right. I managed to escape from death, after all. Oh, sure, I had help, but it's still quite a feat when you think about it.

Here's the thing about being given a second chance: There's a part of you that wants to hold onto it and be greedy. I mean, I was dead, all right. Not mostly dead, not in a coma, not accidentally buried alive.

Dead. Oh, sure, I never had a burial plot or any of that stuff, but believe me, I was dead.

I had a long time to think about it while I was in the state of non-living, and I have to tell you, I wasn't very fond of it. I sure as hell am not in a hurry to get back there, either. So, yes, there's a part of me that likes the idea of being very, very careful about living.

Happily, it's a small part.

All of those thoughts went through my head as I walked along hauntingly unfamiliar streets. Was Millie still alive? More importantly, would she even remember me? Fifty-seven years is a long time not to see somebody, flesh and blood relative or not. There were so many questions I wanted answers to that it was hard to think about anything else.

I felt the need for a distraction, something to let me relax a little before I started walking in circles. The good news is, it's never that hard to find a distraction if you really want to.

What I found to help me relax was the local library on Bleecher Street. That one structure was still standing from when I'd been in the area, though I'm happy to say they'd added a few small wings since then.

The place was almost deserted. I stared around in wonder, because, really, when I was a kid the library always had a few dozen people of all ages sitting inside, reading books or the newspaper or just killing time on a cold day.

The librarian was a middle-aged man with a spare tire and a bald spot growing on the back of his head. He looked up when he saw me come in and moved immediately to help me. I think, sad but true, that he was surprised to see someone of my apparent age in his building.

My apparent age? Well, I guess I need to clarify that a bit, don't I?

If I saw myself walking down the street and I didn't know me, I'd guess I was in my early twenties, tops. I stand six feet tall, and I weigh one hundred and sixty-five pounds. I am a skinny little thing. I have dark hair that I keep just over shoulder length. Most people see it as black, which makes sense, because that's the color I dye it every few days. It's actually very blue. A little dye helps keep everybody on the planet from staring at me, unless I want them to stare. I won't lie and say I don't like to be the center of attention, but like a lot of people, when I want to be discrete a disguise helps.

See, my name is Rufo the Clown, and it's a fitting name. Remember how I said I escaped death? Well, I'm here to tell you that death left a few unusual scars to make sure everyone knew who was boss. Back when I was just Cecil Phelps, I had short, dark hair and I was just as skinny. Now, I have long blue curly hair and skin that matches the makeup I used to put on every day for working the rubes. I used to put on makeup to be seen, and now I put it on to hide myself. A small price to pay for being born again, but a little inconvenient when it comes to walking down the street.

Depending on my mood as much as anything else, I can look healthy and hearty or like I just crawled from the grave. Believe me, that little talent can be handy, too. No one wants to mug a walking dead man.

I was going for the casual look when I entered the library, so I was wearing my flesh tones and dressed in regular clothing. The librarian still seemed surprised to see me.

"Did you need help finding anything, sir?" He smiled as he spoke, and he had a warm pleasant voice that was probably perfect for reading to kids.

I thought about that for a moment and decided that maybe I didn't need a computer to get a little help with my quest for Millie. "Yes, please. I was wondering if there's anything I can do to look up an old relative of mine who used to live in the area."

The man looked at me for a second and I could almost see the gears go to work in his head. Here was something more challenging than finding a copy of Paradise Lost for another school report. What? You don't think I had to do book reports in my time? I said I'm older than I look, I didn't say I was ancient. I just felt that way sometimes.

He nodded his head and motioned me to come with him. Five minutes later, the hunt was on properly.

"Elizabeth Ariana Montenegro, Hispanic female, age according to her identification, twenty-six." County coroner Lance Sweeney spoke softly, but as there was no audience except the recorder and his assistant Leslie, he had no problem being heard. "Weight: one hundred and seven pounds. Height: sixty-seven inches. External examination of the deceased shows substantial decay, congruent with the reported location of the body upon discovery. While not definitive, I'd guess the postdating on the package where she was found is close to the actual time of death, seven days ago."

Leslie shook her head and tried to look calm. She wasn't quite making it, but Lance really couldn't blame her. They'd gotten the corpse in one of the worst stages of decay, when the bodily fluids had rotten through the body.

"The deceased was found carefully wrapped in plastic, sealed inside of a package delivered to the 'Circus of the Fantastic.'"

"Carnivale de Fantastique," Leslie corrected him.

"Whatever. Let the record show it was the 'Carnivale de Fantastique.' In any event, the deceased was found after having missed three scheduled appearances, adding to the belief that she was shipped in the packaging to the latest performance site.

"Preliminary cause of death appears to be mutilation. There are multiple lacerations covering the torso, the legs, the arms and both hands."

Lance paused and looked down at the blade that the police had been good enough to leave in the wound through the performer's chest. Moving very carefully, Lance pulled the blade out, making sure not to actually touch the handle, even with his gloved hands. It wouldn't do to ruin potential evidence.

"The weapon used was left in the victim's chest, forced through the sternum and puncturing the heart. The weapon in question is..." He took out his ruler. "A knife, rather antiquated in appearance, but sharpened professionally by the looks of the blade. Said blade is ten inches in length with a four-inch handle."

Leslie leaned down to look at the weapon, her eyes squinting.

"No apparent manufacturer's label, nor is there any indication of a serial number."

Leslie shook her head again. "Is that a throwing knife? Like the ones they used to use in circuses?"

Lance looked at the weapon again and studied the hilt. It was definitely not a standard-issue hunting knife. The pommel at the end was smooth from apparent years of use and the tip was slightly blunted, though the entire weapon was obviously well cared for.

"Good call. I wouldn't be at all surprised if you're right."

"So maybe it was someone at the circus?"

"Didn't you say it was a 'Carnivale'?"

Lance rubbed at his eyes while Leslie stuck her tongue out at him.

It was going to be a long night.

"Finishing the external examination, it appears the deceased was tortured. Most of the wounds, while deep, are superficial."

Tia Natchez looked at the letter and smiled. Then she set it down, thought about it for a few seconds and looked at it again. This time her smile was accompanied by a squeal of delight. She quickly covered her mouth and looked around her apartment to make sure that absolutely no one had heard the sound that escaped her lips. Her parents weren't home yet, so all was well.

After that, she read the letter one more time and did a furious tap dance across the floor of the living room, still stunned by the good news. She'd tried out for the Carnivale of the Fantastic months ago and received the letter that said they'd notify her of any openings. As she had been one of over 500 people trying out at the time, she assumed that meant they had no openings and probably wouldn't have any openings.

Sometimes it felt so wonderful to be completely wrong. The excitement grew instead of dwindling as she started grabbing the clothes she would take with her. There was so much she wanted to pack and so little she could actually fit in her two suitcases.

She'd barely finished packing when her mother came home. Dora Natchez was a slender woman, with dark hair that was starting to silver and the same café au lait skin as her daughter. She did her best to hide the sadness she felt when she heard the good news, but Tia knew and understood. Tia was her little girl, but she was also the little girl who'd been going to dance and gymnastics classes for most of her life in preparation for this very occasion.

"Mom, I'm going to be the stand in for the lead role!" She had to wipe at her eyes to get the start of tears to go away. God, it was so much to take in, barely out of high school and the best she'd been hoping for was to be a background dancer or maybe even an acrobat. Stand-in wasn't perfect, but it was a paying gig and she got to see the show for free, so what the hell.

"Your father is going to be so proud of you, honey." True words, but he'd be just as miserable as her mom. They didn't want her to grow up and move away. They wanted to keep her at home. She knew that, but didn't want to live her life for them. Besides, the show would be coming back to New York in a month or so, so she wouldn't even be gone all that long.

Still, despite all the excitement, there was an undercurrent of fear. On her own for the first time was bad enough, but on her own in different cities all over the country? Scary.

She was looking forward to it and the opportunity to be a part of a show as spectacular as The Carnivale. The reviews for this year had been astounding, and even if she only performed a few times, it would look damned good on her resume. She was also not happy about the idea of living out of hotels for the next six months, at least.

Any doubts evaporated when she looked at the letter again, and the contracts that came with it.

In so many ways, her life was just starting.

Life on the Road: Part Two

I made it out of town before I got distracted. I was tired and I was hungry, but I knew my father well enough to understand that he'd come after me. He'd be worried sick and, bills or no bills, he'd come looking.

I was two days away from home when I heard the elephant call out. Not exactly the sort of noise you expect to hear when you're walking down the dirt roads of Illinois. I went to investigate.

There were seventeen trailers set up at the end of a long farm field, lined up near the edge of the land, right next to a small creek. All of them had outlandish signs on the sides, proclaiming about the wonders to be found within them. I still think my favorite at the time was the illustration of a dog the size of a bear, with the words: Beware The Hound of Hades painted above it.

I may not have been the brightest kid on the planet, but I knew a circus when I saw one. The other big hint was the army of people working to put up the tent where everything was supposed to take place.

I think every single performer that could had to help with raising the poles and tightening down the canvas and ropes. I saw one of the elephants actually pick up and move the center post of the whole affair, assisted by people to help keep the thing balanced. I guess that post must have weighed at least four hundred pounds.

I was tired, and I had almost no food left, but I decided it was the perfect place to settle in and have my breakfast. I opened the roll of clothes I'd brought with me and fished out the three apples I'd pilfered from one of the farms on the road, and sat Indian style to watch the show.

The day wasn't too hot yet, but I thought it probably would be after the sun was straight above me. My shadow reached out toward the group of people working their asses off, and I could see them all clearly as they worked. They didn't look much like I had imagined circus folk would look. None of them wore sequined outfits or had on makeup. They just looked like regular folk, and I guess right around then was when I started wondering if I'd made a mistake. If circus people just looked like farmers and laborers, where was all the magic?

I munched on one apple and juggled the other two in my left hand, as they raised that gigantic pole. There were actually three poles all told that were bound together with clamps. The bottom one had been sharpened to a proper point and men took turns pounding it into the soft soil of the field. Even with half a dozen guys working, it took a while. By the time they were done, I'd killed off the second apple.

I was down to the third piece of fruit when the dwarf came my way. He was maybe four feet tall, and walked with a weird gait, caused by one leg being shorter than the other. He was also the most muscular human being I'd ever seen. His head was bald, but his lower face was buried under a few days' worth of beard growth. He had a rucksack in one hand that swayed and slapped against his leg with every step he took. He wore a hat that made me think of my father when he was working the fields, and that smile that crept across my face was pure nostalgia.

Without saying a word, he sat down in front of me and reached into his sack. A moment later he was offering me a canteen filled with water.

I nodded my thanks and took a sip. The apples were a bit tart and I swear even with the juices that came out with every bite it felt like my mouth hadn't had anything liquid in it for a week or so.

He eyed the apple in my hand and I tossed it his way. The man nodded his thanks and pulled out a knife that was almost as long as his forearm from the depths of his old sack. Next he pulled out a wedge of cheese wrapped in wax paper. I swear to you, my stomach made a noise as loud as the elephant had earlier when I saw that cheese.

We shared the water and the cheese. He ate the apple alone.

That was how I met the man who taught me everything I needed to know in order to be a circus performer.

Chapter Three: Looking for Millie (Part Three)

The librarian's name was John. He was polite and efficient and he answered my questions to the best of his ability. That counts for a lot with me.

Try to remember, I was fifty years gone from the world. A lot of the modern technologies escape me. The idea of computers like the ones they had in that library amazed and intimidated me. Hell, I remember the first time I heard about cell phones I was nearly stunned speechless and at that particular moment I was busy trying to kill everyone in a town.

I have a cell phone these days, but I don't use it often. I'm not known for giving out my phone number.

I'm letting myself get distracted, sorry about that. It happens a lot. John the Librarian was amazing. He sat down at the computer and started hitting keys. Using the information I had—my old address and my sister's name, he started searching the Internet for information about her. While he didn't get much, he did manage to find an address for her, as well as three separate news articles that brought up her name. The first news article was archived in the local newspaper. Apparently someone decided the best way to save up old papers was to take pictures of them and put the pictures up on the Internet for people to look at whenever they wanted. Once again, technology amazes me.

I don't remember all of the details, but the article was an obituary for my mother. According to the paper, she died seventeen years after I did. She got cancer. The rest is history. The article said the only known survivor was my sister, Millie. I wrote down the name of the cemetery and promised myself I'd pay my mother her final respects.

My mother was a good woman. She took care of me and she took care of Millie. She made the meals, mended the clothes when there wasn't enough money for newer outfits, and she made sure we got to church every Sunday morning. That's the way it was when I was a kid.

She was not confrontational, but neither was she weak.

Sometimes, I think she wanted to kill my father. Sometimes I think she loved him. It depends on the day and the memory. She was not a fighter, but she also didn't allow the man to walk all over her. She had a quiet strength.

I can remember one time when he came home after a bad day in the fields and started yelling at my mother. The old man liked to yell when he was under pressure and he was almost always under pressure.

She took it. She let him have his piece. But only one wall separated my parents and me when I was a kid and I heard the quiet argument that happened after Millie and me were supposed to be asleep.

He didn't win that part. Before it was done, he was the one apologizing.

Ruth Ingrid McArthur Phelps. She died at the age of sixty-three. Her last name in the obituary wasn't Phelps any longer. I assume that means she got married and lived happily ever after until the day she died.

John was good enough to find something else to do for a few minutes as I read the article and got teary-eyed. That was good of him. I owe him for that. I always pay my debts; you can go to the bank on that.

The second article mentioned little Millie getting married. That was unsettling. It shouldn't have been, because in my mind I hoped and prayed that she had a good life and was still having one. In my heart, however, she was still a child of ten. She'd gotten married at the age of nineteen. The man she married was a doctor.

I always knew Millie would be a heartbreaker. There was a very grainy picture that hadn't come across too well. It showed a woman with most of her face hidden by her veil. What I could see of her was beautiful. Her husband looked well to do and the wedding itself was a posh affair if you can judge by the decorations.

The last article mentioned the birth of the family's first child. A girl named Cecilia. There was no accompanying picture for that one, but my heart swelled anyway.

Cecilia. Not that far off from the name of her uncle.

I took the address I was given and I thanked John for his time. He was very good to me and there was no reason for it. Oh, you can chalk it down to good customer service, but I know better.

John the librarian was just one of the good people. The sort we tried not to rob too blind back in my carnival days. There were always a few of them. They made up for the ones we milked dry.

I miss the carnival. I miss the lights and the sounds and the screams of excitement from the mouths of children and adults alike.

I was missing them then, too, and knew I'd have to find one soon enough, but first I had a few clues to work with, solid links to Millie.

I intended to see my little sister again, and the Lord help anyone who tried to stop me.

There were always problems with following a murderer across state lines, but they were made worse when the possible suspects were traveling. Because of the unusual nature of the case, the police were bogged down with arguments about jurisdiction and state laws.

Add in the fact that Elizabeth Montenegro was a celebrity—she'd been interviewed in multiple magazine and newspapers and her face had graced the cover of US Weekly and People Magazine alike. There were even tales that Playboy had offered her a very tidy sum to be a centerfold—and things got a lot uglier and very fast, at that. There were arguments aplenty to go around and in the end it was decided that the FBI might be the best group to handle the situation.

The paperwork was gathered and the questioning began.

And in the meantime, the Carnival de Fantastique kept making money. They moved up the east coast slowly, and settled in for a stay in Arlington, Virginia. The shows were sold out. They'd been sold out months in advance.

As was almost always the case, advertisements were placed in the local newspapers. Laborers were needed. The stars got paid well for their parts in the show, but behind the scenes the roadies just barely made due. It was easier to hire new help than it was to keep begging the same old workhands to stay around.

That's where Kyle Cummings came into the picture. Kyle was in charge of the whole set up. In the long run, he took care of dismantling and assembling the sets and made sure the packages got where they needed to go. He'd have preferred to keep everyone happy, but understood that what he paid wasn't always going to be enough to convince people to leave their hometowns and go on the road for six months or more. So it was time to hire some new blood.

The interviews were the worst part. Every damned one of the kids who came through wanted to be a star and thought they could make it in the back door. At least half of them he sent away. Why the hell would someone who couldn't even figure out the business end of a hammer want to work backstage?

Still, there were a few hopefuls. The kid standing in front of him had potential. A little skinny, but he claimed to have experience.

"What sort of work have you done?"

"Well, I worked a carnival for a few years. Had to help with pitching the tents, putting up the booths, that sort of thing. And I did some work as the backstage manager back at my high school, you know, making props."

He looked the man over a second time. Tall, lanky, didn't seem too interested in the spotlight, which was a plus.

"You have any problem with traveling?"

"Like I said, I worked a carnival. I get it. Lots of moving and lots of packing. I even have my own tools."

The kid had a slightly crooked smile but he was relaxed about it.

"Let me see your hands."

The kid held them out and Kyle looked them over. Sure enough, there were calluses, hard ones, from hard labor.

"Okay, here's the deal. We have a show starting tomorrow. There's a lot of work to be done. Pays by the hour, fifteen dollars an hour as you have experience. I'm going to give you a trial run. Let's see what you've got. If you don't disappoint me, you've got a job as long as we're still going, and this show never really shuts down."

John Booker smiled back at him. "I've been looking to be around a circus again. Close enough for me, and the pay is better."

"Great. You'll need to fill out some paperwork, but after that I think we're set."

Booker held out his hand to be shaken and Kyle took it. "Looking forward to it. Thanks for the opportunity."

Kyle watched the man walk back out of his office and frowned. There was something about his accent that was puzzling. It was familiar, but not common. In the long run he let it slide. There were more interviews to take care of. Even as he thought it, another kid came in with the graceful walk of a dancer. The boy was practically walking on his toes and from ten feet away he could smell the cologne on the kid.

"You know this isn't try outs for the show, right? This is for working on building the sets."

The kid immediately looked disappointed.

It was going to be a long day.

Tia met up with the producers and had a long, long talk. She listened as intently as she could, wanting to absorb every detail of what they wanted from her. Mostly, they wanted her to work her ass off, which was exactly what she'd expected.

They were paying her outrageous amounts of money, too. Crazy money, though part of it would have to go to covering her expenses on the road. That part they made clear. They would make reservations for the performers, but the cost of a hotel room was hers to foot. Just to make sure she could cover it, the first payment was delivered to her bank account by electronic transfer five minutes after she'd finished filling out the paperwork.

Tia was the understudy for the main female lead, a character named Ramona. According to the story they'd printed in the program book, Ramona was a runaway who'd hooked up with the circus and taken on the duties of a proper mystic. She read tarot cards and told people their fortunes. Unfortunately, in the story, Ramona also starts having visions of an icy death for the Carnivale de Fantastique and while she tries to warn people, no one wants to listen. The story didn't make much sense, but as there were no spoken parts, except for the narrator, it didn't really much matter.

The first thing they wanted her to do was relax and enjoy the show. She'd be watching from the front of the stage the first night and already had a seat reserved for her. While she was excited, she'd also been warned in advance that the special treatment was a one-time thing. Enjoy the show now, because she was going to be in the show the next night. Unless and until she was needed for the leading part, she was going to be an extra, dancing several small numbers in the background. She was out front to observe and the next day she'd start rehearsals.

As soon as the meeting was over and the papers had been signed, Tia was taken to meet the cast. There were a lot of people to meet and she hoped she wasn't supposed to memorize any names. Three people stood out for her. The first was Leslie Dobbs, a tall, willowy girl with dark brown hair and light skin. If she'd had to guess, Tia would have put the girl at no more than a couple of years older. Leslie was currently playing the part of Ramona. She'd only taken the role over a few weeks earlier, when Elizabeth Montenegro disappeared.

One look at the girl and she knew they'd be friends. Leslie was from Canada, and had been professionally trained. Tia was from New York and had also been professionally trained. They spent fifteen minutes comparing notes on the teachers they'd had and how much they missed being at home. Neither of them would have gone back on a bet though. This, the show, the dancing, the traveling, was what they'd been working toward for years.

Leslie was the one who introduced her to everyone else.

She was right, there were too many people to meet and not nearly enough time to meet them. It wasn't a social so much as a chance to see what happens backstage.

The performers were all getting ready, some in their regalia and others still stretching out for the night on the stage. In less than an hour, the matinee performance would be taking place.

The choreographer, a short, manic man with a crew cut and exactly no body fat on his body, grabbed her by the arm and hauled her to the side.

She didn't even have a chance to catch his name before he was talking even faster than the average New Yorker in a bad mood. "Okay, Tia, right? Right. Here's the thing. I know you're good. That's why you're here. I don't pick anyone but the best. Now that we have that out of the way, I want you to enjoy the show tonight, because when it's done, you and me are going to go over every scene."

"I-Okay."

He shot her a look that shut her up before she could start talking.

"Leslie's going to join us and we're going over ever scene. It won't take all that long, and as soon as we're finished, you can go back to your room and relax, but it's crucial that we get you up to speed as quickly as possible. I don't like the idea of ever going on without a backup performer. Believe me, honey, it's best to learn it now instead of trying to learn it after there's been an accident, God forbid!"

He kept talking a mile a minute as he led her toward the actual auditorium where the people would soon be gathering for the show. "You're not dressed as well as you could be for the show, but screw it, it's Arlington. Go grab your seat while you can and relax."

Without another word he was off, moving like a rabbit on crack cocaine and already calling to one of the performers.

Tia sat down and stared at the stage. Her mind was a whirlwind and her body felt almost as energized as the choreographer had been.

It took a while for her to realize she was grinning from ear to ear.

The smile lasted throughout the show as she drank in the performances on the stage before her. The reviews hadn't done the Carnivale justice. She'd never seen anything like it in her life.

Life on the Road: Part Three

I had stumbled unknowingly into my second family, just for the record. Alexander Halston's Carnival of the Fantastic, which promised, among other things, the most amazing freak show ever seen, and thrills and chills to delight the entire family.

It looked to me like a big farm field, a lot of lumber and canvas, and a lot of people breaking their backs to make it into something else. Of course, that was before the magic could start. It was just people working.

The short man I met—I think he just missed technically being a "dwarf"—introduced himself as Carter Seward. He was a jack-of-all-trades and as I learned in due time, a damned good one, too. He's the one who convinced me to hang around for a while.

While we ate together, he prodded me with a few questions. "Where are you coming from, kid?" His voice was higher than I expected, but not really feminine. More like puberty forgot to change his voice.

"Chicago."

He nodded and cut a slice of apple for himself. "Why are you running?"

"I'm not. I'm looking for work. I need to help my family out."

I remember him looking at me hard, reading me, I guess, and finally nodding his head.

"So what can you do?"

"What do you mean?"

"I mean what are you good at? You have to be good at something before you can make money at it."

"I want to be an escape artist, like Harry Houdini."

"Tough call. You any good at it?"

"I've been practicing a long time."

"Yeah?" He looked at me again. "We could maybe use an escape artist. We can always use a couple of strong hands. Want to try your luck?"

"You mean audition for you?"

"Well, I could just tie you up and see if you got out, but maybe showing what you can do to the boss would be a better way to see if he's in a hiring mood."

"Well, I was on my way to New York, to see if I could get work."

He was good to me. He didn't laugh in my face.

"One step at a time, kid. Why don't you see about getting some work here, and save up some money on your way to Broadway, okay?"

"Is the pay good?"

He chewed a piece of apple before answering. "No. It's shitty. But we'll get to New York sooner or later and maybe you can make a little dough on the way, instead of stealing apples from a farm or two and trying to ride the rails all the way to the east coast."

I nodded my head and we finished our meal in silence. When we were done, Carter stood up, gathered his rucksack together and motioned for me to follow him.

Alexander Halston was an unusual man. He was the boss, sure, but he was right in the middle of things, dirty and covered in sweat, and working just as hard as the people around him to get the big tent pitched.

He wiped the dust from his hands with a handkerchief and shook with me. His grip was strong as steel. He was as tall and lean as me, and his hair was just as dark and curly, but that was all we had in common. His nose was long and hawkish, his jaw tapered down to a point, with a cleft at the base. His eyebrows were thick to the point of looking ludicrous and his mutton chop mustache was in need of a good trimming.

He also had crooked teeth.

He was also a pleasant man when he was by himself and not doing business. When it came to me giving a demonstration, he put that on hold until the tent was done and didn't ask me, but rather ordered me to get my hands dirty. The work was hard, and before it was done I was sweating along with everyone else.

When it was done, Halston pulled up a folding chair and settled himself in the spot that would later be the main ring of the circus. He lit his pipe and blew a thick plume of smoke into the stifling air.

All around him other members of the circus sat on the ground and talked quietly until he cleared his throat.

"Ladies and gentleman," his voice was deep and melodious, and every head turned to him when he spoke. "We have with us today one Cecil Phelps of Chicago. He'd like to join us."

No one spoke. Instead, they merely waited for him to say something else, or watched me as I stared at the lot of them.

"Bert, Carter, do us a favor and help Mr. Phelps get ready for his demonstration."

Without another word Carter and a heavyset man who had to be close to six and a half feet tall came forward and showed me the rope they planned to use. For the next four minutes I stood still while they tied the rope around my waist, my hands, my ankles and knees. Before they were done, I was all but cocooned in heavy netting designed solely to keep me from escaping.

Just to make things fun, they laid me down on the ground and tied another thick rope around my ankles. Two minutes after that, they were hauling me into the air and I was looking down at Halston and everyone else as they watched me.

My little sister tied tighter knots.

Five minutes after they'd lifted me up, I was done unraveling the puzzle they'd made and the audience was cheering me on.

It was a good feeling, doubly so because I hadn't been sure until they had me up there that I could possibly escape without killing myself.

Alexander Halston himself welcomed me aboard, but only after he got the approval of several other people. We discussed how much I would be paid, which was minimal, and what was expected of me, which was a lot. That night was too soon for me to work out a routine for escapes, so something else had to be done with me.

Bert Calhoun and Carter Seward sat me down in front of a mirror and handed me a box of grease paints. Until I could work out a full routine for the escapes, I was going to be a clown.

Bert spoke in one big breath, covering everything he thought I should know. "Three things to remember, kid. First, every clown is different. You come out looking like another clown and there's gonna' be hell to pay. I'm not kidding. Second, being a clown is more than the makeup. You have to keep the audience busy while the next act is being set up. Carter says you know a few magic tricks? Great, that'll help a lot. Third, you have to come up with a name. My clown name is Dexie the Dunce. I do a lot of pratfalls."

I nodded and looked at the makeup. My fingers went into the white and I started covering my face. It was a weird sensation, burying myself under the thick paste. It was weirder watching how much it could change the face I knew into something else entirely.

The blue came next. I drew in large triangles under my eyes, and from my eyebrows up almost to the hairline. I put dimples high up on my cheeks, and then I grabbed the red paint and painted a smile that stretched almost all the way to the dimples. As an afterthought, I put a single red dot on the tip of my nose. Sometimes I added the last part and sometimes I didn't. Either way, when I was done and looked in the mirror, I barely recognized myself.

Dexie gave me his approval when he was done putting on his own face. "I seen a lot of clowns, kid. The face works. Keep it."

Not far away, Carter was finishing with his own face, which was mostly red and white. He had circles around his eyes and wore a bulbous fake nose. He put on a wig, too, a massive red poof of curls, and a pointy hat. His clown name was Tumbles. Watching him hit the center ring and start his series of crazy rolls and handstands let me know why.

I looked in the mirror for a few more moments and finally had my name.

Rufo the Clown. I just liked the way it sounded.

Chapter Four: Looking for Millie (Part Four)

The address I had for Millie was still in Illinois, in a little town called Lakewood Shores. It wasn't much to look at, but it was exactly the sort of place I could see having a certain appeal to Millie. It was small, intimate, and had enough open spaces to make her feel comfortable. I know she was never happier than when she was on the farm. I think living in Chicago made her feel a little claustrophobic.

Getting there wasn't much of a problem. I took the bus as far as I could and then I started walking. I'm good at walking. I've had a lot of practice over the years.

By the time I finally got there, the sun had set and I was bone weary. I didn't know if I could find her place in the dark and I wanted to be in better shape before I tried my luck, so I found a hotel to stay in. A lovely place, really. I was almost certain the sheets had been changed within the last week.

I didn't want anything to go wrong with my visit to Millie, so I was a good boy and actually paid for the room. After a shower and a good night's sleep, I headed down the road to find 381 Crab Apple Avenue. According to the information I had, that was where I would find her.

It was a nice house; two stories, with a well-tended lawn and beautiful flowers in the garden. It was, frankly, exactly the sort of place I would have loved when I was growing up.

My heart was racing, because I was finally going to see my little sister. I stepped closer to the front door and hesitated for a moment. Not out of fear, though there was some, but because there were no curtains inside and I could see the empty hallway and its well-polished hardwood floors.

And in the living room I could see the same thing, emptiness.

I stared through the window for a while, trying my best to imagine what the furniture should have looked like, what my sister would have looked like after almost sixty years. Was she old and stooped, or still thin and spry? Did she dye her hair an atrocious color of red? Or was she going gently silver? Did she smile? Or were the lines on her face the marks left by bitterness and disappointment? It was hard to know, because I had no point of reference. My mother was still a fairly young woman the last time I'd seen her, under forty and in good health.

All I could see was the light gently reflected by the hardwood floors and my reflection in the glass of the window. I didn't look much like myself. I hadn't in a very long time. Oh, I'd done my best when I escaped from the great beyond, but there were a few problems to consider. When I was growing up my hair was short and straight. Not so anymore. I seem to remember my face being longer, but that had changed as well. Everything about me was just to the left of what it should have been, but that was the price you paid when you escaped death, I suppose.

I turned around when I heard the sound of feet on the sidewalk. There was a man standing behind me, a tentative expression on his round, withered face. If he was a day younger than eighty, then mimes are some of my best friends.

"Are you looking for Millie?" his voice was as skittish as his expression.

"Yes, I am. I'm an old friend of the family, but I've been away for a while."

His expression changed several times. First there was doubt. Mostly, I suspect, because I didn't look old enough to be an old friend. What followed was sorrow as he shook his head.

"I'm sorry to tell you this, son, but Millie passed away a few months ago."

I know I stared hard enough to worry the old timer. I couldn't help it. I'd been back for a while, close to two years, but I hadn't even thought to look for my sister until two weeks earlier. I'd had no special plans, no particular challenges to face in that time. I'd just chosen not to think about my little sister.

There are very few times when I've felt like a monster. Hearing that I'd missed my last chance to see my baby sister when she was alive was one of them.

My legs grew weak and I sat back against the front door and slid until my rear-end kissed the concrete.

The old man moved closer, his eyes showing concern for me. "Are you all right?"

If he knew the things I'd done in the past, he'd have run from me. Instead, he offered me a hand up and I took it.

"I'm sorry. I was hoping for better news." It was all I could think to say.

"I'm sorry for your loss, son. Millie was a good woman. A dear friend."

"Can you tell me how?"

"She died in her sleep. I think they decided it was a heart attack." He had a kind face, old and weathered, but a smile that made him younger. He smiled not because of my sorrow, but because of his fine memories. As quickly as the expression surfaced he pushed it back under again. "I wish I could tell you more, but that's really all I know."

"Do you know what happened to her possessions?"

"I think her granddaughter collected all of them. Or she had them put into storage."

"Her granddaughter?" I know I must have sounded stupefied. I was. Despite all the evidence, Millie was still ten years old in my heart.

"I think I have her address, if you think that would help."

I smiled again, a real smile for the simple kindness of a stranger. It wasn't something I'd ever gotten used to.

"I think that would help a lot, sir. And thank you."

He waved the thanks away as he headed back to his house in the very next lot. I stayed where I was and looked back at where my sister had ended her time on earth.

One more chance to see my little sister, to apologize for lying to her. It hadn't seemed that much to ask after all I'd been through.

The old man came back, waving not one piece of paper, but two. "I found her address! I also have a different address for where Millie's possessions are. I was wrong about that. Her granddaughter had them put into storage, because she's been on the road."

The man handed the two scraps to me and I took them as if they were the finest treasures I had ever found. Here, at least, was a connection to Millie.

"I can't thank you enough, sir. You have no idea how much I wanted to see Millie again."

"Well, I like to keep this sort of thing around, just in case somebody does come along who needs to know." He smiled and made himself younger again. I wish I could tell you how much I envied him that smile.

Before I could make another comment, the sound of screaming tires came around the corner. I could hear a booming bass coming from the car that cut into the road at high speed, even over the thunderous roar of the engine.

I'm not good with cars, forgive me. Most of the ones I know are as old as I am. Whatever the vehicle was, it was heavy and it was loud and it was large enough to seat the six youths inside of it with room to spare. The music coming from the speakers was filled with obscenities, and both my new acquaintance and I looked at the car as it came toward us.

I was raised in a different time. Try to remember that. I was brought up to believe that you didn't "share your musical tastes" with the people around you unless they wanted to hear them. I was also brought up to believe that you were supposed to respect your elders, at least until they proved themselves unworthy of respect.

A teenaged boy, who probably wouldn't be shaving for another two years, stuck his face out of the passenger's side window and screamed, "Hey, Old Man Walker! Eat my dick!" The other kids inside the vehicle laughed like it was the funniest thing they'd ever heard and from the back passenger's seat a soda can came rolling through the air, spilling its contents into the air and across the lawn as it soared for the old man's head.

Did I mention I've been known to juggle? Hand-eye coordination is a big plus for that. I snapped the can out of the air and sent it back the way it had come without much effort. I missed the window, but the can scraped along the side of the car and left a smear of soda and a few scratches for my efforts.

The car's tires locked and the entire contraption stuttered to a halt in the road. Both of the younger heads I saw on the passenger's side were looking at me as if I had committed a cardinal sin. The boy in the driver's seat opened his door and moved around the car, his face already reddening. He wasn't ashamed of how he'd let the passengers act, or how loudly he was playing his music—and I can barely qualify the noise as music, believe me—instead he was angry.

"What did you do to my car?" His narrowed eyes shot accusations my way as he moved closer to the scratches.

I pointed toward the boy in the back seat. "Don't blame me, he's the one who threw it."

"My dad's gonna' fucking kill me!" And right then I understood his dilemma. He didn't look old enough to drive down the street. He also didn't look like he'd ever worked a day in his life with his soft gut and baggy pants. Listen, I speak as a clown here. I know that fashions change, but half the boy's ass was hanging out of his jeans and the other half was only kept in place by the belt he used to hold the pants up. I have no idea who decided the look was fashionable, but they were very, very wrong.

"Did you hear what I said?" The kid was looking at me, the anger clear on his pudgy features.

I shrugged. "Heard. Don't care."

I don't think I'd ever seen a kid gape so blatantly before. I guess I was supposed to feel sorry for his dilemma, or maybe offer to pay for the damages, but I thought about the old man next to me who'd likely have gotten himself a black eye at the very least, and I couldn't make myself sympathize.

"You need to pay for this!" He pointed to the scratches in the paint with a trembling hand.

"No, I don't see that happening."

He gasped, as if I'd surely condemned him to death, and I smiled. I couldn't help it. I've always liked to smile, and I've always loved to watch the occasional rube make an ass of himself.

Before he could find something to say, I gave a suggestion. "Maybe you should talk to your friend in the back seat. He threw the can in the first place."

"Maybe you should go fuck yourself!" He took two steps in my direction and came no further. But he would. I knew that as surely as I knew my own name, because you have to read people when you work for a carnival. You have to know how they work.

The old man made a nervous noise and I looked his way. "You should go now. Thanks again, Mr. Walker."

"Should I call the police?" His face was pasty and I shook my head.

"No, that's all right. I think I can handle the situation." He looked at me with a doubtful frown on his face. "No reason to get the lad in trouble. His father will see to that, don't you think?" After another moment, he nodded his head and moved for his house.

I looked at the boy standing near me, still contemplating whether or not he could do me harm without getting himself in trouble. He might not have tried his luck but the other boys with him were climbing out of the car.

Now he had an audience, and there aren't that many young men who can resist an audience when it comes right down to it. I know. I speak from experience. I was around the same age when I joined up with the carnival.

He just had one problem he hadn't counted on.

I like an audience, too.

Gary Peck was a standup guy, at least according to most of the people who knew him. Oh, true enough, he was a gossipmonger, but that's hardly a crime and most of the time he was just passing on what he'd heard from others. Perhaps the sin he was most guilty of was liking to hear himself talk. Not surprising, really, as he'd spent several years doing voiceover work before deciding he wanted to work on the stage instead of with the microphone. He still did the recordings from time to time when money was tight, but he much preferred the lights of Broadway as it were.

He bragged regularly that he could have recited every line from the show by heart, and it was true. That didn't stop him from studying the text every day just the same. He didn't want to screw up any of the storyline, especially since he still wanted in on the recorded soundtrack that was due for production around the same time the show got back to New York.

The deal was already in place for the recording, but the producers were contemplating getting Patrick Stewart or possibly Sean Connery to do the voiceover in his place. They were known for their voices, and they were damned good. But if Gary could just keep everything going the right way, there was a chance he could still get the gig. As the only voice in the entire show, he felt he deserved it, but there were always a few big wigs that wanted to improve on what was already a sure thing.

He just had to convince them to leave well enough alone and that meant not screwing up a single line. Ever. Or at least until the contracts were signed and the checks were cut.

The royalties off the soundtrack would be huge, and he could always use the money.

The prop guys had done their job and set everything up the way it was supposed to be set. The lighting in the area came from several high wattage overheads that left pools of twilight between them. It had taken him a while to find the right spot where he could sit in peace and do his readings, but he'd managed well enough. There were two separate sections for the finale sequence—massive fifteen-foot-long walls of plastic and glass that looked like an enchanted forest of frozen trees—and the way the back area was arranged, there was only one location to put the massive displays where they wouldn't get hurt. Between those two sections were three support posts and it was in between the posts that he had pulled up a chair, an ashtray, and a decent reading lamp.

He liked to pause from time to time and look at the frozen trees, and the illusion of glacial mountains in the distance. His little oasis was comforting and private enough to let him have the time he needed to study.

Right up until the time one of the new prop runners came into his area and leaned against a plastic tree. Youngish, mid-twenties at most, long, curly hair and a Braves Baseball team hat that covered most of his face with shadows. The guy walked into Gary's study hall, stopped in the dusky area between the lights and crossed his arms, smirking as he listened to Gary reading his lines softly.

When the man's presence made him stumble across one of the lines he finally set down the pages of dialogue and glared. "Is there something I can help you with?" He tried to keep the irritation from his voice, but didn't quite succeed.

"You're Gary Peck, right?"

Perfect. Just what he needed…a fan. "Yes I am. What can I do for you?"

The man held up one open hand with wide spread fingers. There was nothing to see. But a moment later, with a flick of his wrist, the stranger tossed a small piece of paper in Gary's direction.

He watched the stiff, index card sized paper arc through the air and gently roll until it landed on top of his script.

Gary picked up the photograph and stared long and hard at the image printed on the front of it. He knew the girl, of course.

"Is this supposed to mean something to me?"

The man stepped closer, a tight, thin smile playing at his lips. "We're going to have a talk, the two of us, about that young lady. I want to know everything that you know about her, Mr. Peck."

"She was with the tour last year, I think. I remember seeing her a few times." He shrugged as casually as he could.

"Now, I doubt that. I bet you know a lot more than you're telling me." The voice was cold and condescending. The stranger reached up and plucked the baseball cap from his head, shoving it into the back pocket of his carpenter's pants.

"That's a bet you'd lose." His voice didn't quite tremble, because he was very good at what he did. Without even thinking, he carefully marked his page on the script and pushed back from the small makeshift desk he'd set up. He knew things were about to get bad. He could feel it in his bones.

The man stepped closer and Gary saw his face clearly for the first time. Was that makeup he was wearing? Yes, either that or he was an albino. No one had skin that white.

And there was something wrong with his lips.

The man came closer, and his smile broadened. Perfect white teeth, straight enough to make any orthodontist jealous of the workmanship. And his lips? They were red, crimson. Christ, he was done up as a clown. What the hell?

"Is this some sort of joke?" Gary stood up, angered now.

"Do I look like I'm joking to you, Mr. Peck?" The man stepped directly under one of the spotlights overhead as he came forward and revealed the rest of his face. The dark blue triangles above and below his eyes, the small red dot on the tip of his nose, dimples painted above a broad painted grin, the eyes Gary had seen before, that looked as cold and murderous as the steel on a knife. The smile was gone from his mouth, his lips peeled back in a snarl of clenched teeth. "Do I look at all like I'm joking?"

"You're kidding, right?" There was a tremor in his tone this time, a revelation of the growing anxiety in the pit of his stomach.

"The girl. Tell me everything you know about her." It wasn't a request.

"I barely even knew her."

"Why don't I believe you?"

"Look, why don't you get your stupid clown face out of here before I call security?"

"Well, you could, but the security guards are in a meeting right now. Orientation time for the new guys. It could be a while before you get a response." The smile started creeping back. "And because there's a cast party being held over at the Hilton; time to interview all the dancers and jugglers, even the acrobats." The man tossed something in the air that flipped and wheeled in an arc. He caught it with his other hand threw it back in the air, only now there were two somethings. Both moving too fast to be clearly identified. Another toss and there were three. After that they simply moved through the air with the skill of a long-time juggler. "I'm not part of the cast for this little show. I wasn't invited."

He'd forgotten all about the casting party. His stomach dropped a bit as he thought about it. He was supposed to be there, but he'd lost track of the time.

"I have to leave."

"You were invited, weren't you, Mr. Peck?"

"That's why I have to leave. Maybe you can catch me later and we can discuss the girl you want to know about."

Three hard rubber balls flew toward him, one after the other, and slammed into Gary's face, his left shoulder and his solar plexus. The first one struck above his right eyebrow and staggered him back as easily as a haymaker from Muhammed Ali. The second reduced his left arm to a numb, useless lump of meat. The third knocked the wind from him and Gary stumbled before crashing back to the concrete floors.

"Poor Gary. Finally invited to a party and he forgot to attend…"

The clown stepped closer as Gary tried to gather his wits and stand back up. The shoe on his foot was old and scuffed, with heavy treads. The man brought it down and stomped Gary's fingers hard enough to break the nail and bone of the index and middle digits.

Gary let out a scream that was little more than a gasp as the pain washed through him.

"Too late for parties, Mr. Peck. Tell me everything you know about the girl, before I have to start getting inventive."

Gary looked into the face above him and started talking.

He knew a lot more than he intended to tell the stranger. In the end he told the man everything. He'd have told the stranger anything at all to make the pain stop.

The clown got very, very inventive.

Tia finally started learning names around the same time she saw the cast being interviewed. She couldn't believe how many people had come to the party. Hell, she couldn't believe the spread of food and the free drinks.

Her body still ached from the hard session of learning routines, but it was a good pain, the sort that meant she was accomplishing something. Not just dreaming, but doing. It was a wonderful thing.

Leslie had been there right along with her, making sure she learned every step and being as patient as a saint while she was at it. She'd heard stories about how catty performers could be, and she wasn't naïve enough to believe the tales weren't true, but it was nice to not deal with that in her first ever show.

The press was all abuzz with questions, most of which revolved around the disappearance and later confirmed murder of the star of the show. While there were a few photographers who wanted to take her picture, Tia knew she was not the main attraction for the night. That was Leslie, the new female lead and the only thing that seemed higher as a priority than getting as much information as they could about her, were the rumors of what might have happened to Elizabeth Montenegro.

The stories were everywhere and most of them were asinine. There were tales that she'd somehow gotten involved in the mob, and a few tall tales about her being murdered for drug money she owed. According to Mark Blake, one of the jugglers who was on stage for all of five minutes every night, the girl had been a coke fiend. Anything was possible, she supposed. As horrible as it sounded, the only thing the woman's death meant to Tia was a chance to become a part of the show, and that was still a staggering change in her life.

There were more people moving with the show than Tia would have guessed. In addition to the main characters of the story, there were half a dozen women who dressed up as cats for the lion tamer, easily fifteen different people dressed as clowns, and a score of secondary characters to add color and flavor to the entire affair. There were several actual acrobats who performed the sort of stunts that would have made her pee herself if she even considered them, and what amounted to enough stage performers to populate a real circus. Then there were the people behind the performances, an on-call doctor, two trainers, the choreographer and his assistant, a fairly large group of musicians, the stagehands, a lighting crew, and on and on. She'd never had any idea how big the Carnivale was until now and the scope was damned near staggering.

And she loved it. She might never get to know all of them, but she didn't care. There was magic on the stage and some of it seemed to carry over into the atmosphere around her. Even dealing with a bunch of reporters and being at a party where the microphones and cameras were everywhere and practically rabid with questions, she felt energized.

She also knew she had better enjoy it while she could, because later, she was supposed to go over the entire routine again.

The choreographer—and she still couldn't remember his name to save her life—smiled in her direction and Tia smiled back.

"Sometimes dreams come true." She was speaking to herself, but one of the reporters walking by heard her and smiled.

"I'm going to quote you on that." He winked as he walked past and Tia laughed even as her face flushed with surprise. She had no idea anyone was listening to her as she spoke.

He kept his word. The next day there was a picture of her on the front page of the entertainment section in the Washington Post along with a quote.

From that moment on, Tia's life went into a whirlwind of activity and a sudden plunge into the waters of celebrity.

Someone decided she was photogenic, and the quote, along with the picture of her and Leslie standing together and smiling, caught the attention of the media. Within a day, she was a media darling. Within a week, she would have her first performance on stage.

Right after Leslie had her accident.

Life on the Road: Part Four

My first time on the stage was something else. There were about ten of us dressed as clowns, and most of the others had a lot of time and practice behind their moves. Dexie the Dunce was a bumbling idiot on the floor, falling on his ass and rolling across the ground in ways that seemed impossible. Tumbles was the exact opposite, moving with insane grace as he did rolls, splits and tumbles that would have been hard for a lot of professional gymnasts. They were the two ends of the spectrum and they both got laughs like there was no tomorrow. I watched them for a few minutes before finally getting the nerve up to walk out into the ring.

Next to the rest of them I looked like a fucking amateur, which was fair, because that's exactly what I was. Every step I took in the ring was exactly the wrong one, and half the time I wound up scrambling to get out of someone's way. I guess it worked well enough for the audience, who was laughing at every move I made, but I didn't much like it and I know the other clowns were annoyed. So, I decided to do something different. I walked out of the ring and started doing a few simple magic tricks. Listen, when it comes to the easy stuff, it's all sleight of hand. Once you get that down, it's just a question of what you use to keep the rubes entertained. I used a few quarters, a long runner of scarves I'd tied together before the show, and four wild roses I'd picked from the field behind where we were set up for the show.

It was better for me out of the ring, and that's where I started staying. None of the other clowns minded at all, and a lot of the locals thought I was something pretty special, especially the girls who got the roses. You know how you pick the right girl to give a flower to when you're a clown? Simple. You pick the one who isn't smiling. They need them the most. My choices usually came down to the sad-faced girls or the ones who, for whatever reason, made me think of Millie.

After the first time out, it became easier to be a clown, and Halston not only liked but also encouraged my forays into the audience. I think he'd always been afraid someone would react poorly to a clown up in the stands, but it never happened on my watch. Well, once or twice, maybe, but that was later, after I died.

When we were traveling, I practiced my routines. They needed a little work, but I was already a pretty damned good escape artist. Within a month or so, I was ready for the big time as it were.

But before I could go on stage in that capacity, I had a month of time as a clown to deal with. It got comfortable very quickly, that makeup. Every town we went to, big or small, started with building up the tents and stands—most of the stands were owned by individuals who took care of them alone or hired someone to help, but everyone worked on the canvas tent—and ended with a parade through the town proper to advertise our presence.

I'd always assumed people would be happy to see a circus, but that wasn't always the case. In a surprising number of towns, people came out to cheer and to watch as we did a few tricks, but in just as many, the people who looked at the Alexander Halston Carnival of the Fantastic scowled and merely stared as if they were watching a funeral procession.

I was a little taken aback, but Carter explained it to me. "It's the religious folk. A lot of them see us as a temptation."

"Temptation? What? To laugh and have fun?"

"We aren't like other people, Cecil. We live on the road and we don't attend church regularly."

"So because we don't wear our Sunday best we're bad people?"

Carter shook his head and I could see his smile even past the one he'd painted on his face. He stopped for a moment and did a spectacular series of backflips and I took the cue from him and started juggling four throwing knives I'd borrowed from Lou Hawkner, who also did a show involving sword swallowing and some amazing work with knives and moving targets. Carter was definitely more impressive.

When he was finished, we started walking again, heading down the main street of Alberta, Illinois, where the cheers and jeers over our arrival were a fairly even mix.

"Okay, Cecil. I'm going to point this out, because maybe you're not getting the whole picture. After this, we don't talk about it. It's something that happens, but we don't discuss it, understood?" I nodded my agreement. "There are girls here who perform with snakes, and do exotic dances, and read fortunes and all sorts of other stuff, right?"

"Yeah."

"Some of them make money on the side." I stared blankly. I had no idea what he was talking about and I said as much.

"They sell their services." I'll admit it; I was rather ignorant. It must have shown on my face. Carter sighed and leaned in closer. "Ten dollars on the side and the men get to fuck them."

"You're kidding me."

He shrugged. "It's how they make a living. Sometimes working on the road isn't so easy, okay? It's not all the girls, at least that I know of, but it's what they do to make ends meet."

"So people get upset with them for it?"

"People always get upset when a woman sells herself. You have the men, who buy it, deny it and condemn it as the devil's work. You have the women, who are angry because their husbands are sneaking off to be with strange women, and you have the losers who look at any girl with a nice rack and take it for granted she's there to spread around discontent and maybe herpes."

I shook my head. I'd barely met any of the girls on the tour with me, except as a nodding acquaintance. I wasn't exactly a ladies' man. Frankly, they scared the hell out of me. I never knew what to say or do, so I avoided the situation when I could. Still, I couldn't imagine any of them selling themselves. Well, actually I'd had a few fantasies about one or two of them and didn't much take to the idea that any man could have them for the right money. It went against the way I was raised.

"Don't be that way."

"What way?"

"You're being a rube." Carter's voice was soft.

"What's a rube?"

"Someone who doesn't understand the circus. A mark, a shill, a rube. Someone who comes in all smiles and happy, and leaves the circus just as happy but a lot poorer."

"I don't get it."

"They leave poorer because they're naïve, Cecil. They come in thinking the world is black and white, and it isn't." He stopped talking again and we both went into our routines. There was a certain rhythm to it and I was gradually picking up on it. The people on the street stared at us and a lot of them were smiling, delighted by the distraction from the tedium of the day. "You're an escape artist. You're also a clown when you have to be. Miriam the snake charmer is a snake charmer and a dancer; she's also a whore when she needs to be. It's the way it's done and the way it's always been done. That doesn't make Miriam any different than when she's being a snake charmer."

He'd pointed out Miriam because he knew I already knew her. We'd talked a few times and somehow got stuck working together on putting up the tent. She was a nice lady, maybe ten years older than me, who was pretty when she was helping pitch the tent and absolutely beautiful when she was fully made up. Yes, I'd had a few thoughts about her, even knowing that she was much older, but I'd have never considered doing anything about them. When I was around her she was just Jane Hanover, from Massachusetts and when she was working she was a different woman entirely.

I nodded my head and gave thought to what he'd told me. We were all out there to make a living and so far, the pay hadn't been spectacular. I could see where a woman might be tempted to do whatever it took to make ends meet and to set some aside for the future.

I could also see where it would cause problems in some towns. Chicago might have been tolerant of prostitution, but the farm area where I was raised? They'd have driven anyone guilty of that sort of activity out of town in an instant and half of them would have been quoting the Good Book along the way.

Sometime later, when we were back in the field we'd rented for the circus, the atmosphere was different. Most of the people who showed up were glad to have a chance to spend a little money and have a night out. I suppose the only entertainment otherwise was the cinema I saw in the town proper, and the movie they were playing there had been out on screens for a long while. The people came in droves, and I did my part to entertain them.

The weather made it a little harder to do, however. There were violent storms in the area and the winds were enough to make the walls of the tent rattle and snap like the sails on an old wooden ship.

Because the weather was so bad, several of the sideshows were moved under the big tent, shoved into corners and placed wherever they could fit. A few of the others were forced to stay outside, and in most cases they went ahead and closed up.

I saw the freak show for the first time that night. I'd known it was there, and I'd seen a few of the attractions as they walked along and ate, but I'd only been with the carnival for a few days and I still hadn't met everyone.

The freak show was in a smaller tent, jet black, and oddly intimidating in the middle of the light and splendor. Admittance was only permitted to adults or kids who had supervision. Even then, there were parts where anyone underage was forbidden access.

I spent my off time—between the main attractions in the center ring handling their performances—near the entrance to the freak show. My curiosity had gotten the better of me and I wanted to see the wonders that the signs proclaimed. I wanted to see the Succubus and the Hound of Hell. I wanted to know exactly what the Amazing Snake Man looked like, and what made the Ape Man of Darkest Africa so special. It was simple curiosity, of course. I'd lived a very mundane life and even after seeing some of the more unusual specimens out in the open, there were plenty I had not had the chance to observe.

Curiosity has always been one of my biggest flaws, or greatest assets, depending on whom you ask.

After my seventh time hanging around the outside of the tent, the man who ran it—his name was Ames, I believe, but it's been a long time—smiled at me and gestured for me to come closer. "Listen, kid, you work here. So no charge if you want to go through, just always ask first, okay?"

I thanked him and he nodded his head. The lion tamer was on stage and would be for a while, so I slipped inside with Ames's blessing. I walked from the world I knew into a place of terrible magics.

Chapter Five: Looking for Millie (Part Five)

Riding down the highway in a car beat the hell out of taking the bus, so when I was finished with the boys, the car came with me. Oh, I'm not quite dumb enough to think it wouldn't be reported, but there were a few hours at least before that became a serious problem. I'd stashed the bodies in the trunk, and I knew enough to understand that the world hadn't changed completely in the fifty years since my death. Kids still broke curfew and their parents still let them.

I would try the girl's address soon enough, but before that I wanted to see what Millie had left behind in her storage room. I wanted to know my sister.

I can't lie and tell you I cried when I heard about her death. I'd been prepared for that, you know. I'd been dead before. I knew what was out there, or at least some of it, and I knew she was probably at peace. If not, I also knew there wasn't much I could do about it without help. It's one thing to get away from death yourself, and quite another to help somebody else escape from beyond the grave.

I thought about that a lot on my way to the storage place. I had the time, because I got lost for almost an hour. Little towns might be little, but they can have their share of secrets. In this case, I couldn't find Everett Street to save my life.

So I thought about my death, and I hoped Millie's was more peaceful.

And I thought about life after death and wondered if Millie would want any part of it. I didn't know. I guessed then and still believe that a lot of that would have depended on the life she lived.

See, mine was cut short. I died badly, burning to death while some of my dearest friends screamed and burned with me. It wasn't my time. I didn't get to live a long, happy life. I didn't get to settle down with the girl of my dreams and have a few kids and watch them grow up while me and the missus grew old together. I got robbed.

I didn't want that for Millie. Not ever. I had to know if she had a good life. A good death. A happy existence before the final bow and curtain call. Then, maybe, I could accept her death.

And if not, if someone hurt her and she left evidence of that pain anywhere among her worldly possessions, well, then something could be done about the situation.

After stopping at three different service stations, I finally managed to find the right street, a little two-lane road that rolled along for almost five miles before I found the storage units.

I didn't bother with the office manager. I just went back to unit number 712, the one that Mr. Walker said held Millie's life within its confines. The place was snazzy as far as a storage place goes. Two stories tall and "environment controlled" according to the sign out front. Turns out that meant the building was air-conditioned. It was also locked tight, with steel doors and padlocks on every single unit.

Okay, here's the thing: The principle for escaping from a confined space isn't that different from the one used to gain entry. I had the lock picked inside of twenty seconds after I first held it in my hand. After that, it was just a matter of building up the nerve to see what my sister had left behind. I'd last seen a ten-year-old girl. Now, I was about to look into the other fifty odd years of her life and the idea scared me a little.

Mostly, I could overlook the things that had changed in the world since I died, but this? Might as well ask me to get over being murdered. Some things aren't as easy to shrug off as others.

The storage room was what you'd expect: furniture covered with boxes and then buried under more boxes. Mounds of cardboard stacked to the ceiling. The only good news was that someone had taken the time to label all of them. I started with the ones labeled "bedroom" and moved on from there. The clothes were set aside carefully, reverently, and as I sorted through them I caught the first scent of my sister's cologne. Every person has his or her own smell, I suppose. She smelled of old woman, and that sent the butterflies moving in my stomach. She was supposed to smell of summer and youth, not of age and ointments. She was supposed to be ten, maybe as much as twelve, but no more than that.

I'd been robbed of my sister as surely as I'd been robbed of my life. I took my time, carefully examining the world my sister had made for herself, an archaeologist sifting through the sands of time to find out everything I could about Millie. I had to move carefully, not because the room was cluttered, which it was, but because if I lost control then, I'd have set the entire building ablaze and I couldn't allow myself the luxury of rage.

After the bedroom boxes, I moved through her bathroom toiletries—neatly layered into two boxes of perfumes and powders and slightly musty towels, and from there into the remains of her living room and family room. I spent most of the afternoon and into the early evening staring at the items she'd found significant, and alternately holding them close or shoving them away.

I held them close because they were Millie's. I shoved them away because they belonged to a woman I'd never met. Still, I kept sorting the treasures until I grew too tired and had to rest. I made a nest of her bedclothes and slept where she had slept before. And I dreamed as I slept. I dreamed of summer fields and Millie's voice as she laughed and as she cried. I heard her challenge as she coaxed me on when I wanted nothing but to surrender from the challenges of the ropes and canvas traps she'd built around me. I'd forgotten how many times I wanted to give up on my dream of being the next Houdini, how many times she'd been the sole purpose for going on even when I felt like casting my ambitions away.

Then I woke and sorted through the rest of her life.

There were things missing. Small things, mostly. I could have convinced myself that Millie's daughter or granddaughter had taken them. I could have made myself believe that no one in this world would violate her memories, but the things that were missing weren't always what should have been taken by a grieving loved one.

Her jewelry boxes were there; simple wooden cases that still held sentimental treasures, items collected through the course of a lifetime, valueless to thieves, but priceless to loved ones. One piece in particular caught my attention. It was a golden medallion on a simple golden chain. I would have thought nothing of it, but I could see where someone had bent the piece, scratched at it to check if it was really gold or simply gold-plated. It was plated. I swear to you, there were tooth marks in the metal. Other pieces had been cast aside in the bottom of the box where the jewelry rested. A strand of plastic beads with Mickey Mouse's head as a centerpiece and several other pieces of cheap sentimentality lay on the bottom, cast aside instead of placed with reverence inside the boxes. Whoever had packed everything in the boxes had been careful, I could not believe that they would have only been careless with the things my sister held as special in her world.

I felt a nervous tick in my eyelid, felt my lips peel back from my teeth. Still, I kept looking. In the farthest corner of the mountainous stacks of neglected belongings I came across a box that had been opened and tossed to the side. It only took one look at the contents to make me strip away the face I normally show the world.

The box contained photo albums. The tape had been torn off of the treasury of my sister's life and then been discarded as rubbish. No care was taken to replace the books and memories. No slight effort taken to make sure the contents were safe.

Trash.

Garbage.

My sister's life!

I managed one last time to calm myself. I carefully gathered the books and placed them back in the box, finding along the way a large stack of letters and three separate diaries.

I wanted to stop and look them over, but it wasn't the right time.

First I had to pay a visit to the proprietors of the Safe and Sound Storage Facilities.

I checked on my way out of the storage room. I looked carefully at the lock I'd picked to gain entrance, and at the locks on neighboring units. They matched. They were all from the same company, and had the Safe and Sound logo on them.

I always double check. I'd have felt bad about killing the wrong people.

The office was at the front of the compound in a small house. I knew the type. The odds were good that whoever ran the place also lived in the upper floor of the building. I was a little too early for the place to be open, so I let myself in.

The stairs were creaky, but I didn't let that bother me. I doubt the people in the rooms above would have heard me anyway, because whoever was up there snored louder than an elephant breaks wind, and that is not a sound you easily forget, believe me.

I found two people sleeping in the same room on the upper-level apartment. Both of them were in their early forties at a guess and between them they must have weighed in at close to seven hundred pounds. Unfortunately, they also believed in sleeping in the buff.

Despite a desire to run screaming from that much bared flesh, I stood my ground.

I saw myself in the mirror on the front of the closet door. My clothes were still the same, but my face had changed.

When I came back from the dead, I discovered that Rufo the Clown was the one who mattered most to my benefactor. The makeup I'd worn professionally was part of me now, and very permanent. Oh, it's easy to hide, but sometimes I don't much feel the need. There were a few modifications. I didn't have a big red nose, just a red dot that showed up sometimes and now and then didn't. That was the only part that changed regularly. It wasn't present that day. But the dark blue triangles above and below my eyes, the red dimples and the red smile were where they belonged. The white of my face, as stark as freshly fallen snow, almost glowed in the light of the rising sun that came through the window. The markings on my face were highlighted enough to see that they'd been cut into the skin. I let my fingertips dance over them, feeling the deep wells where flesh should have been.

I must have been particularly angry that day, because I wasn't well fleshed out at all. Another odd side effect of resurrection; sometimes I look healthy and others I look like I've been dead for a while. I could see the angles of bone under skin that felt too tight. I could barely see my eyes past the deep shadows that still marked me.

My smile was in place.

It was show time.

"Hey, rubes…"

The two slobs in the bed in front of me didn't move, though the man doing the snoring snorted and stopped his loud musings.

"Hey, rubes…"

The woman opened her eyes and blinked in confusion. She looked to the man she bedded down with and saw he was asleep before she looked my way.

I felt my smile spread across my face. It wasn't a happy smile.

She sat up fast, gasping, and slapped at her man to get his attention. For a moment he fussed and tried to brush her away, but finally he woke up and then sat up on his bed amid a chorus of groaning springs.

"What the fuck? Who are you?" His voice was slurred by sleep, but alert in tone.

"I am Rufo the Clown, and at least one of you has been naughty."

"Mister, you better get yourself out of here before I call the police!" The woman's voice was shrill and nervous and she tried to cover her ponderous breasts with her flabby arms, as if there would ever be a way I could find her attractive. She could have been the most beautiful woman I'd ever seen and she would have remained vile and repugnant to me after what she had done to Millie's possessions.

"I'll leave as soon as you tell me what happened to my sister's jewelry."

"What?" One word from her, but I could see the shift in her eyes, the sudden guarded expression that fell over her face. That was all the admission I needed, but I have always liked a little amusement.

"Unit 712. Somebody broke in and took my sister's valuables. Then they locked it up nice and tight with a lock provided by you."

The fat man stood up, not even bothering to cover himself. "That's it. Susie, you call the goddamn cops. I'll take care of this."

Susie reached for the phone. Porky reached for me.

I grabbed the fat man's wrist as I avoided his clumsy grab, and then I twisted and pulled. Several wet reports followed, meaty popping noises that told me I'd broken a few vital connections inside his hand as easily as his scream did.

Some people react differently to pain. In Tubby's case, he got angrier and pushed forward. I could respect that. I could understand it. That didn't mean I was going to be any nicer about how I handled it. He was already off balance as he came my way. I merely helped him into the closet door and the mirror it held. The door collapsed inward, breaking under his weight. The mirror broke too, and lacerated his face in the process. Broken glass, wood and oversized man all fell into the closet in a heap.

Before he could rise, I was on him, my fingers grabbing his skin and drawing back the heavy flesh hard enough to tear it. The man screamed, bucking wildly, and I stepped back as he sought to stop the blood flow spilling from the back of his head.

The fat woman screamed and dropped the phone she'd been dialing as I moved closer to her. I knew the man would be up in a minute and ready for another chance to kill me. That only left me a few moments to get to the woman and I intended to make the most of them.

I jumped onto the bed and leaned down over her, smiling brightly as I reached for her face.

"Tell me where the jewelry is and I'll go away."

The woman blubbered, her face collapsed into a wailing mouth and eyes that were squinted almost shut with fear. For one second I thought I was wrong, that I shouldn't have attacked these people and demanded back what had been stolen.

"We pawned them! We sold them for money!" Her voice was shrill, her breath stank and spittle from her fat lips touched my hand.

I thought of Millie.

The rest was easy.

"Possible Serial Killer. Eight bodies found in bizarre murder case." Brad Lowman read the headline and tsked. "What the hell is the world coming to, anyway?"

He was supposed to be assembling the stage units for the Ice castle, but there was no hurry. The show didn't start again until the next day and there were plenty of extras these days, including John Booker, who was working his ass off hard enough for both of them.

Booker looked down from the post he'd scrambled up and tilted his head quizzically. Brad sighed. The kid was always curious. Served him right for reading aloud.

"Okay, let's see... 'Eight bodies were discovered yesterday morning at the home of Martin and Susan Burke, the proprietors of the Safe and Sound Storage Company in Lakewood Shores, Illinois. In addition to the owners of the rental facility six additional bodies have been counted and added to the list.'"

He cleared his throat and took a sip of his flat cola before reading any more. Booker had climbed down to the ground and was listening, his long face almost expressionless.

"'Police Chief Floyd Heedner of the Lakewood PD was speechless at first, but in a candid moment told reporters that "It might take a little while to identify the bodies, they'd been mutilated. The nature of the mutilation is unknown as is the motive for why the individuals in question were killed. Sources inside the Lakewood PD have let slip that the remaining six people were believed to be from around the area and might be a group of young men who were reported missing almost two weeks ago.'"

Booker shook his head and shrugged before heading back toward the ladder.

"What kind of sick fuck kills eight people, and six of them kids?" Brad shook his head.

"World's full of sick people, Brad. You should know that." Booker's voice was a little teasing, but held no accusation. Still, Lowman felt his skin go red. Booker had caught him scrawling the Internet for under-aged porn earlier in the week, but had said nothing to anyone about it. He might not have just sent Brad a verbal bitch slap, but then again, he might have.

"Whattaya' mean by that?" Last thing he needed to do was take shit from some little asshole.

"It's not a new thing is all. I've seen bigger body counts on the news. Think about it. We're setting up the stage for a show about what happened to fifty-seven people who disappeared from the face of the earth."

"Fifty-seven?"

"Yeah. That's how many people were in the Halston circus."

"How do you know that?"

"I was there."

"Bullshit!" Brad laughed. He knew when someone was yanking his chain.

"Well, there might have been a few more, but it was fifty-seven that died in the fire."

"What fire?"

"When the circus was destroyed. Pay attention, Brad."

"Are you fucking high?"

"No." Booker climbed out on the thick cable that held the pieces of the stage set together. Brad watched him and felt his balls try to shrink away. He hated heights and could never understand how anyone who was sane would willingly walk across a piece of one-inch-thick cable suspended thirty feet in the air. Okay, maybe only fifteen feet, but still, it was a terrifying notion.

"Jesus, be careful!"

"I'm fine, Brad." He looked around from his bird's eye position and then hunkered down on the wire like it was solid earth instead of a metal cable high enough up to cause broken limbs. "Listen, what you were doing the other day...does anyone else know about it?"

Brad thought his face would catch fire he flushed so hard.

"No, and please keep it like that, okay?"

Booker smiled. "No worries. I was just curious, have you ever...?"

"You mean with a girl that age?" Brad licked his lips and looked at the man up above him. The answer was yes. He had. He didn't mean to, not really, but the opportunity presented itself and he took it. The girl never told anyone and he hadn't either. But looking at Booker, he was beginning to think he'd found a kindred spirit, someone else who understood the beauty of making love to a little girl.

Booker nodded.

"Maybe yes, maybe no."

"What was it like?"

Brad smiled softly, his skin flushed again but for a different reason. Remembering the feel of her soft skin, the sounds she'd made, was getting him aroused.

"Like magic. The most amazing feeling in the world."

Booker moved a few more feet to his left and looked down at Brad. Lowman was almost directly under the man's shoes and started to get up. If he fell from that height, he'd kill them both.

Booker stood up and stepped away from the wire that held him in the air.

"John! Watch out!"

Booker came straight at him and moved too fast for Brad to get away. The man's shoes slammed into his face and drove Brad into the floor with the force of a falling anvil. The impact didn't kill him, but it left his spine ruined. Agony flared in his neck and head but didn't seem to make it down to the rest of his body. Not far away, Booker was standing up, brushing himself off.

He moved closer and squatted next to where Brad lay on the ground, wanting desperately to move and failing.

"I had a little sister around that age once, Brad. And I saw a few little girls who ran into the wrong sort of man."

Brad tried to speak, but he couldn't get his mouth to move the right way. It felt like his lips were doing their own thing and that didn't involve listening to his commands. Also, there was blood spilling down the side of his face and running into his ear.

"I've done a lot of bad things in my time, Brad. Probably more than you ever did, but that? To a little girl?" Booker's hand reached out and blocked off Brad's mouth and nose. Something must have been wrong with his vision, too, because Booker was all pasty white and looked like he was wearing makeup. "Nothing personal, Brad. But you disgust me."

Brad would have fought the suffocation if he could have, but he couldn't even move his head. He could only watch the face of the man above him as he was smothered to death.

―――――

Everything had been going well and apparently for a little too long. It was inevitable that something go wrong. Still, Tia hadn't expected murders to be among the issues.

One of the stagehands found two bodies hidden in the corners of the set. That was on the Tuesday afternoon, as the stages were being disassembled. Gary Peck, the narrator, was one of them. She'd met him briefly and he seemed like a really nice guy, but beyond that she knew nothing about him. And also a stagehand, one of the small army that had to make everything run smoothly. Both of them were as good as strangers to her, but that didn't make it any easier to accept.

People were dying on the sets, at least three that she knew of, and it was scary stuff.

More importantly, it was going to slow down the show. There was a small army worth of men in police uniforms looking the place over, and she doubted they'd be allowed to leave before the entire group was supposed to be in the next town; Philadelphia in this case.

Somehow the media had been left out of the picture, but she doubted that could last for very long. Sooner or later the same people who'd showed up for the press party were going to come back and start asking questions.

Which was why the entire staff was sitting in the auditorium seats and listening to three suits talk about how to avoid getting trapped by the reporters. They were also being told what would happen to their job security if they did talk. From what she was gathering, it would be a very bad move for her career if she talked to anyone without permission and got caught in the act.

The orders had been given and now it was down to people asking questions, a few of them obviously trying to find out if there were loopholes that would let them get away with speaking to reporters. Tia had already decided she liked her new job too much to risk it for any reason. She felt herself starting to drift, her mind wandering away from the morons who wanted to find ways to get fired, and slipping back toward the rumors about the bodies they'd found earlier.

"So, once again, no one talks to reporters or anyone but the police about the unfortunate incidents. Anyone caught doing so loses his or her employment, and any and all bonuses that have accrued. It's in your contracts, people. Don't think we won't enforce the contracts, because we will."

Tia sighed and flushed with guilt simultaneously. Yes, it was frustrating having everything put on hold, but two people had been murdered and she'd have to accept that things were going to be delayed.

Next to her, Leslie shook her head and muttered for a moment before brightening. "Hey, at least we'll have a few more chances to practice before Philly, right?"

Tia smiled gratefully. "Yeah! I need it, too!"

"Jamie says you're doing great." Jamie! That was the choreographer's name. "Besides, I can always use the practice myself." Leslie shook her head. "I don't know how some of these guys do it all."

Tia knew what she meant. There were several of the performers who had to move between scenes and change every aspect of their appearances. It would have been possible to have a cast of three hundred with as many small roles as there were, but in the long run it made more sense to have some of the bit performers switch costumes. The only problem was, that meant more than a change of clothes, it also meant a change in demeanor and the nature of their performances. One of the men she'd met, Brandon, was on stage as much as any of the leads, but in ten different costumes and doing ten different things. He juggled, he climbed on a high wire—well, relatively high, it was only fifteen feet off the floor, but still—as well as several dance routines that were complex enough to make anyone panic.

"Has anything like this happened before?" Tia asked the question without thinking, and a second later felt herself flinch at the idea that the big bosses might have heard her. They'd just had a long speech about not starting rumors and what was she doing?

But Leslie shrugged it off. "People quit sometimes, but nothing like this. I mean, you know how hard the routines are, Tia. Some of the performers can't keep up with the drill, so there's always a couple of them that end up walking away."

"Not me, not ever."

"Same with me, but you know what? I'm probably going to take a few days off after Philadelphia, because I can feel it in my ankles."

"Really?" She couldn't keep the excitement out of her voice. If Leslie took time off, she got to be on the stage.

"Seriously. I was talking with Jamie about it. He said you were ready, and he's with me, no reason to kill myself if there's a backup ready to go, right?"

"What if I freak out?" Her stomach sank at the idea.

"So the first couple of times, I'm there and ready and if you can't handle it, I step in." Leslie shrugged. "I did it for Liz a couple of times, too." Her face wrinkled into a smile and she winked. "What? You think this week was the first time I ever went out there? I'd have pissed myself."

"So we have until after Philadelphia and then I go on stage?" She wanted to make sure she was hearing the words properly. That meant there was a real chance she'd be able to perform for her family, not just sit on the sidelines and let everyone else have time to shine.

"New York City, Tia. That's when you get on stage and I get to go out shopping."

At least fifteen uniformed police officers moved into the room, ready to take statements from every single member of the show.

Tia watched them and felt her heart sink again. "Yeah, we just have to get there first."

One by one, each member of the troupe was taken aside, moved to a different part of the massive auditorium, or even backstage, where the props that could be packed away had already been taken care of. Each of them was asked questions and then signed off on statements.

Most of them had a longer interrogation than Tia, who had only been with the show for a week. For the most part, the people in the room cooperated. The few that tried to be funny about things or that had something they wanted to hide soon discovered that a forgotten speeding ticket was hardly a good reason to argue with the local police. Several people were dragged away in hand cuffs.

The end result of the investigation wasn't known, but that the delays would be substantial was becoming more and more obvious by the dragging moment.

And all Tia could think about the new changes was that they were good. The more the next show was delayed, the better her chances of having the part down perfectly when they got to New York.

Life on the Road: Part Five

You don't think much about circuses going year round, but in the case of the Halston Circus, that's exactly what happened. We started off in Illinois and moved east until the weather started going sour. Then we were on our way to the south, and whatever towns Halston arranged for us there.

The road never lost its magic for me. A lot of people in the troupe hated the traveling, but I thrived on it. There were always new places to see and new people to meet, though in truth, I'd met the one woman I was certain I would someday marry.

Her name was Doreen Miles, and according to the signs, she was a succubus. It took me a while to find out what that meant. She was supposed to be a demon from Hell, one that specialized in seducing men into willingly giving up their souls. I have to tell you, I think I would have been tempted if she'd ever asked any such thing of me.

I wish I could tell you how she looked, but unlike most of the people I traveled with, I only remember Doreen a few features at a time. Her hair was dark, though I couldn't say anymore if it was blond, brunette, or even red. I just know it was dark. Her eyes were hazel, except sometimes they were green. Her nose was small and straight and fit the rest of her face perfectly. Her lips were perfect.

Want to know the scary part? No one else who met her could have told you what she looked like very well, either. I know, because it's one of the things my roommates and me talked about sometimes, late at night when we were riding the rails.

I met Doreen in the Freak Show. Last place I would have expected to meet an angel, but you never know what life has cooking, do you?

I'd gone past the scariest dog I'd ever seen, almost as tall as I was and that was while it was sitting down, with eyes that glowed green and steam coming from its nostrils every time it breathed. I'd gone past the fat lady and the strong man—both of whom I'd already met, by the way—and I'd made it past the snake man, who really did have a human torso and the long sinuous body of a snake. I thought I was done until I saw the crowd of men staring at one last cage, a heavy affair with thick steel bars and a lock that would have taken a few shots from a cannon before it gave out. The men stared raptly, and it took the brute next to the cage poking them with sticks to get them to move on to the curtains that put them back in the main tent. I think some of them would have protested even then, but he always reminded them that their wives and girlfriends were waiting outside. That normally did the trick.

Finally I looked at what was the source of so much attention, and I understood why they might want to fight.

At first there was only the darkness in the cage, and a scent like lilacs, and then the light above the cage grew brighter and revealed her to me, one secret at a time. Perfect face, perfect body, supple wings that stirred in their own gentle breeze, and horns that rose from above her perfect eyebrows and curved gracefully back away from her face.

I blinked, and the wings and horns were gone. I shook my head and they were there again, but only for an instant. She looked into my eyes, and I saw her sweet, full lips play at a smile.

Again, she was beautiful. I couldn't tell you much more than that to save my life, but she was enough to make me hold my breath and stare. I was afraid that if I exhaled, the gust of wind would make her evaporate like a mirage.

Her eyes spoke to me, promised me a hundred pleasures from holding hands, to kissing to so much more. The bars between us annoyed me, and I reached for them, determined to bend them, no matter what, so that I could hold her in my arms.

The feeling of wood cracking my knuckles brought me back to the real world in a hurry. I looked away from the girl and toward the oversized fat man who held the stick and for one moment, I swear I was ready to snarl at him.

He smiled and winked. "Time to go back to work, lad, before Alex decides to cut your wages."

Reality came back to me then. I looked into the cage again, but the light had gone out, and there was no sign of the girl.

The rest of that night seemed rather pale in comparison. I went through the motions, but my mind was always on the woman I'd seen for only a few moments.

Later that night, I talked to Dexie and the rest of my roommates about her. She seemed to have that effect on every man she met. At least I wasn't alone in my misery.

We moved on, and while I enjoyed the travel time, I kept thinking about the girl. When I couldn't stand it anymore, I asked Carter about her.

Carter smiled knowingly and stuffed his cheap pipe with tobacco from a pouch. "Doreen Miles, the Succubus," he chuckled. "She is a beauty, isn't she?"

"Why do they keep her in a cage?"

"They don't."

"But I saw her."

"You saw her act, Cecil. Her routine. She stays in the cage as long as you stay in your greasepaint."

I stared at him, having trouble believing what he'd just told me.

Carter laughed and patted my shoulder good-naturedly. "Relax, boy. She's not a prisoner. None of the freaks in the tent are prisoners. They're here by choice, same as you, same as me." He winked. "Still, if there was ever a damsel worth saving, eh?"

"Where does she hide when she isn't in her cage?"

"She has a trailer, same as you and me. Only hers is a little better decorated and a lot more private."

I had no answer to that, so I sat in silence for a while. Later, when his pipe was snuffed and I thought Carter had long since drifted off to sleep, he spoke softly to me. "The only way you'll get to know her, my boy, is if you approach her."

"I could never..." I trembled at the very idea.

"Why on earth not?"

"She's..."

"Too beautiful?"

I nodded my answer.

"How lonely the rose that sits on a hill unadmired." Carter sat up and cast a wink in my direction a second time. "She spends all of her time in that room, and almost never speaks to anyone. But she's been known to pass the time with me and do you know why?"

"No. Why?" I asked because I was genuinely curious.

"Because I take the time to say hello."

That was the last he said about the matter. It was the last he had to say to make his point to me. I made plans to talk to her, if only to say hello, when we reached the next town.

Of course, there were other things to do first, like pitching the tent, gathering my supplies and preparing for the parade through town. I'd sewn extra pockets in my jacket and hidden a few inside of my shirt as well, the better to do a few tricks for the crowds, and it took time to make sure everything was concealed the way it was supposed to be and that my makeup was just so. I always spent that time with Burt and Carter, learning from them and now and then teaching them a few simple tricks.

Then it was parade time, and for the first time ever, I noticed the men on the streets and the way they looked at the women around me. More than one looked like he was on the hunt.

The shows went well, and two things happened that changed my worldview. The first was that Halston got himself in trouble. The second was that one of the girls, Miriam, the Snake charmer, got raped.

It was at the end of the second night when we heard Miriam screaming. Listen, whether people want to believe it or not, there's a real sense of family in the circus life. You work with the same people every day, you sleep in the same room with a few of them and you even share meals when things are rough. After a while they become a part of your world. I know for a fact that everyone was exhausted, because we'd done three shows to handle the crowds. That didn't mean a damned thing when we heard Miriam.

I was off my cot in a flash and I was slower than Carter and Burt, both of whom were out the door by the time I was halfway to the floor of our trailer.

By the time I got outside, half of the crew was already there, and Halston was standing in front of a man who was quivering, his pants around his ankles and his arms wrenched behind his back by Walker Kincaid, the strong man of the circus.

The man was a blubbering idiot and he had a good reason. Alex was holding a knife with a blade that was at least a foot long and aiming the point directly at the man's erect penis.

Miriam was trying to cover herself and several of the other women were surrounding her, shielding her from any more harm.

Alex spoke softly, but he was heard very clearly by everyone.

"Miriam said 'No'. That should have been enough for you."

The man in question was a slob, dirty and drunk. I could tell by the clothes that he was probably a well-respected member of the town, and I could see the wedding ring on his left hand. It didn't take much to connect the dots.

"I paid her! I gave her five dollars!" The man was trying to sound indignant, but it wasn't working out very well.

Alex smiled and I have to say, that was the first time in my life I understood that a smile could be filled with hatred. "So, if I have Walker here fuck your ass and give you five dollars, that makes it okay?"

Oh, how that man paled at the thought. "No!"

"Well then, why don't we just give Miriam her pound of flesh?" He jabbed at the man's penis with the knife and the man soiled himself. All around me, the people I'd come to know laughed. It wasn't a happy sound at all, but more like the low warning growls of a pack of feral dogs.

I should have stayed put, but I couldn't. "Alex! Let the sheriff take care of this." I was pleading, because I knew where they were going with this and I didn't want us in trouble with the local law. I didn't want to see the people I was growing attached to thrown in jail cells.

Halston looked at me, his hawkish nose wrinkled up like a wolf's muzzle. "Cecil, you'd do well to keep your tongue."

"Report him to the sheriff! Let the locals take care of their own, and let's just go on."

"Ask Miriam if she wants to let it rest!" Alex's face was livid. He pointed with the knife, the edge of the blade inches from the throat of his chosen prey. "You ask her how she feels about this sick fuck walking away from here with his cock where it belongs!"

Miriam collapsed in tears and tried to make herself smaller than she already was.

I should have fought harder, I suppose, but he got me with that comment. Miriam was a good woman, and didn't deserve whatever the local had done to her.

Alex nodded when I looked away. The stranger was uncircumcised when Alex swung the blade. He could have been Jewish by the time Alex was done.

They let him go after that, and he did his best to run away, one hand over his penis and the other trying to pull up his pants, even with the shit he'd soiled them with.

No one laughed, no one cheered.

The women took Miriam with them as they went back to their tents and trailers. The men stayed behind, and without a word, several of them prepared for whatever the night might bring.

It brought the police around the same time that the sun rose. And after a very brief conversation, the police left, taking Alexander Halston with them.

As they were taking him away, Halston looked at me and said with his expression that he knew I was right, had known it all along, but that he could not, would not, let the rape of one of ours go unpunished.

They'd taken him most of the way to the squad car before they stopped. After a moment's conversation Halston called out to me and I went over, half expecting to be locked in chains myself. I'd done nothing wrong, but I felt the guilt just the same, perhaps because a few of the people around me might have thought of me as a traitor.

"Cecil, I'll be occupied through the rest of the day. No one in town has heard about what happened, and it's likely to stay that way. We're going to have business and the show must go on and all of that nonsense."

I nodded my head, but had no idea where he was going.

"I need to you to lead the show for me. Be the ringmaster."

"What? Me?" My heart was in my throat.

"You." He shrugged as best he could while wearing handcuffs.

"Why me?"

"You have a decent voice and a good sense of showmanship. Also, you can fit in my tux."

He left a moment later, and I stared long and hard after the police car had gone.

Later, as I was trying to get myself into costume, Carter explained the facts to me.

"Alex will be out in a couple of days." He looked at my reflection next to his as we both put on makeup.

"You think so?"

"He didn't castrate the man. He just cut a little skin and made the asshole know not to try anything else that stupid." Carter shrugged. "It's not the first time he's done it and it won't be the last."

"So what? They'll just let him go?"

"They won't have a choice. They won't like it, but they'll let him go."

"Why?"

"The man he cut will drop the charges."

"That's not possible."

"Of course it is. He either drops the charges, or he has to tell everyone what happened to his dick and *why* it happened."

I thought about that and slowly nodded. That made sense. If he had to go to court, the circus had to go to court. His word against one man might not mean much, but his word against twenty or more people who say that he raped a woman, shit himself and got his dick sliced open? That's a different story. Especially when you considered that he had a wife at home, and maybe even a few kids. Divorce wasn't a regular thing back then and believe me, most of the smaller towns looked at a divorce as a scandal.

I nodded again and looked at myself in the mirror. I took off the bulging red nose. It didn't look right with the tuxedo and top hat.

I thought I should have been nervous, but the makeup helped. It wouldn't be me talking to the rubes when the time came. It would be Rufo the Clown.

Ten minutes later, I headed for the center of the main ring and squinted a bit as the spotlight glared down at me.

I smiled and listened as the audience grew still.

Alex used a microphone and I used the very same one as I spoke. "Layyydieees and Gentllllemennnnnn! Boyys and Girrrrrls! Welcome and I'll be your host tonight!"

They ate it up. I could barely see the crowd out there, but I could hear them as they started to clap and stomp their feet.

They wanted to be entertained, and that was what we were there for.

And like the boss man said, the show must go on.

Chapter Six: Looking for Millie (Part Six)

I wish I could say I took no satisfaction in murdering the fat couple that robbed my dead sister, but I'd be lying. They deserved to die and I enjoyed every moment of it. I laughed while they screamed.

And when it was done, I carried the boys from the car's trunk and placed them in the house on the upper floor, along with the owners of the storage facility, and I locked everything up nice and neat and left a note on the door that said Out To Lunch, Back in Two Hours.

Then I left, driving to the west, because I needed a place to relax and I decided on Delavan, Wisconsin. I'd never been there, but I understood that was where the Barnum and Bailey circus got its start. Curiosity was my only reason for heading there.

Along the way, I stopped at a diner or two and occasionally picked up a hitchhiker who looked too miserable to keep on walking. None of them tried anything stupid and most were grateful for the chance to rest a while and get where they were going at the same time.

When I got to the town, I was a little disappointed. I guess part of me wanted to see clowns and celebrations of the Greatest Show on Earth. I stayed at a place called the Delavan Motor Inn and parked myself in a room where I could lie down for a while and read my sister's history.

I looked at photographs first, starting with the oldest, most worn albums and slowly moving forward. In that first volume, I saw a life I knew all too well. I saw my history and that of my family before I left and broke apart the world I'd grown up in.

There were old, cracked images of me at ten holding the toddler my sister would become. Old black and whites of my mother and my father, the sort that I don't think get taken often these days. They were smiling, of course, because they were being photographed and they knew it, but there was a look to them, a hunger beneath the surface of their smiles, which most people never see these days. You can't be truly hungry if you've never been starved, and both of my parents lived through the Great Depression and understood what it meant to live on nothing but shriveled grains that had fought hard to crawl from the arid soil. The people I've seen in most places in the U.S. these days, they've had food. Even if they haven't had a lot of it, they've never starved. There are people that call this country the Land of Plenty, and they aren't wrong about that. There's plenty to be had if you want to work for it. Those that don't want to work for it get pushed to the wayside. I don't know, maybe that's my father talking. Sometimes it's hard to say.

I looked at the pictures and toward the back of the album, I saw the newspaper clippings. Every report she found about the Alexander Halston Carnival of the Fantastic, my sister clipped from the papers and glued in her book of memories. There were also three letters I'd written from the road, each of which had been wadded up at one time or another and then carefully pressed flat again before she put them in their final resting place.

I could remember each of the letters clearly. I'd written them after all. Written them, folded them around whatever money I could send, and then mailed them off. At least I knew the family got the money. That was something. Back then, it was all I had.

There were more pictures, of course. Candid shots of my sister growing up, posed family shots, and everything in between.

God, I don't think I've cried that much in years. I can't say whether they were tears of sorrow or of joy; probably a little of both, I suspect. I flipped through all of the books of pictures and stared at my sister as she aged in stills that were cut from her life. I saw her at twelve, and then at fifteen. I saw her at her sixteenth birthday and smiled because she was surrounded by family and a small army of friends. She was beautiful, just as I knew she would be.

I studied her face, her life, the smile that almost never left her, even when I could tell that times were lean. I saw the man she married, who had kind eyes and always had a hand on her, gently, as if to reassure himself that she was real. That's the way it should be, I think. So in love that you have to check whether or not you're merely dreaming.

I read her journals, diaries from different times in her life and the tears came harder than before. There were good times, yes, but there was grief and anger as well. I read of my father's death, which took place well after I'd shed the old mortal coil, and I read of my mother's passing a few years later, eaten away a pound at a time by cancer.

I had known for a long time that my parents were dead, had sensed it, I suppose, or maybe just done the math. Fifty years is a long time to be gone and the odds of them being alive weren't the best. Still, I thought about the good times, about my mother's gentle hands, and my father's rare and precious smiles. I thought about the farm and the dingy house we rented later, and how much I loved both of them.

How much I missed them, even after half a century.

I read entries about me, too. I read her worries about her older brother, her hopes that I was okay. I read how much she missed me and I hated myself for ever letting her down. There is so much in the world we make for ourselves that we can regret, and I had a great deal of regrets right then.

But damned if there wasn't joy, too. I looked on a life filled with happiness, read of Millie's triumphs and tragedies alike. She loved her husband and he loved her, too, until he died in Viet Nam. She loved her daughter, and was loved in return, at least for a time.

Mostly what I did, really, was examine the evolution of my sister from child to adult and finally to her golden years, a history written in ink, but one that showed the changes in her world just the same.

I read her life for the next two days, learning in bits and pieces how she'd grown and how she'd changed. I wept with Millie when she learned that her husband was dead. I laughed with her when her daughter, Cecilia, first walked and spoke her first word.

I learned about Cecilia's growing troubles as her life progressed. A somber child from the beginning of her life, I learned that she blossomed into a beautiful girl and I saw the pictures that proved it.

I read about Millie's second marriage and the man who left her one night and never came back. Believe me, I read that carefully and I wrote down the man's name. Should I find him while he's alive, we'll have a long discussion about how he treated my little sister.

I read about Cecilia's troubled adulthood. The angry young girl became an angry young woman, and then a starlet in the sorts of movie no young girl should ever be a part of. She had her share of celebrity first as a model in a few legitimate magazines, but the offers of quick money became too much for her and she wound up in the types of movies that used to only play on the seedy side of town in theaters that didn't bother with selling snacks.

Cecilia came home to her mother and brought along a daughter born out of wedlock. Her name was Meaghan, and when Cecilia left a second time, she left Meaghan behind as a parting gift. Millie became a mother for the second time, even if she was only a mother in name. She raised her granddaughter as her own, and maybe this time she was wiser, because the second time around she did a better job of it.

There were pictures of Meaghan, too. She looked enough like her grandmother to almost be her twin. She had the same smile, the same wild mop of dark hair. She even had the same patch of freckles that grew on her face whenever the sun touched her skin.

She had high hopes and bold dreams, Meaghan did, and so Millie did everything she could to make those dreams come true.

I read about my family, the ones I loved and the ones I never knew. It was enlightening, heartbreaking and I'll even say it was cleansing, like a good rain after a few weeks without; the air smelled cleaner when I was done.

Millie was dead, but she'd died after a long and happy life. What possible reason could I have for wishing to change that except for personal greed? None, so I left her in peace and I mourned the loss of her in my world, as I'm sure she'd once mourned for me. I didn't know what the afterlife held for her, but I knew it had to be better than the hell I got stuck in for half a century.

Cecilia could be anywhere in the world, alive or dead, but in time, if I could, I'd look for her. I had pictures of her, all of the ones that Millie collected over the years, and I thought I could find her with remarkably little effort if she was still alive. But she was a lower priority.

I wanted to know about Meaghan. I wanted to see what she'd made of her dreams and ambitions, and I knew where to look thanks to the journals my little sister had kept of her life and the lives that touched her the most.

In her own unusual way, my grandniece had joined the circus. I intended to find her and meet her. Perhaps after that we could discuss the past and the woman who raised her.

In the meantime, I was off to a different sort of circus, one that was based, oddly enough, on the life and times of Alexander Halston and the second family I had come to know and love.

———

Detective Michael Carver stared at John Booker and tried to read the kid in front of him. It was harder than he expected. The cold, blue eyes that looked back at him offered nothing. He didn't act nervous, didn't even seem overly concerned about the fact that he was being interviewed, but there was something about him that set off alarms in Carver's head. After seventeen years with the police, he'd learned to trust his instincts, but he was the first to admit they led him wrong from time to time.

"Did you know Gary Peck, Mr. Booker?"

"Not really. I saw him around, but he was one of the stars. I just build stuff." Booker shrugged his shoulders as he spoke.

"How about Brad Lowman?"

"Yeah. We worked together a few times." Nothing. His facial expression didn't change in the least.

"What did you think of him?"

Booker shook his head and sneered just a bit. "Kind of a pervert, if you must know."

"Why do you say that?"

"I saw him looking at pictures of little girls on his computer. Naked little girls."

"Did you report him?"

"No."

"Why not?"

"I'm new. I didn't want to make waves."

"You understand that child pornography is against the law, don't you?"

"Of course."

"But you didn't feel the need to report him?"

"Have you ever worked behind the scenes at a show like this, Detective?"

"I can't say as I have."

"You do a lot of work that puts you in dangerous positions."

"What do you mean?"

"I mean things like standing on a ladder while working with a power saw and leaning out until you're barely able to hold your balance."

"What does that have to do with anything?"

"I think a lot of people liked Brad Lowman. I think they liked him a lot, because he was always cracking jokes and glad to let you bum a cigarette." Booker stared at him now, and Carver did his best to stare back. The man's eyes were unsettling, not merely cold in color but in their lack of emotion. He could have been staring at matching marbles for all the expression he got off the man.

"And?"

"And I have to work with those people. Would you want to report somebody who was well liked and then have to trust somebody you barely know to hold the ladder while you're leaning out and cutting away with a power saw?"

Carver nodded his head. "Good point." He leaned back in his chair until the two front legs were off the ground and stared hard at the man in front of him. "Did you kill Gary Peck or Brad Lowman?"

"No."

"Did you want to kill either of them?"

"No."

"Do you know anyone who wanted them dead?"

"No."

And there it was, the end of the interview. There was nothing else to ask the man in front of him.

"How did they die, Detective?"

"I'm sorry?"

"How did they die? Maybe you should be looking at that instead of just trying to guess."

"There's not much to go on, but what I do know I'm not at liberty to talk about."

Booker nodded. "Just seems to me that if the deaths are connected, there should be an underlying reason for the connection."

"Like what, Mr. Booker?"

"Beats me. I'm not a detective." Booker smiled for the first time. It was a tight, closed-mouthed little smile.

Carver stared long and hard, still without any proof that the man he was looking at was dirty and still with a deep sense that something was wrong with him just the same. He might not have done anything lately, but he gave off a vibe that said he'd done bad things before and maybe would again.

"Thanks for your time, Mr. Booker."

Booker nodded and stood up in one fluid motion. He didn't say another word as he left, but he hummed a tune that was familiar.

"That song, Mr. Booker. What's it called?"

Booker turned back and smiled. "Tears of a clown." With that he was gone.

Carver had a dozen more people to interview, but he wrote down Booker's name and circled it three times. On a whim, he called one of the uniforms, Josh Wilkins, over and handed him Booker's name and pertinent information with a request to find out what he could about him. He needed to look into the man. Something there, he knew it, but just wasn't sure what that something was.

He was halfway through interviewing an attractive young woman who was the stand in for the female lead when the officer came back to him. The girl noticed Wilkins had returned.

"You have a guest."

Carver turned around and saw Wilkins. "What do you have for me?"

Wilkins leaned in and spoke in a whisper. "The social security number you gave me belongs to Lawrence Oliver of Queens, New York. It's a fake."

Carver stood up. "Can you excuse me for a moment, Ms. Natchez?"

The girl smiled and nodded, relieved to avoid being questioned any more. Seemed that was almost always the case when the person being grilled was guilty or innocent. Maybe that was what had set off his alarms about Booker. The man didn't seem to care one way or the other.

He looked at Wilkins. "Find Booker. Now."

The dark-haired cop nodded and took off at a fast walk. Carver picked up his cell phone and called Captain Jeffries, the man in charge of the massive interview session.

"Jeffries." The answer was terse. If Carver had to guess, Jeffries was as sick of talking to suspects as he was.

"John Booker, one of the backstage guys, is running around with a false ID."

"Grab him."

"Already working on it."

"Excellent. Get a few uniforms to help you look and get him now."

There was no guarantee that Booker was connected to the murders, but a false ID was almost a guarantee that he was doing something he shouldn't have been.

"I'll keep you posted." He hung up the phone and headed for the hallway around the same time the screaming started.

Carver turned to the left and saw Wilkins staggering backward, heading straight toward him and away from John Booker.

Booker was grinning ear to ear and shaking blood from the blade in his left hand.

Wilkins lost his balance and fell down, which was when Carver saw the open wound across the officer's face. A hard slash had cut the uniformed cop from the left side of his hairline all the way down to the right side of his chin. Loose flaps of skin were held apart by the blood flow and the man was trying to cover his face.

Carver drew his weapon and aimed it at Booker. "DROP IT!" His voice boomed down the corridor and several of the people coming to investigate the first scream backed away as soon as they saw the pistol Carver was aiming.

Booker raised his hands over his head and opened the fingers wide. There was no knife. Carver had seen it a second before, but now the hands were empty, though the left was still covered in blood. "Drop what?"

"Don't you move! Don't you fucking move!"

Two more cops were coming up behind Booker now, and they moved with the proper caution. Booker never blinked, even when they pinned him against the wall and started frisking him. The grin on his face grew even wider, if anything.

Carver grabbed for his radio and called in that an officer was down. Booker looked his way, the cold blue eyes that had unsettled him earlier for their lack of emotion now showing a wild amusement that was completely inappropriate.

"Guess you found out about the fake name, huh?"

"Read that asshole his rights!" Carver leaned down over the fallen officer and pulled on a set of gloves. Sometimes it was good to be prepared for investigating a scene and, in this case, it meant he could try to hold the wound together with sterile hands.

"Don't move, Wilkins. I've got an ambulance on the way."

Wilkins tried to speak but the severed sections of his mouth wouldn't form the proper shapes. Carver hushed him and then looked around for something, anything, to staunch the flow. The girl he'd been interviewing handed him a thick wad of tissue papers. She'd stepped into the hallway when he wasn't looking. He nodded a thanks and started pressing the tissues to Wilkins's ruined face. Wilkins let out a few screams and Michael couldn't blame him.

He got luckier than he expected. He'd forgotten there were medics already on the scene, but somebody had alerted them anyway. One of the men he'd been questioning an hour earlier and another man he'd never seen before urged him and the dancer aside and pulled open a first aid kit they brought with them. Chalk one bonus point to the show.

Wilkins let out several screams as they began working on him, and Carver looked away. He wasn't normally that squeamish, but when the victim was someone he knew it unsettled him.

"Go back into the room, please, Ms. Natchez." She nodded her head, her eyes as wide as saucers, and did exactly as she was told.

He looked back toward Booker and scowled. There were other cops around, or he might have seriously considered just shooting the bastard and saving everyone a lot of paperwork.

"What the hell is wrong with you, Booker?"

"Not a thing." The smile was still there, unsettling in its intensity.

"Why did you attack Wilkins?"

"He started it."

Carver could feel his blood pressure surge and saw the edges of his vision sliding into red. "Get him away from me."

The two uniforms nodded and started to drag Booker away. Before they'd gone four paces, both of the cops let out startled gasps.

Carver had been checking on Wilkins, watching the medics as they worked, but he looked back at Booker and his escorts just as Booker stepped away and revealed the handcuffs locking the two offers together at the wrists.

"Who's got the most guns now, Detective?" Carver swallowed and looked at the two service pieces aimed in his direction. Before he could so much as open his mouth, bullets were flying through the air around him. The wall to his left exploded as missiles slammed into it. Another bullet whizzed past his head as he started to duck. More bullets might have gone past, but he couldn't hear them over the loud cracks of the pistols being fired again and again.

Carver dropped to the ground, his heart pounding as loudly as the walls that took more bullets. The crazy bastard wasn't aiming for him; he was just unloading the weapons.

A second later, Booker dropped both pistols and then started backing away, his grin flashing brightly in the smoke-filled air. Carver scrambled to stand up and to take aim at the man. The two uniforms blocked over half of his view as they cringed down and tried to cover their heads, their arms locked together by handcuffs that Carver had seen on Booker's wrists only a few moments earlier.

How the hell did he *do* that?

Carver shook the idea away and charged, "Duck your stupid asses!" The cops did their best to listen and he hurtled over them in pursuit of John Booker. The man he was after didn't stand still and make it easy; instead he turned tail and ran.

There was no way in hell he could shoot at the man. The hallway wasn't narrow but it also wasn't empty. There were people sticking their heads out of doors in every direction and a few of them were actually stepping into the hall to get a better look.

Booker went around a corner and Carver lowered his head and charged. A moron on his left started moving in front of him and rather than bother with talking he simply knocked the man to the side. He wasn't a big man, but he didn't need to be. He knew how to hit. The guy he hit slammed into the wall with a squawk of protest just as Carver went around the corner.

Booker was waiting for him with his fist drawn back. Carver hadn't expected that, and what happened was his own fault as far as he was concerned. Michael tried to backpedal and never made it. The man's fist slammed him square in his jaw and took all of the fight right out of him. He stumbled backward as he tried to recover his senses, but there wasn't a chance to compensate before the man was on him again.

Booker's foot shot straight up between his legs and slammed into his testicles, hard. Only a second after that, he was down on his knees and Booker was running again.

Sucker-punched and twice at that, Michael Carver tried to get back to his feet and failed as the man vanished around another corner.

There was going to be hell to pay for letting the perp get away, and he knew he deserved every single flame that came along to roast his ass.

Tia waited almost an hour before the detective came back to talk with her. His expression spoke volumes, as did the large bruise growing on his chin. She'd heard the scuffle outside of the room and she might have even gone to investigate, but the sound of gunfire convinced her to stay exactly where she was. She'd almost decided that he was done with her and it was time to leave, but there was still a lot of commotion in the hallway and she didn't want to give any of the officers a reason to so much as look at her funny.

That didn't change the fact that she really, really had to pee.

Detective Carver was average height, with dark red hair and the sort of face that was easily forgettable. It wasn't that he was unattractive, just not very remarkable. The growing mark on his chin and jaw was the most outstanding feature on his face, but his expression, which had merely been bored earlier, was now enough to ensure that she'd remember him for a long time.

"Are you alright?"

He tried to smile for her and failed. "I'll live." He sighed as he sat down in his chair.

"Ms. Natchez, what can you tell me about John Booker?"

Tia frowned. The name meant nothing to her. "I don't know the name, but I haven't been here for long. Was he the man you were arresting?"

The man nodded at her. "I was afraid you'd say that." He did his best with a second smile, but he was already a hundred miles away, she could see that in his eyes. "Thanks for your time, Ms. Natchez. We'll contact you if we have any more questions."

"Is that officer all right?"

"Wilkins?"

"Is he the one that got cut?"

"Yeah. We don't know much yet. They took him away in an ambulance."

She still had to pee, so finally she nodded her head and scurried out of the room and down the hallway. She didn't let herself stop and look at the bullet holes in the walls, floor and ceiling. She'd seen enough of them growing up, anyway.

The closest restroom was public and clearly marked for women, so she was surprised when she opened the door and saw the pile of men's clothing on the ground.

Tia stepped closer to the jeans and shirt and then stepped back. Even from ten feet away she could see the blood on the front of the shirt and the other things she tried not to remember.

Two minutes later, she was bringing Detective Carver to examine the clothing. He brought a few extra uniforms with him to help in the investigation.

She wasn't supposed to hear, she wasn't supposed to know anything, but one of the men in blue let it out before Carver or anyone else could stop him. "Why would he take off his clothes?" The man looked closer at the pile of fabric and frowned. "Is that skin?"

Carver looked in the man's direction and snapped "Shut up, Palmer!"

Tia took the look the detective sent her way as a hint and left the room.

It wasn't that far to the next restroom, and she knew if she tried really hard she could avoid messing in her pants.

She made it, but just barely.

Life on the Road: Part Six

Funny how word gets around, isn't it? We left the town where Miriam was assaulted and Alexander Halston left with us. It was like Carter said, no one could press charges against Halston but the man who made the initial claim and after a very small amount of time, he realized how much he had to lose if he decided to seek indictment.

We moved on, and in the process, I got to know Doreen Miles a bit better. On the second night of traveling, I made a point of investigating her trailer. It was a modern affair, and nondescript. Most of the trailers had posters of the different performers, or something to let you know that whosoever was inside was someone to be admired. Doreen's was simply covered in sheets of aluminum.

I must have stood outside of her place for half an hour, trying to get up the nerve to introduce myself. Oh, you can bet I got spotted and you can believe it when I tell you there were a few comments made. Everyone at the carnival knew who owned that trailer and I don't doubt a few men had tried to get to know the woman inside a bit better.

After staring at the closed door for far too long, I lost my courage and turned away.

From inside the trailer, I heard her voice for the first time. "I don't bite, you know."

I stared at the door for a moment and willed it to disappear. I didn't know quite how to answer her.

"I-Hello."

"Hello yourself."

She opened the door and I stared at her like an imbecile. She was exactly as pretty as I remembered. My tongue promptly tied itself into knots.

"Um."

"You're Cecil, right?"

I nodded, mostly because it seemed safer than opening my mouth.

"I saw you the other day, when you took over for Alex. You were amazing."

"I was?" I felt the blood rush through my face.

Doreen smiled, and I swear to you, I heard birds singing.

"You were. You looked so confident!"

"It was the makeup." I looked down at the ground because then, at least, I could stand to speak to her. "It's not me they're looking at, it's the clown."

"I should try that some time." Her voice was a little rueful. I could see where the problem came in.

I smiled and nodded. "Maybe you should. Then you could, you know, get out more."

"Yeah? Got any spare makeup?"

I nodded my head. "Yeah, hang on and I'll go get it."

Five minutes later, I was in her trailer and standing next to the most amazing woman I'd ever seen. I didn't touch her. To be honest, I think I was afraid I'd burn if I touched her. Instead, I showed her how to put on the makeup and I told her that each clown face had to be unique. She smeared her face with the titanium white base and then added on comically full lips that did nothing at all to hide how perfect the lips underneath them were. She added thick eyebrows of blue and painted on a series of tiny stars under each eye. To finish off the face, she borrowed my red, bulbous nose. In the end, she looked preposterous, and I found I could look at her and talk to her like she was just another person.

She didn't scare the crap out of me.

We were due in the next town the following day, and unlike other times, she decided she would walk down the main street with the rest of us. I don't know who was more excited, her or me.

Strange how things turn out sometimes, isn't it? In the long run it wasn't Doreen that caused the troubles in Hapsburg. It was just the town itself.

When we arrived in Hapsburg, Ohio, I felt the tension in the air. There were few people who looked at all happy to see us. Even the few who showed a little excitement at the idea of a circus tried to hide the fact.

Carter did his tumbles and I did my tricks, but there was no applause from the people who watched. Doreen, who had been so very excited about being a clown lost the smile under her painted lips and replaced it with a puzzled frown. Most of the rubes watching us looked away and in a few cases they even closed their shop doors on Main Street, as if we might somehow be contagious.

When the parade was done winding through town and had returned to the fields, Alex stood outside the tent and shook his head. He stared in the direction of town several times and frowned more deeply each time.

Finally he spoke. "Take it down. We're not staying."

I was stunned. Oh, I'd felt the unusual tension in the air, but to take down the entire tent and never see a single customer? It seemed like madness to me.

I opened my mouth to say something and was rewarded by Carter's elbow striking my side sharply. When I looked his way, he frowned and shook his head. I got the message.

Tents always go down faster than they go up. We had the entire affair stowed away before the sun set. Unfortunately, that was all we managed to do before darkness slipped in and held us prisoner.

We were given a quick dinner of half-warmed stew and told to watch ourselves. A lot of folks locked themselves in their wagons and cars and called it done. Not all of us. Some of us sat out and played cards, instead. Others, myself included, took to practicing our tricks as quietly as possible and looking out into the night.

I didn't know what to expect, and I didn't feel like being surprised.

I didn't know what had happened in the town before, or what they'd heard about us, but something had the locals riled up, and I, for one, didn't like the feeling at all.

The night was dark and the sky was gloomy with low lying clouds that hid away the moon and the stars. The air was still, and the only sounds we heard for the first few hours were the insects in the fields and the noises of seventy odd people sitting in the stillness. There were a few laughs, but only a few.

It was unsettling and I felt myself get more and more agitated, because I knew something would happen before the night ended and, damn it, I wanted whatever was coming our way to get to us and be done with it.

I had to wait until midnight before we heard the trucks coming our way. Not one or two, but a dozen, and each of them carried men in white sheets and hoods. I knew the Ku Klux Klan. I knew their methods and I understood their reasoning. Despite what anyone might have heard, the Klan didn't just exist in the southern states. They were everywhere, or close enough that it didn't matter. The Klan believed that the only way to save their way of life was to drive anyone who caught their attention out of their back yards. Blacks were taking jobs, so they had to go. Asians were guilty by association: they could be Japanese and therefore enemies. World War Two was done, but the end of the war left a whole slew of people who were as scared of the Yellow Scourge as they were of the Communists who could be hiding anywhere, even in the house next door. I can't explain it better than that. The Klansmen believed they were protecting themselves and their neighbors. I knew their type all too well, and I could remember the occasions when my father had come back from meeting with his friends and then pulled out the white sheet he'd had altered for when he had to make a point.

To hear him talk, it was the blacks who had ruined his finances and cost him the farm. It didn't matter that the only people of color in my hometown had worked the farm a few miles down the road since before he was born. They became his scapegoats.

All I can say is, I guess the Klan in the area needed scapegoats, and a bunch of clowns and circus freaks seemed like as good a target as any to them.

They came bearing torches, and several came armed with rifles. I didn't know why they were there, but I knew they had no intentions of welcoming us to their town.

An eerie silence had fallen over those of us who stayed outside, a silence that had nothing in common with the outward calm.

I was raised to believe that all people should be met as friends until they prove otherwise. I was also raised with an understanding that you don't back down from trouble unless you have to.

Alexander Halston must have been raised in a similar fashion. He came out of his trailer with a loaded shotgun in one hand and four extra weapons to pass out to the men around him. By the time the Klansmen had climbed out of their trucks, easily half the men in the circus were waiting with weapons of their own. I never even guessed once that any of the people around me carried firearms. It never even crossed my mind, because to me the circus had always been a place of magic and in my naiveté I had assumed the rest of the world felt the same way.

Maybe most of the world, but there were exceptions, and they wanted to have a talk with us.

The men in white sheets stood around for several minutes before one of them came closer. "You need to leave here!"

Alex shrugged his shoulders. "You can see we've packed the tent and supplies. We'll be gone as soon as the sun rises."

"You'll be gone right now if you're smart!" The voice was filled with anger and righteousness, as if our mere presence on the planet was reason enough to be outraged.

"We've done nothing to you and we paid good money for the right to camp here and hold a show. We spent the morning raising the tent, the afternoon in town and the evening taking the tent down. We need rest, and we'll leave in the morning." Alex's voice brooked no argument.

Unfortunately, the same was true of the man under the hood. I didn't see any way out of a fight and I'd be lying if I said the idea didn't terrify me. But I was raised to never back down from exactly the sort of nonsense that was going on and I wouldn't have run in a million years.

I've heard it said that great minds think alike. I guess angry mobs do, too. The Klansmen wanted us gone from their town and wouldn't let us wait for sunrise. Alex Halston wanted to settle in until the morning came, and so did his people, including me. It was ludicrous, but guns were being pointed and I had no doubt in my mind that we were, all of us on both sides, perfectly willing to die for our beliefs.

Doreen changed that. She came out of her trailer wearing nothing at all, except the flesh she was granted at birth. All of us turned and looked at her.

I was struck by her beauty again but it was a different beauty this time, a terrible, powerful thing. Her looks had not changed, but their impact most certainly had. I wanted to look at her, wanted to be with her, but at the same time, I feared stepping too close to her, the way a wise man fears to reach into a furnace that's blazing hot. Several of the men around me averted their eyes from Doreen Miles, and more than one actually cringed.

Doreen turned away from me, from Alex, from all of the others who stood their ground against the hooded men, and faced the Klansmen. I looked at the shape of her body, the delicate muscles that moved under supple skin, the curve of her hip, her buttocks, her legs, and was, I think, relieved to not have to stare into her face.

She spoke only one word, "Leave," and the men who faced her trembled as they backed away. She stayed in the exact same spot, an unmoving statue with a petrifying gaze, as the Klansmen climbed back into their trucks and hastily drove away.

Sounds silly, doesn't it? A little girl terrifying a small army of angry rednecks. But that's what happened. I saw it with my own eyes, felt a touch of what they felt, and for a moment, I was terrified of the same girl I'd helped into her clown costume the day before.

Without another word, Doreen turned to head back into her trailer. Most everyone averted their eyes rather than look at her, but I stared, too drawn to her to look away and too petrified to move.

The following morning, we were on our way, driving away from the town of Hapsburg and heading further down south. We couldn't drive fast enough for me. No speed will help you escape fresh memories.

Chapter Seven: Looking for Millie (Part Seven)

I spent three days and nights in that damned hotel room. Reading about Millie's life consumed one of those days. The rest of the time was spent thinking about what I'd learned and contemplating what to do next.

I spent a lot of time sleeping, losing myself in dreams and memories and everything in between.

I've had two families in my life. I lost one when I ran off to join the circus. I lost the other to fire and deceit. Much as I would have rather avoided thinking about either of my families, they were on my mind more and more and I had no idea how to stop them from haunting me.

I had a grandniece. I studied the few pictures left of her again and again and I looked at the photos of Millie. They were hauntingly alike and completely different. I could see that they were related, could catch certain expressions in the pictures and know they shared blood, but that wasn't enough to make me want to become a part of Meaghan's life, was it? The girl was probably happy. Very few of the people I've ever met and befriended or loved could say the same.

Oh, I know it sounds like I was wallowing in self-pity, but not really. It's just a fact. I abandoned my family to make money for them. I meant to return and never did. The people I grew to love in the Alexander Halston Carnival of the Fantastic died. They were murdered and even if a few of them survived, the same problem came back to me again. They'd been alive fifty years ago and the odds were better than fair that they were either dead or so decrepit that they'd never even know I was in the room with them if I could somehow manage to find them.

I watched the television a lot while I was in that room. A lot. There was nothing else to do that wasn't too distracting, and the sound of voices kept me from going too stir crazy.

I was watching the local news when I heard about The Carnivale De Fantastique. The name was similar enough that it took me away from my internal musings and drew me back into the world around me for a moment.

An anchorwoman was talking about the latest show and how some people were claiming that the Carnivale was the next best thing to magic. As she spoke they switched to shots of the show, a couple of scenes that were nicely laid out and colorful to say the least.

Three clowns did a crazy dance while a girl in a scanty outfit with more glitter than cloth pirouetted across a high wire. All of them were young and athletic and flexible enough to be made of rubber. I'm a circus man. Naturally it caught my attention.

I listened to the report with slight curiosity until I found out the mythology behind the show: The stories were based off the "alleged" disappearance of the Alexander Halston Carnival of the Fantastic.

Alleged. I felt my teeth grind together.

All that I had experienced, all that had happened to me and my second family came down to a footnote about *maybe* having existed once upon a time and *just possibly* disappearing one day, never to be seen again.

I felt the smile growing as I contemplated that. Not a happy smile. I have to be honest; most of the people who've dealt with that smile are dead and a lot of them by my actions.

While I was in that room, I saw a documentary on chimpanzees. According to that film—which I think has certain elements of hogwash—the smiles that chimps show in the wild are signs of intimidation and challenge. It was that sort of smile that played across my lips and face. I watched the flesh on my hands peel away and show the white underneath.

I didn't leave the room. I didn't dare. I think if I had, I'd have killed almost as many people as I did in Serenity Falls. And believe me, I killed hundreds in that particular town.

No. Instead I stayed right where I was, staring at the television set and grinning like a chimpanzee. My body rocked back and forth on the bed where I sat watching, and I took the comforter into my hands and tore it into strips of fabric, all the while watching an hour long special about the Carnivale de Fantastique and contemplating what I would do next.

I think I might have gone after the owners of the show with a hatchet, but seeing Meaghan's face stopped me.

Meaghan, my grandniece. The last member of my family. The legacy left behind by Millie.

She was in the show.

Not the star, but oh, for me she shined so very brightly.

Millie's ghost haunted me again, only this time she was made flesh. Her smile, her mannerisms. The girl my sister had raised and this time she'd gotten it right.

She was not Millie's ghost. I know that and I knew it then. She was something better. She was family.

I had Meaghan's address. I knew where to go to find her.

Finally, I would meet my remaining family. Maybe, somehow, I could make it right again, I could just be Cecil Phelps, a man with a reason for living beyond the need to kill.

Maybe I could live again. Really live.

I had a purpose. I had an address.

I sat carefully, looking at the clown that smiled back at me from the mirror. Cecil Phelps was dead. I knew that, too. He'd died in a trailer, locked in with other performers five decades earlier. I just had his mind and soul. The body belonged to another person entirely until I took it.

Still, I could have a life. I could have a family. I kept thinking those thoughts as my body grew another layer of flesh, the mask that allowed me to hide when I was out in the world where the rubes ruled.

Family. It had been so very, very long since I'd had a family.

The term "clusterfuck" came to mind. Certainly it was the word the captain had used not once or twice but roughly fifteen times during his long, drawn out rant in Michael Carver's face. He didn't even try to defend himself. As far as he was concerned, everything that went sour happened because he didn't think the man he'd cuffed was really dangerous. Bad mistake, and one he wouldn't make again if he got the chance to go after John Booker or whatever his name really was.

Thinking about the smarmy bastard made him clench his jaw.

Booker had played him like a fiddle and then escaped. Worse, he'd maimed a cop in the process. Wilkins lost his eye. There was no chance in hell he could keep it, and it looked like the doctors would have to do a few reconstructive surgeries before he'd ever look right again.

Personal? That would have been an understatement. It was very personal. He wanted the bastard in a cell at the very least, and if he were honest, he wouldn't mind beating the man into a coma.

Mike kept his poker face on through the entire reaming, never once letting himself lose his temper. Every spray of spittle was another reminder that he'd screwed up.

Aside from three possession charges and a handful of outstanding warrants for everything from traffic violations to armed robbery, Booker was all they had to go on. He was the most likely suspect on the murders, but that connection was weak at best. There was no evidence aside from the fact that one of the workers said Booker and Lowman were working together right before Lowman was murdered and that information came from a man they'd had to take in for outstanding drug warrants in Florida.

And Lowman, there was a character. He'd had links to a hundred different porn sites, almost all of them dealing with children, on his computer. The FBI had already taken the laptop because they were better equipped to take care of a ring of pedophiles. If Booker was responsible for Lowman's death, he'd done the world a favor, as far as the detective was concerned, but that didn't make the other murders any more acceptable or legal.

The captain finally wound down and moved on to the next police officer he intended to ream. Two of them actually, the ones Booker had managed to handcuff together. Michael had no intentions of defending them either. They'd screwed the pooch on their own and they'd face the captain the same way.

There was the other body to consider, of course. The one that had been shipped up from Atlanta. He'd have to look at the files, see what he could find out about who had been added to the cast and crew after they moved up to Baltimore. One of the cast members was the victim. A girl if he was remembering properly. He hadn't been assigned to that case, but there was always a chance that there was a connection. Now he just had to remember the name.

"Elizabeth Montenegro." The name clicked into his head and he nodded to himself. There was a real possibility that there was a connection. He made a note to call the Atlanta PD and find out who was working that case, if anyone. He still wasn't quite sure exactly who was supposed to be in charge of that one on either end.

"What?" Jeffries turned on him and snarled the word. Mike made himself stand still and even avoided flinching.

"Elizabeth Montenegro. Is she a part of this investigation, sir?"

"The dead girl that got shipped here?" The man still scowled, but Mike knew him well enough to understand that he was thinking now, and not just pissed off. "Maybe. Who's assigned to that one?"

"I think you gave it to Koslowski." Actually he knew the man had assigned Koslowski. All the other detective had done since then was bitch about being overworked and underpaid, like that was a news flash.

"Not any more. Add it to this case and get all of Koslowski's notes."

Mike nodded his head. He didn't need the extra work, but if there was a connection he wanted to know about it. Still, now he had to call Atlanta and then, just to add to the grief, if there was a correlation, he'd have to call the feds. Technically it would be their show if they decided to take over.

Maybe that would be for the best. Mike didn't like the way this investigation was going so far.

Tia walked slowly, wincing at the aches moving through her legs and stomach. Despite the pain, she was still smiling. She'd gotten down all of the parts. Now all she had to do was remember them when the time came and an audience was watching her every move.

Leslie walked next to her, wiping sweat from her face with a towel that looked big enough to cover a station wagon. "You did good. Really good."

"Think so?" It was a serious question. Leslie was the one in charge of making sure she was good enough to be on the stage, and Leslie was also the one person she was looking to as a real friend at this point. They'd spent a lot of time together, and now they had matching bruises from a few of the maneuvers they had to do on stage.

"Yeah. You've got the goods." Leslie smiled and waved at one of the cast members. Tia did too, but she still couldn't have told you the man's name if pressured for an answer.

The props were all in place now, and the stage was amazing. Tia felt a sudden need to soak it all in again and stopped where she was.

The final set for the performances was a frozen wonderland, walls of ice and snow that towered into the air, with a castle in the distance that also glittered in shades of white and blue.

The idea of the story was that the head of the circus fell in love with one of the performers, a gypsy fortune teller named Ramona—played by Leslie and Tia alike—while she in turn falls for John, the lion tamer. Even as all of this is going on, the circus is visited by strangers who watch and dance around the periphery until one of them, a beautiful woman, also falls in love with John. The woman is the queen of a frozen fairy land, and when the final fight between John and Alex, the head of the circus takes place, John is gravely injured. The Fairy Queen then offers to save him, but only if he's allowed to stay with her. Everyone agrees and the entire troupe is carried away to the frozen paradise, leaving little to prove that they ever existed. As complex stories went, it was weak, but the performances made up for the lack of in-depth tale. Besides, it was hard to go into too much detail when none of the performers actually spoke or sang.

Leslie stopped with her, and smiled. "Pretty cool, isn't it?"

"I can't get over it, you know? I've wanted this my whole life..."

Leslie put an arm around her and rested her head against Tia's. "See? That's why I like you. You stop and look and it still makes you smile. Half the people with the show couldn't care less. They're just here for the cash. You? You love to dance."

"I almost went out for that show, the one on Fox. 'So you think you can dance.'"

"Why didn't you?"

"I was too busy worrying about the audition for this." She knew how lame that sounded, but it was the truth. The Carnivale wasn't just big, it was huge. The money, the publicity generated, it was the sort of thing that could make a whole career.

Of course, the show on TV was getting pretty big, too.

"I wanted to try out for it too, but I'd just gotten the part on here and I wasn't going to risk it." Leslie slipped her towel around her shoulders and did a long slow stretch, touching her hands to the floor in front of her. Tia thought about it and joined her. She didn't much feel like it, but knew stretching was all the difference in whether or not she managed to keep all of her muscles where they belonged instead of letting them get torn to pieces.

One of the stagehands came by and let out a wolf whistle. Without even looking, both girls raised one hand in a one-finger salute. It was automatic after a while. The calls were mostly good-natured, and the response was given in the same spirit.

Something moved at the corner of her vision and Tia responded automatically looking toward the movement to her right. Someone was moving behind the plastic ice wall. She couldn't make out many details but she could see that he was looking in her direction. Dark hair, pale face, tall and lean. For a moment she thought he could be John Booker, the person the police believed was behind the killings, but she shook her head at the very notion. If the man had half a brain he was in Canada or Mexico by now.

She looked away for a second as Leslie started speaking. "So I was thinking, we have the shows starting tomorrow, but maybe we can work out a switch. I'll check with everyone, of course, but how would you feel about doing a couple of the scenes on stage tomorrow as a practice run?"

"Like I was ready to pee myself."

"Oh, come on. You're ready! And this way, you can actually get a little comfortable with being on stage with an audience."

"Maybe just a small scene or two?"

"Of course." Leslie shrugged. "I don't want to throw you to the lions or anything."

Tia looked back at the ice wall to gather her thoughts. Whoever had been behind it was gone now.

"Okay. If you get all the permission and stuff taken care of."

"Piece of cake. Believe me. They want you cool and relaxed when the time comes for you to step out on the stage."

"You know, I still can't believe this is all real." Even to her own ears, Tia's voice sounded small.

"I'm finally getting used to it." Leslie laughed. "It's probably the bruises."

"Oh, those feel real. No problem there."

They finished their stretches in silence and headed for their dressing rooms.

Behind them, the clown-faced man nodded his head. They'd do. One or the other. He didn't much care which one.

Life on the Road: Part Seven

I don't know if time has muted my memories or if I just got bored with my lot now and then. I have few recollections of the year that passed except as a sort of marker in my mental calendar. I was with the troupe for over a year, I know that much. During that time I spent hours and hours practicing my routines and I wound up being the ringmaster for no less than once a month. Alexander was always getting himself in trouble with the local law. It seemed to come with his job as the owner of the circus.

Life on the road was seldom easy. Most days we were traveling and when we weren't there were tents to pitch and routines to practice. I worked hard at my routine as a clown and at least as hard at my escape act. Alex had promised me that when we reached the north again, I'd have a chance to perform at least a few times to see how people reacted.

Alex was a man of his word. After almost a year with Carter, Burt and even Doreen helping me with my routines, I got to do an escape act. I got to do it as Rufo the Clown, because that way if every stunt went completely wrong, I still could milk the situation for a few laughs.

Nothing went wrong, and I have to say the sound of applause was amazing. Clowns get laughs. Escape artists get applause. Ten minutes after I was done with my routine, I was back in the audience and getting admiring smiles from more than one of the people who'd watched me escape from a straitjacket while hanging fifteen feet off the ground.

From that day on, I was still Rufo, but I had more time on stage and I became part of the draw for the circus. I didn't let it go to my head.

Oh, I probably would have, but Carter and Doreen stopped that from happening. They reminded me that at the end of the day, I was just a person, not the makeup I wore.

Rufo was the escape artist. Cecil was just one of the gang. I think I liked it better that way. I'd seen a few of the performers who thought they were something special, and I'd seen the way they were treated for it. Royalty, or the attitude that you are royalty, has no place in a traveling circus.

We'd done most of the circuit again before we finally headed for the Northeast. The reasoning was simple enough, you really couldn't get a lot of people to head into a circus tent in the winter months and a lot of the upper states tended to stay damned cold for a long time. So it was May or June before we hit Maine and a few weeks after that when we came to Serenity Falls, New York.

Serenity Falls was a pretty town. I remember seeing it as the train let off the cars for the show, and I looked out the window of my trailer as we were hauled up a mining company's access rails to the site of the Pageant Farm.

We set up the same way we always do, and we had our show the same as we had in every other location, but the fun times didn't happen this time around.

See, it was in Serenity Falls that I was murdered.

I guess I should try to explain that a bit. We pick up strangers from time to time, provided they met the approval of not only Alex, but the majority of the troupe. That's how I came to be a member of the circus family and Alex never changed that particular rule. If he thought someone had merit, he was certainly within his rights to decide if they could become a part of the proverbial family, but instead he let everyone have their say.

One of the people he picked up and we agreed to let stay around was a man named Billy Raker. Billy was a clown by trade and a damned good one. He had a routine down that left people speechless with laughter. Have you ever seen a person laugh so hard that tears came from their eyes and they couldn't catch a decent breath? Billy saw it all the time and he was the one responsible for it.

Despite that, I didn't like Billy very much. He had a certain air around him that was well…slimy. I wanted to wash my hand after we were properly introduced and shook. I wasn't the only one, either. But he was a draw, and Alex promised that if he kept getting the people in there, he'd not only agree to let me leave when we hit New York City, he'd also introduce me to a few of the right people to know.

Did I still have plans of being a big star on Broadway and having my name as well known as Harry Houdini's? You better believe it. I'd miss a lot of the people at the carnival, God, how I'd miss Doreen and her sweet smiles, but I'd have left just the same. I was quietly in love with Doreen but as time went on I realized she thought of me only as a friend and nothing would change that. I'm not quite masochistic enough to want to spend my life pining away for a woman who doesn't love me back. I might have been, but there was my family to consider as well, my real family, and Millie, who deserved so much better than she had at home.

I wanted to be a star and I wanted to be rich, so yes, I'd have left.

I never got the chance.

Instead, the new clown and the man who'd recommended him, a loser names Lonny Whitaker, snuck out one night and killed five children. I learned about that later, of course. After I died. Before that, all I knew was that the first show went very well. We had a grand old time as they saying goes, and we got more than a small amount of applause.

It was business as usual, in other words. After the show I got together with Doreen and Carter for a few rounds of poker with a penny ante. Nothing too major, but a chance to relax a little with my friends. I made it a point not to look too closely at Doreen. It was easy to get drawn into her, even if you were trying not to let yourself. We'd already gone through a few times when being around her had made me act stupidly. Not too dumb, just like what I was, a kid with a serious crush on the pretty girl who lived in the area. I'd never gotten obsessed. I was too busy dealing with other things to get that involved in how I felt about her.

Besides, there's nothing quite as distracting as being smitten when you're trying to save yourself from death by stupidity. Thinking about pretty girls would never have worked out well for me when I was doing the straitjacket routine. And of course, I'd be leaving when we hit New York.

I had thought of a thousand reasons not to fall in love. Most of them almost made sense at the time. In hindsight, they were all foolish. We'll get to that later.

The first day was a good one. The night of poker was pleasant and left me only a few dimes poorer than when I started. Then, the next morning, we heard about the five children from the Pageant farm that disappeared.

Want to know something? No one was surprised when the people of Serenity Falls started looking at us as the source of their troubles. No one.

I was a little surprised by the group of men who came to see us, but only because they had the guts to actually show up in their regular clothes instead of in white sheets.

Their leader was a big man in his mid-forties, I guess. Like most of the blue-collar types in Serenity Falls, he had a crew cut and a broad face. Not ugly, but the expression on his mug when he showed up could have been carved from the granite they quarried in the area.

I wasn't there when the screaming started, but I got there quickly enough. It was a show day, so I came out of the trailer wearing my clown makeup and ready to perform. The locals weren't much in the mood for me or anyone else who was trying to be peaceful. After one of the rubes got close enough to Alex to spit in his face, I stepped in to try to calm things down.

I slid in between the ringleader of the mob and the ringmaster of the circus, facing the bear of a man who was screaming accusations. "Listen, whatever's happened, we didn't do it. We're a circus, folks. We're just here to entertain." To make my point, I handed over an elephant head made of balloons.

Maybe the guy had a problem with elephants, because his face turned red and his hand wrapped around the central part of the peace offering and he squeezed until I thought for sure my fingers would break. I tried to pull back, but he held on tightly.

Finally I defended myself. I kicked the man in his testicles as hard as I could. He dropped down fast, groaning and coughing, and I stepped back, trying to see if he'd done my hand any permanent damage.

I didn't go far before the man who owned the farm had a shotgun pressed to the side of my face. I felt the barrel slide along my cheek, then up my nose until the red ball at the tip got knocked away.

I stopped moving. Everyone stopped moving. I don't think anyone there really expected the situation to get out of hand. I know how weird that sounds, but there'd been none of the odd sort of vibe we all got from time to time, the warning bells going off and telling us it was going to be a very bad day.

I don't think anyone there that morning was expecting more than some chest beating and maybe a few fists. And out of nowhere, the man who we'd paid to allow us on his property was shoving a very intimidating weapon in my face and asking, just as cold as you please, "What happened to my little ones. Tell me, please."

The man was looking at me with eyes that were worried not for his own safety but for little children. I think that was what stopped everything from going crazy. That and a few of the townsfolk who maybe didn't want blood on their hands when they weren't even sure a crime had been committed.

Another of the townsfolk calmed everyone down, and despite the tensions, we all agreed to help look for the little kids. All I could think of was how desperate I would have been if Millie disappeared like that. There were plans to head back toward Illinois in the not-too-distant future, and I made my own plans. If New York didn't work out, if I didn't get a crack at serious money and stardom, I would drop by the homestead and see my family. I had just sent them most of my earnings for the last few months, and I wanted to see how they were. Despite the distance between me and my father—physical and emotional alike—I was even starting to miss my old man.

The show was put on hold. We spent the afternoon looking for the missing children without success. The night's performances were cancelled as well and we considered pulling stakes and leaving the area, but in the long run it was too late in the day.

The only good news was that the carnival's efforts in searching seemed to take care of a lot of the tension between the rubes and my second family.

At least it seemed that way until I felt the flames.

I awoke to the sound of Bert and Carter screaming, along with Markus Chambers and Lou Crompton. Just five clowns, that's all we were. Five guys eking out a living and thinking of better days, maybe, or a brighter future.

Our brighter future came in the form of fire, yellow and red tongues of flame that blackened the trailer's walls and sent thick coils of smoke into the air. Tears burned in my eyes and smoke tried to claw down my throat. I coughed and gagged and looked on as Carter tried to extinguish the flames running up his long sleeves. He never made it. The fire spread too quickly, devouring his flesh and clothes alike. Poor Bert tried to extinguish him, but it did no good. I think Lou was already dead by the time I woke. I think he died in his sleep only five feet away from me. Markus lived longer, but he couldn't do any good for himself or anyone else, trapped as he was, and burning in the blankets he'd covered himself with.

I tried to give us an out. Broke out the single window in our trailer and tried to unlock the door from the outside when I realized it wasn't budging from the inside.

My fingers reached through the window and struggled to get to the doorknob, but it was useless. My arms weren't long enough.

I coughed and hacked and spit at the foul tastes scorched into my mouth, they wouldn't go away.

Bert screamed when Carter died. I was trill trying to reach the door.

I saw the other members of the Carnival of the Fantastic outside the trailer, saw them trying to reach us, but the flames were too high, too hot.

They were still trying to reach when my hand started burning. I remember pulling it back inside and looking at it, wondering why it didn't hurt more. I guess that was because by them my legs were already on fire, and you can only feel so much pain at any given time.

Oh, I wish I could explain how much my body hurt, how much my soul burned, too. Not with pain, but with rage.

I burned and I howled for as long as my lungs would let me, and in the end, it meant nothing. In the end, I was dying, and dying, and then I was dead and the flames kept licking at my roasting body as my spirit slipped away from the corpse I had become.

I died in flames. Four other men joined me.

I used to believe in Heaven. I used to believe that if you tried to live a good life, you would be rewarded in the afterlife.

I had perhaps a full minute of freedom outside of my body before I felt the pull of dark hands, dragging me down and into a different place that never had anything to do with a benevolent God.

I died and I went to my own special kind of hell.

Rage? Oh yes, there was rage and there was pain.

And then, ladies and gentlemen, I pulled my greatest escape trick of them all.

Chapter Eight: Looking for Millie (Part Eight)

I took a bus to see my grandniece. I couldn't very well take the car, you see, because it was starting to stink a bit. Summer heat and raw flesh don't go so well together.

The bus let me off in a little town outside of Baltimore, and from there I walked to the apartment where my last flesh and blood lived. It wasn't much to look at, but it was better than I could afford.

I stared at the building for a long time, trying to get up the nerve to knock.

Then I left, found a hotel and decided to try my luck the next day.

The second time around, I finally got up the nerve to knock at the door. There was no answer.

A little after that, I realized she was on tour with the circus that had made me so angry, and I cursed myself for my stupidity. Thing about the TV is, I didn't have one growing up. The few times I'd ever watched one it had been something of a special event, and it was as big an affair for the family as going to the movies. Somehow I'd gotten it in my head that the events on the screen were always filmed before they were seen, even the news.

It wasn't too hard to find out where the Carnivale de Fantastique would be playing. I found out the name of the city and I got myself on another bus.

Miami had changed a lot since I'd last been through the area. Really, the whole world has changed so much I sometimes can't even recognize it, but Miami? I may as well have been on foreign soil.

It took me a while to find the theater where the Carnivale was performing. The crowds were huge and the excitement from the people waiting in line was electrifying. I could remember the feeling of having an audience that was excited to see a show, and this dwarfed the sensation.

I didn't have the money to gain legal entry, but that had never stopped me before. I made my own way inside the show and settled in to watch the performance. There were clowns, people in bear outfits, men and women dressed for work on the high wire, and everything in between. I looked at the clowns first. None of them would have made it in the real world. They all looked too much alike.

Meaghan would be dressed in a different outfit. She would be dressed as a female demon of some kind. According to the program book I lifted, she was one of the seven demonic enchantresses that sent the Carnivale de Fantastique into the show's title: Infernal Temptations. Apparently in this version of their story, the entire troupe was lost when Halston made a deal with the Devil. I looked at the names of the succubae and was a little surprised to see that Meaghan played the part of D'ReAnne. Not that far off from Doreen. Was it a coincidence? I contemplated that question and then decided that I really didn't care one way or the other.

My grandniece was playing a demon from hell. That was just fine with me. It was all make believe, right?

I watched the show without saying a word. Most of the audience was a lot ruder. A few times I heard people's cell phones ringing, but most of them had the good grace to turn them off quickly. One young man not only didn't turn it off, he had the gumption to answer it and start talking. He sat two rows away from me and I heard almost all of his conversation with a girl named Heather before he finally shut the thing off.

Has the world gone mad? I mean, honestly, who needs a phone in the middle of a night out with friends? Seems the height of rudeness to me. I decided I'd have a talk with the boy about his manners when the show was done.

I was more impressed than I'd expected to be; believe me, I went to the Carnivale with every intention of being disappointed. Yes, I was there to see my only remaining family, but since I was there, I decided to judge the show against the life I had lived. They got it all wrong, of course, but I didn't much care. The performers were all top notch. There were a few stunts handled on that stage that I would have bet good money couldn't be done before I saw them with my own eyes.

But the story of being seduced by the devil and his handmaidens was a bit of a stretch for me and there was a bit too much dancing. This was supposed to be a circus, not a damned ballet, and yet, dancing, dancing, and more dancing, with a few truly spectacular feats thrown in to keep things moving.

The clowns weren't bad. Not great, but not bad. A few of them even moved into the audience in what the reviews were calling an "interactive and cinematic experience." So, apparently a few clowns moving around makes a show more of a movie production for some people.

Again, it was fun. It also wasn't a circus. Not that I would have said anything of the sort to Meaghan.

I watched the dancing demon girls with their tight red outfits, their horns, tails and wings and tried to decide which one was my niece. They wore too much makeup on their faces, red paint and glitter, for me to know. When the show was done, I left the building along with the crowd and took the time to teach the boy with the cell phone a lesson in etiquette. I snatched the phone from his hand and smashed it into the ground while he looked at me with shocked eyes.

"What the fuck are you doing?" He stepped in my direction, ready to swing on me.

I dragged him away from his friends and into the alley behind the theater as he fought back and the group of people with him stared on slack-jawed. One of them finally decided to follow along to see if he could help his friend, but by then it was too late. I'd already broken my new toy and dropped him in the corner.

While the man came down calling out for "Randy," I slipped back into the theater and made my way behind the stage. Sounds challenging, doesn't it? Slip in unseen and get past the security guards, make my way to the dressing rooms and look for my niece. It's nowhere near as hard as you think it is, especially if you're any good at climbing. I went up into the rafters and made my way from room to room with ease, trying not to let myself get distracted when I saw a few of the performers stripped down to their birthday suits. One thing about circus folk who do hard work, they normally have the bodies to show it.

I found the demon girls with ease. I couldn't tell because of their faces, but because they were all washed clean and their outfits were set to the side, hung up with care or draped over any convenient surface.

Meaghan was not among them.

I checked twice to make sure, and when I was absolutely certain, I left the place. Not by the same method I used to get in, but through the front door. By that time the alleyway was overflowing with cops and emergency vehicles. I decided it was best not to get their attention, so I left the area quietly, but not before I noticed the man who'd followed me to protect his friend being questioned by the police. If he saw me, he didn't recognize me.

The news that night had three stories about the Carnivale. The first was an overview and a positive review. The second dealt with the murder of Randall Pearson, murdered in a botched attempt to steal his cell phone of all things. The third mentioned that one of the performers, Meaghan Phelps, was missing, having vanished three days earlier.

The couple sent along by the FBI looked far too young to actually have finished their training, but Carver kept that to himself. No need to piss off the people taking over his case, especially since the Feds had helped him more than once in the past.

Agent Gary King was sleek, slender and spent too much time trying to look good for his counterpart. Agent Holly Cantrell was probably just as high maintenance, but looked good enough in her suit that Mike was willing to forgive her a few sins. The end result was worth the effort.

Both of them were purely business and courteous, too. It wasn't what he'd expected, but he was grateful for it. After the recent reaming, he didn't really want anyone so much as looking at him funny.

They'd gone over what little evidence there was, including the fingerprints that Booker had left behind and forensic evidence that was still being sorted by the labs.

The only thing that didn't suck was the fingerprint, not that it was doing them much good. A criminal had to be on record somewhere in order to have their prints in the system.

"How certain are you that this John Booker of yours was responsible for the murders?" Cantrell spoke softly, and Carver had to strain just a bit to hear her. If she was capable of raising her voice over a whisper, she had yet to prove it to him.

"Well, he didn't confess or anything, but as we've already discussed, his actions, both before and after we questioned him, point in that direction."

She nodded. "Pain in the ass when they hide well, isn't it?"

Her partner chuckled. "Not if you like your job, Cantrell."

She rolled her eyes, but there was a smile on her face as she did it. They had a chemistry that he envied. Seemed like most of the detectives he'd worked with were too busy trying to play catch up to consider actually developing a personality. Or maybe it was just him.

The time hadn't come for serious introspection, so he moved back to the case at hand. "Do you think the body shipped from Atlanta is a part of this?"

"I think it's a real possibility." King shrugged. "We'll probably find out soon, too."

"Why do you say that?" Carver frowned, puzzled by the comment.

King shook his head. "Because the odds are good this show is going back on the road in a day or so. We can't keep them here for the investigation, much as we might want to."

Carver nodded. He'd been the one to request an injunction to stop the show from going any further. Apparently a murder investigation or three wasn't enough to stop the show from moving along its chosen path. He hadn't held out much hope for stopping it, but he'd held out some.

"Well then, I guess I should give you folks all the information I have and leave the case in your hands." He felt his jaws wanting desperately to clench. The notion that the investigation was being taken away before he could actually get involved properly was frustrating.

King shrugged. "Well, it's your choice, but we were thinking about starting a task force, and maybe keeping you involved."

"Seriously?"

"Of course. If the body from Atlanta is involved, then we're dealing with a multi-state killer and if he isn't done yet, we need to make sure we have each of the states covered. Besides which, we might have a couple of agents going undercover and it's better if we can have them call a number that doesn't actually go to the FBI offices."

"Okay, but why me?"

Cantrell was the one who answered. "Don't go feeling all special or anything, Carver. We just want to make sure there's some muscle we can trust if we need back up."

"What?"

King had pity on him. "We're the undercover agents." Carver must have looked like a complete moron, because King actively laughed out loud. There was nothing nasty or snide in the sound, just genuine good humor. "Oh, come on. You didn't really think the two of us were picked for our people skills, did you? We're both trained gymnasts. We'll be joining the troupe. It's already been arranged."

"Well, that's great, but I still don't see where I come in."

"You're already involved in the case. You've already dealt with Booker, and we managed to insist that a representative from Baltimore PD be allowed to follow along with the show as it goes, allowing you to continue your investigation."

"So, technically, I'm an observer?"

Cantrell nodded. "Yes, technically. Look at it as a chance to see more of the show than anyone ever wants to."

"Look at it as a chance to see Cantrell here in a unitard."

Cantrell rolled her eyes again and Carver smiled. She was a good-looking woman, and he thought he could survive staring at her in a skintight outfit without any trouble at all.

"So, I know you've probably had this discussion with half the police force, but go over Booker with us one more time, will you?"

Carver stared at King for a moment and nodded. "He seems normal enough, but he gave me the creeps. You know how some people just sit wrong with you? He was one of them. He was, I don't know, cocky. That's it. He was cold and cocky at the same time."

He was interrupted when King's cell phone buzzed. The younger agent held up a hand to stop his words and apologized with his eyes even as he answered. He almost immediately walked out of the room.

Carver stared after him, not sure whether he should be offended or amused.

"He does that. It's nothing personal. I think his hearing is going to hell and he doesn't like to admit it." Cantrell crossed her arms and stared after her partner.

"No worries. I was just a little puzzled."

"We're waiting for half a dozen calls on this case alone. I hate cell phones. He wins by default."

Cantrell shifted in her seat and put her legs up on the table. She was wearing black slacks that did nothing to hide her shapely form, but he didn't bother staring. His mother had taught him better and his father had taught him that getting caught ogling by any woman was a bad way to get a relationship going or, if you were in one, to keep it steady.

Not that he was looking for a relationship. Or a relationship with a woman who was ten years his junior. Or with an FBI agent. Nope. No thanks. Well, maybe just a one-night stand…

King came back into the room with a puzzled frown and saved Carver from the thoughts that had been slipping into his head.

"Seems like the fingerprints got a match after all."

"Yeah?" that was enough to make Carver focus.

"Yeah. Marco DeMillio. Disappeared from the town of Serenity Falls, New York back in 2003. Juvenile record as long as my arm, but never anything too serious. All petty theft and the like."

"Never heard of him." Cantrell sounded disappointed. Carver understood where she was coming from.

"Of course, if this is DeMillio, he's not aging well."

"What do you mean?"

"Booker claimed to be thirty-two. DeMillio would just be hitting legal drinking age."

"No way in Hell." Michael shook his head. "I saw him, I talked to him. That guy was nowhere near twenty-one."

"Maybe he's good at looking older." King shrugged. "No one ever said he had to be a pretty boy. Fact is, the fingerprints you got off Booker's job application match DeMillio."

"Who's been missing for over four years?"

"Yep. Which leaves us exactly where we were."

"So, where's the next town for this show, anyway?"

"Philadelphia, I think."

Mike stood up and stretched. "I need to make a few calls and get a suitcase ready."

"So you're coming with?" that was Cantrell. Despite himself, he smiled at the eagerness that was either in her voice or his imagination. Probably the latter.

"Hell yes." He smiled. "I could use a trip out of town."

King nodded his head and then slipped his phone away. "Excellent. We'll let the bosses know."

"Let them know?"

"Yep." The agent smiled. "We were hoping to work something like this out, actually, but none of it's written in stone yet."

"But you said..."

Cantrell tsked and looked his way. "That's some of the phone calls we're waiting on. Don't worry. It'll work out the way we want it to."

"You sure about that?"

"Oh yeah. They want us going undercover. We get to at least whine until we get a few concessions."

He couldn't argue with the logic, so he didn't even try.

———

Four minutes can completely change a life. The lines were longer than she'd expected, and the idiots from the cable company that she dealt with on the phone refused to expedite matters.

Jeannie Westingham was not used to being kept waiting and she especially didn't like it when some little strumpet behind the counter couldn't remember her drink. She took an extra few minutes to let the bitch know it. She drove a Mercedes, damn it, and that counted for something! The stupid cow probably drove a Toyota from the last century. What the hell did she know about being important?

When the manager came along and asked Jeannie to leave, she opened the lid on her medium-sugar-free-caramel-latte-with-skim-milk-cinnamon-and-chocolate-drizzle (no hotter than 140 degrees, because she didn't like to risk burning her tongue) and slowly dumped the drink all over the floor.

That was when the prick actually said he'd call the police on her, forcing her to leave before the situation grew embarrassing.

She'd parked at the curb to expedite matters—the lines at the drive thru were too long—and she slipped into the car after she shot her middle finger at the manager and the stupid cow that had screwed up her order in the first place. She'd be calling the district manager in the very near future and that was a promise to herself that she meant to keep; he lived in her subdivision.

She stopped thinking about her rapidly forming plans for revenge at the same time that she saw the empty baby seat where Hunter should have been.

Jeannie looked carefully, her hands twitching and her eyes nervously seeking an answer to the riddle of where her baby boy might have gone to, not letting herself panic yet, because it had to be a mistake. Nothing would happen to her baby boy, because she wouldn't let anything happen to him. Jeannie firmly believed that if she wanted something hard enough, she would get it and that philosophy had always served her through the years.

Only now, she wanted Hunter back more than she had ever wanted anything in her entire life and he still wasn't there.

Jeannie climbed out of the car and double-checked where she'd been parked. There was no sign that Hunter had ever been there.

Her hands flew into the purse she carried over her shoulder and reached desperately for her cell phone. Once in her hands the damned thing refused to behave. The phone slipped from her numb fingers. She watched the battery pop free and bounce under the rear tire of the idling vehicle she'd been happily driving just a little while ago. She bit her lip to stop herself from screaming.

There had to be a rational, reasonable explanation, there just had to be!

The wind shifted and she noticed the fluttering slip of paper that danced frantically under her windshield wiper, practically waving for her attention. Grateful for any possible hint, she reached for it and snatched it in trembling fingers.

The handwriting was precise and prim. The note read: Mommy, I have found someone else to love me as you seem to find me inconvenient. Perhaps you will love your next child better.

Jeannie read the page again and again until her vision blurred and the scream she had been holding in exploded from her mouth.

The manager from the coffee place led her back inside and asked her questions. The fat girl who'd taken her order was good enough to shut off her car and get her a drink—done right no less—while they waited for the police. Several people in the café stared at Jeannie with looks of contempt and pity, but no one else came to her aid.

The police were efficient, but they were not kind.

They felt that somehow she was at fault for leaving her child unattended.

For the first time in her life, Jeannie thought that maybe someone other than her was actually right.

Life on the Road: Part Eight

I died. I have to tell you, it wasn't everything it had been cracked up to be. There were no harps, no angels, no clouds covered with more angels. There was just pain and rage followed by the cessation of anything like a feeling.

Listen, we've all been in a dark room. We have all, at one time or another, had to deal with the lack of sounds around us, or even had a cold bad enough that nothing tasted like much of anything.

You haven't been stuck in nothingness before. It's death. No pain, no light, no sound, no color, no taste no sensations at all. Nothingness, capital N. Oblivion is not a nice place to be.

I saw an article about isolation chambers once. They're these metal contraptions designed to isolate a person completely from the world around them. They strip you down to your underwear, lock you in a soundproof, lightproof room that's been filled with water at body temperature. Either it's supposed to let you feel like you're back in the womb, or it's supposed to make you feel like there's nothing around you at all. No sight. No touch, no sound, no smell, no taste.

I understand they do a pretty good job with it. According to the article, a lot of people find the experience therapeutic. All they have to do is deal with their thoughts while they're in there. It's supposed to help you reconnect with yourself or some such nonsense.

Weird, isn't it? You'd think that would be a wonderful thing. So why do you suppose they suggest patients spend only an hour or so inside of the damned things? Maybe it's because you aren't supposed to be alone with yourself too much. Maybe if you are, you start thinking about things a little differently.

I felt nothing. I knew nothing. I saw and tasted and smelled and heard nothing. Not even my own heartbeat. On the bright side, there was no more pain. On the darker side, there was no more anything.

I remembered dying. For a while I almost convinced myself that I was only asleep, but eventually I had to let go of my fantasies and accept that I'd been murdered. I didn't really have any choice. See, you can lie to yourself for a long time if you want to, but without life to distract you, eventually you have to face the truth about every decision you ever made, about the way the people around you treated you, and about every feeling you've ever had.

I came to a realization. I was really never meant for bigger and better things. All of my life I'd let myself be a victim and that wasn't changing very quickly. Hell, I'd become the ultimate victim, a murder victim, and look where it got me.

Then, after I can't begin to say how long, I came to another and far more important realization. I had an opportunity. Harry Houdini was fixated with life after death to the point that he swore to his wife that he would come back if he could.

I'd spent my life wanting to be like Houdini. Why should I change my ways just because I was dead?

Instead of looking inward, I decided to escape. I had nothing but time on my hands, figuratively speaking. I wasn't really sure I had hands anymore in a real sense.

You can't move when there's nothing to touch and use as a method of locomotion. How do you feel when there's nothing at all around you? How do you see when there isn't even darkness? I had to struggle with those questions for a long, long time, but again, I had nothing else to do except look inside and tear my memories into shreds, looking for any truths I might have missed.

If you are reading this in the hopes of an epiphany about how to escape from death, don't waste your time. I had to work for the answers, so will you. I managed it though. It took a long time, longer than I expected, but I managed it.

Well, sort of. When I finally got a chance to experience any sensation again, it was overwhelming. Light burned. Sound shattered.

Even the smallest contact felt like a violation. Sensory deprivation does not prepare you for the world, people. Want to know why babies cry? It's because everything they experience is painful and terrifying. Every new sensation was an assault until I recovered from my time in the nothing.

The world around me was dead. Everything that had frightened me upon escaping the nothing was faded into shades of gray, a wasteland. I found the others. Carter and Bert, Markus and Lou were there with me. They were curled in on themselves, and nothing I did could make them move, could make them so much as whimper. Eventually, I gave up trying to deal with them and set about understanding my surroundings better.

There were a lot of bodies, most of them just as frozen in time as the four men who'd died with me. There were men, women, children and all of them in the same situation that I had been in, dead and gone. Aside from that, there was nothing. No homes, no land, no clouds in a blue sky. I knew then that I was still dead. The biggest difference wasn't that I had escaped my surroundings. I think the difference was that I had escaped myself.

There was another difference: this time I could see the way to escape without having to grope around blindly. So I set about doing it.

Remember how I said I wasn't going to tell you how I did it? Well, that's still true. But I have to give you something, don't I? If only to make you understand the situation I was in. For lack of a better term, I was in a sphere. More spheres, like layers or an onion, surrounded that sphere. I can't explain it better than that. I had to find the weak spots on each layer and then I had to escape. I didn't try to count them, because I'd already been through worse when trying to get away from the nothingness.

Here's the thing about escaping from a place: Once you understand how it works, the rest is easy. Oh, you might have to take a few minutes, but you learn the weak spots and nothing can keep you down for long.

It took time, but again, I had plenty. Eventually I slipped free from my prison and wound up at the edge of a farm, the same one I'd been at when I was murdered. The sun was down and the moon was up. Snow was falling, covering the land in a blanket of white that went on as far as I could see, broken now and then by homes and trees and a road that looked like it had been plowed recently.

I didn't feel the cold in the air, or see my breath, but I shivered just the same. When I walked, I left no footprints. When I tried to speak, I made no sound. I walked anyway and spoke as well, if only to have something to do.

Eventually I made it to the town of Serenity Falls. When last I'd been there the weather had been warmer, and I had been alive.

One way or another, I planned to have answers to a few questions. What better place to start than where I had last been alive?

Sometimes you get answers to your questions.

Sometimes you can learn to regret those answers.

I finally found someone who could listen to me.

He was not what he seemed.

Chapter Nine: Looking for Millie (Part Nine)

I went looking for Meaghan. I searched everywhere I could think of, starting with the hotel where she had been staying. It wasn't hard to find, because the entire staff of the Carnivale was still in the same place, occupying most of the rooms in the entire 200-room building.

It wasn't even a challenge locating the room where she had been staying. What was hard to find was any proof that she had ever been in the room. Maybe things have changed since I was a kid, but I'd have thought the room where someone disappeared would have been cordoned off and police warnings would have been all over the place if they suspected foul play. As a matter of fact, I know they would have had that ugly yellow tape up, because I've checked back on a few of the people who offended me and when they found the bodies, there was always yellow tape.

So I had to assume they weren't thinking there was foul play involved. I checked out the room either way. I looked around at her suitcases and her personal belongings where they were tucked neatly away.

There wasn't much to see. A few pairs of jeans, a dozen shirts and a couple of dresses. There was makeup, but nowhere near as much as I'd used through most of my career as a clown.

That was good. No woman should wear that much face paint, not unless she wants to look like a whore.

There was nothing I could use, no hint as to why she might have disappeared, though, let's be honest, I probably wouldn't have recognized a clue if it had jumped out and tried to scare the life out of me. I was never a police detective and Sherlock Holmes would never have to fear me getting in his way. Hell, I'm only starting to get the idea of how far police investigation techniques have come and I'm surprised that anyone ever gets away with anything.

The only reasons I haven't been captured are I never stay around one place too long, and I tend to wear a disguise when I'm in the open. Again, clown faces stands out a bit.

I left her hotel room as I'd found it, except for a necklace I took from her small jewelry box. I recognized the locket; it had belonged to my mother a lifetime ago.

The problem I had was that no one knew where my niece was, not even me. The only people who knew her were the mooks she was working with, and that was a problem because they were always on the move, sliding from one hotel room to another and then doing their performances.

I needed to get answers. I needed to know who was responsible for making Meaghan disappear.

And I needed to know if my last family member was alive or dead before I decided how I was going to react and who, exactly, I was going to be dealing with.

It wasn't an inconvenience. That's what I need to make clear here. I wasn't exactly angry, because, really, I didn't know if I should be angry. All I knew for certain was that the girl I'd come to find was missing. She was blood, but she was not family. What I wanted to see was if we could be family.

I know that now. I understand it better than I could have just then as I walked out of an anonymous hotel room and back onto the street not far from where I'd killed a man the night before.

Did I deserve to have a happy ending? Was I supposed to have a family and friends and something that resembled an ordinary life?

I didn't know, but I had been trying very hard to have one. I think my niece was my last chance for that. I think that was why I was so desperate to know where she was.

I took the stairs down from her room, circling down the long flights of steps without any conscious thoughts in my head. I wasn't capable of thinking, of feeling anything beyond the echoing desire to know something about where Meaghan might have gone.

I took the stairs because I didn't want to kill everyone around me. I think I needed that time to calm down, you see. Since my unusual resurrection, I have been much, much quicker to lose my cool.

And I have to tell you, it's never a good time for the people around me when that happens.

———

There was nothing about the day that was going the right way. The Carnivale de Fantastique was packing up their show and heading to Philadelphia. Carver should have been halfway to there already. He'd packed all of his traveling clothes (three suits and half a dozen shirts, plus some jeans) and was ready for the road.

Then some asshole stole a kid from in front of a coffee shop and now every available cop was on the road, searching for anyone who might have seen anything.

Oh, and the fingerprints on the note that had shown up? There were two sets. One belonged to the mother. The other belonged to Marco DeMillio, also known in certain circles as John Booker, primary suspect in several murders.

That made it his business. Carver was all for it, provided the fingerprint led to something. What he wanted deep in his heart was a suspect in chains. What he'd be happy with in the meantime was a kid safely returned to its parents.

Jeannie and Todd Westingham were justifiably terrified by what had happened. They were currently stuck in a media circus that wanted very much to talk to Carver, but he'd managed to slip away from the cameras, which suited him just fine. He had enough on his plate without having to answer stupid questions. Besides, his captain was better equipped for that sort of nonsense.

He was driving toward the station when the call came over the radio. The rain was just heavy enough to leave the wipers squeaking as they fought to clear the windshield and the sound was exactly the right type to make Michael clench his teeth. Someone had made an anonymous tip about where the baby could be found. That same someone had also told the parents and said if the cops showed up, things would go poorly.

Carver was not amused.

He set the flashers going to get him where he needed to be faster, but kept the actual siren quiet.

The streets were their normal insane mess of congestion with a side of just wet enough to cause fender benders, but almost everyone had the common sense to get the hell out of his way. Michael was glad of it. His stomach was twisting itself into knots at the idea of a kid being involved in any of the madness. Booker had been good enough not to kill him when he had the chance, but he didn't trust that to mean the man wouldn't kill someone else.

The building at 74 Bleakman Avenue was three stories tall and closed down nice and tight. Even if the police hadn't been alerted to the situation the building would have been sealed as whatever business had been in there was now gone. The entire structure was sealed and waiting for a new occupant or two. That at least made the situation easier to contain.

Michael wasn't in charge of the situation. He was just there because Booker was likely one of the people involved. As a result, there were already several squad cars in place and a dozen police officers with weapons drawn and armor in place. The weather wasn't getting any better, so most of the officers had their visors lifted, allowing them to see past the rain spots falling on the face plates.

He shook his head as he parked. This wasn't what was supposed to happen. He'd wanted a chance to see what was happening, wanted to see if he could spot Booker and maybe get the man to surrender the child and then himself.

Instead there were cars everywhere, there were even news vans pulling up down the road, and in the center of the madness, there were the Westinghams, who were looking as nervous as pigs in the slaughter line. The couple had parked directly in front of the building and was trying to look everywhere at once. Todd Westingham was looking from one cop to the next, possibly trying to determine who was in charge of the situation that was supposed to be a quiet affair. His thinning hair was plastered to the top of his head and the wild look in his eyes was enough to let Carver know the man wasn't at all happy with the media circus forming at the perimeter.

Just a short distance away, a uniformed cop was pointing at a cameraman who had decided it was time to get a closeup of the couple. The two were arguing, but not in a way that promised violence.

Tom Keegan looked his way and shook his head. Carver returned the gesture, silently agreeing with the man. This was a clusterfuck waiting to happen.

"What the hell happened to 'just the parents?'" He spoke softly, not daring the wrath of whichever district was actually in charge of the situation. He'd been reamed enough for the present time.

"Jenkins decided this was the best move. He's got Fire and Rescue on their way, just in case someone should actually show up and be offended by him breaking all the established rules." Keegan's voice was harsh, which was not surprising under the circumstances. Jenkins was looking to win any possible confrontation through sheer intimidation and Keegan didn't think that was going to work. Neither did Carver, who had dealt with Booker and didn't think the man could be intimidated.

The cars and lights had already started drawing a crowd, and Carver looked around until he spotted Jenkins. He headed toward the man, already knowing he was going to regret opening his mouth.

Jenkins was a tough old warhorse. That was the problem. The man wasn't really willing to change. He either refused to acknowledge that criminals had changed or he simply wasn't capable of getting it. Either way, the man in charge of the 7th Precinct had just screwed up as far as he was concerned.

"Captain, are you sure this is the best way to handle the situation?" He spoke the words and part of him was already preparing for the screaming match.

The man's eyes flicked across his face as roughly as a vicious slap. "Excuse me, Carver. I didn't realize you'd been promoted to captain of my precinct." There was open hostility in the man's tone.

"Have you dealt with Booker? The man mangled a cop for getting in his way." He spoke the words and knew immediately that he had miscalculated. The captain bristled.

Before the man could explode properly—and Michael could see the pressure building inside the man—he was interrupted by Jeannie Westingham's bloodcurdling scream.

The woman was looking up at the top of the abandoned building and pointing with one hand while the other raked across her pasty face.

Carver looked up and frowned at what he saw.

Maybe it was Booker up there and maybe it wasn't, but either way things were slipping fast into the surreal.

He didn't know Jenkins all that well—they worked from different police precincts—but he'd have hazarded a guess the man either had officers on the roof or working their way in that direction. If so, he hoped they were working their way up and hadn't yet reached their destination, because the man standing on the edge of the building was going to be a very serious problem.

Booker, or someone who looked a lot like him, stood just back from the edge of the sealed building, his left hand held out and waving a small bundle. That bundle moved, swayed in his arm and fussed with tiny arms and legs. Precipitation had soaked through the swaddled blanket around the toddler and dripped down toward the ground three stories below.

"Hunter!" The infant's mother screamed loudly, her voice breaking.

Carver looked up, his eyes tracking the man on the roof. It was Booker, he was almost certain of it, but he'd changed. The wanted man wore dark gray slacks and a dress shirt, over which he'd slipped an overcoat. His wardrobe was of less interest than the fact that his face had been painted.

Stark white skin, so white that it had to be painted, was covered with dark blue triangles over and under the eyes and a broad, bright red smile painted over his mouth and even painted dimples. The man was dressed as a clown. He'd even dyed his hair the same shade of blue as the mask around his eyes. He couldn't have advertised his presence better if he'd tried.

After Westingham screamed, everyone grew silent.

So it was quiet when Booker spoke.

"What? I wasn't clear enough when I said 'no cops?'"

Jenkins lifted a bullhorn and called out with a deep, powerful, electronically enhanced voice. "You need to step back from the edge of the building. You need to set the boy down on the roof and then you need to place your hands on the top of your head. You are under arrest."

Booker waved the child in his hand over the edge of the roof, eliciting several gasps and a loud shriek from the infant's mother.

"You want me to set him down? Are you sure about that?"

"Noo! Nooooo!" The Westinghams both screamed.

Booker looked at the parents for a moment and then back to the police chief. "Your choice! You back away or I let Junior here bounce!" Carver stared hard, studying the man. The eyes were as cold and blue as he remembered. More importantly, he believed the man would do it.

"You have to back away, Jenkins."

The police captain nodded his head and then turned away from the bullhorn. "I have men up on that roof."

"Men on the roof won't stop him from dropping that baby."

"They'll move in as soon as he sets the boy down. We just have to get him to set the boy down safely."

Booker shook his head. There was no way he could have heard them from three stories up, but that was the impression that sank in just the same.

"I really don't think the dead men on this roof are going to help, Captain Jenkins."

The words chilled Michael to the bone. Either the clown had, in fact, heard him talking with the captain, or he had gotten the man's name from one of the cops on the roof. Either way, it wasn't a good situation.

"Back away from the roof and gently set your hostage down on the roof!" Jenkins bellowed into the bullhorn, the sound distorted and broken.

Booker spoke again, his voice confident and his tone falsely cheerful. "Do you know what my favorite part of choosing the roof is?"

Carver shook his head. This was going to go badly, he felt it in his heart and in the way his testicles tried to hide inside his guts.

Jenkins played the same card again as if it might suddenly work better. "Back away from the roof!"

Booker opened his coat, revealing the assault rifles he'd taken from the police officers on the roof. Carver recognized the make.

"I got new toys out of the deal! Wanna see who's a better shot, captain?"

"Jesus Christ, Jenkins, use your fucking head! He has a hostage."

"I know that, goddamnit!"

"Please! Please, don't hurt him!" The man called out, dropping to his knees and actively begging the stranger on the roof not to hurt his only son. Carver looked at Westingham and shivered.

"Mister Westingham! Just the man I wanted to see. You come on up here, and I'll release your son to you. How's that sound for a bargain?"

Westingham was standing in a flash and heading for the front of the building.

"Stay where you are, sir!" Jenkins barked the order through his bullhorn and for half a moment, it looked like the father would listen to him. Then the man started forward again.

"Not the front door, my good man. Try the side entrance. I left it open." Booker spoke loudly enough for everyone to hear.

Jenkins opened his mouth again and raised the bullhorn. Before he could make a comment, the clown-faced man stepped forward and waved the child like a rag doll. The baby started crying.

"This isn't a puppet, Captain Jenkins! This is Hunter Westingham! He dies if you interfere again, do you understand me?"

Carver leaned forward fast. "Screw catching the man. Worry about the baby. We can catch him another time."

Jenkins didn't look in his direction, but he spoke to him. "I'm not a moron. I'll let the man have whatever he wants."

"Then you should tell your people that." He didn't dare point. Two cops were sliding toward the side entrance.

Jenkins raised the bullhorn without hesitation. "No one moves on the perpetrator. Everyone stand prepared, but stand down!"

The two policemen stopped where they were and Carver breathed a small sigh of relief.

"Good man! We might get a safe baby out of this yet!" Booker smiled and then threw Hunter Westingham into the air. The child waved his arms and legs and every single soul there froze for a moment, terrified.

Before the infant could fall, Booker caught him with his other hand. More water spilled from the wet bundle of clothing and everyone watching held their breaths, fearing what would happen if the bundle were too slick to clutch properly. Below him, Jeannie Westingham broke into tears.

Booker pointed with his free hand, his face angry under the makeup. "Oh, stop being a baby! If you hadn't left him in a running car he wouldn't be here right now! I'd have just met up with your husband later and asked him what I need to ask him." Booker leaned over the side a bit more, dangerously close to overbalancing himself. His face broke into a wild smile. "But this way's a lot more fun!"

Carver looked at Jenkins. The man's hands were shaking. He wasn't surprised to feel his own shaking as well.

Just to make sure everyone was paying attention to him, Booker threw the boy even higher into the air on the second toss and then caught the squirming, screaming infant behind his back.

He held the child there as Todd Westingham walked toward him, red faced, panicky and shaking. Westingham came forward timidly, his eyes wide and worried.

Carver would have sold his soul to overhear the conversation between the two men.

They talked for several moments, and while he could hear none of it, he could see Westingham's surprised expression and then the growing dread on the man's face.

There was more pleading, and then there were tears. He could not hear Booker, but he could just make out the angry tones of the man's voice.

He could see the father drop to his knees a second time and crawl, his hands held out in supplication.

Booker pointed and the man rose and headed off the roof of the building. Booker kept the baby.

Booker was calm as he waited. He stayed that way until he saw Westingham walk out of the building and stand next to his wife.

"Good man, Mr. Westingham. Very well done. But you know what?"

Westingham looked up at the angry voice and shook his head slowly.

"You should have turned them into the police!" Carver shook his head. Something big was being discussed and he needed to know what the hell it was.

Before anyone could respond, Booker drew one of the rifles from his coat and started firing down on the couple who looked up, eager only to have their child returned to them. The bullets struck the ground around them for a moment and then the stream of death moved in the right direction and tore through the husband and wife.

Michael Carver had seen death several times in his career and had caught at least one mutilation courtesy of the man on the roof. Watching the couple die was right up at the top of his list for horrific moments. The two people staggered and shivered and nearly exploded as the bullets slammed through them and into the ground. A few of the bullets ricocheted from the ground in a flurry of muddy explosions and had half of the officers diving for cover.

The cops who stood their ground, including Carver and Jenkins, drew their weapons and focused on the man on the roof.

Booker looked back down at them and smiled, the child in his hand crying and purple faced. He dropped the assault rifle and watched it fall to the ground, not but a few feet from the people he'd just murdered.

"Well now, kiddies, how do you suppose I'm going to get out of this one?" It had to be his imagination, but Michael would have almost sworn the man was looking directly at him as he spoke.

Hunter kept crying as Booker paced along the edge of the building and all of the police officers watched him, tracked him in the sights of their weapons. The roof had to be a slippery nightmare for footing, but Booker never slipped and never seemed the least bit worried about where he stepped. Carver stared, slowly following every step the man made and hating that there didn't seem to be a way to stop him without killing or seriously risking the boy.

Jenkins's breaths came in ragged gasps. Carver looked his way for a moment and had to wonder if the man was having a heart attack. His face was sweating and had taken on a green hue that was very uncomplimentary.

Booker was almost out of sight, but the captain said nothing, did nothing, except stare.

The rain increased, the water falling harder, until visibility became almost non-existent.

And then Booker was coming back at high speed. The clown didn't run at the edge of the building, he raced, his feet striking the roof in long, furious strides that sent plumes of dirty water splashing up from the rooftop. The baby in his hand shrieked indignantly as they approached and everyone on the ground watched, horrified.

Hunter Westingham sailed high into the air, screaming, howling his fright out into the heavens for all to hear. As the infant rose higher, Booker reached the end of the roof and leaped into the open air. The coat around him spread like wings, and Michael could clearly see that the rifles he'd had under his coat before were no longer there. One of them at least was in his hand.

Hunter shrieked as he stopped rising and started to descend.

Booker was screaming laughter as he fell toward the ground below and for one moment that hyena call and the infant's cries were the only sounds. Then the ratcheting coughs of the rifle started and bullets cut the air into shreds.

Michael felt the projectile slide past his ear with a hot humming noise. The sound was so low he felt it more than heard it. He might have marveled over that, and later he would most certainly experience a few nightmares remembering the moment, but mostly he was too busy trying to dodge the blood that splashed his way. Jenkins was not as lucky, you see. He was hit three times by bullets and each of them was a shot that would have killed him.

Michael hit the ground with a splash and scrambled, crawled, sought a new angle, a better chance to help stop the madman.

There was a deep metallic crunching noise that was followed immediately by the sound of people screaming.

By the time Carver could spot the clown again, Booker was rolling to his feet and climbing out of the ruin of the Westinghams' vehicle. He looked cheerful. The sick bastard was smiling past even the painted grin on his face, his teeth wide and perfect and white, his gums the color of blood.

It looked like the man had bounced off the hood and landed roughly. The engine had been driven into the street beneath the vehicle and the deep imprint caused by his weight pounding into hood was apparent.

Even as he was starting to stand, Hunter Westingham landed behind him, his cries immediately silenced.

In the distance the cameramen focused on one image and then another. Several of the people watching stood horrified and looked at the dead child, pale and shaken. Perhaps it was true that gathering crowds liked to see blood, but whatever the case, it seemed their desire for violence had been sated.

Michael Carver looked at the dead boy on the pavement. His shape was wrong, ruined, twisted. He'd landed very close to his parents, who had been killed by the same man in the clown's face. Even as he stared, horrified, he could see the infant's blood mingling with the growing red pool around his mother and father.

Carver looked at the man he'd come to arrest. He had no doubt that John Booker was the person under the makeup.

Carver reached into the small of his back and pulled a different weapon than his service piece.

He took aim and fired, shooting to kill.

The first bullet pounded into Booker's chest and staggered him back. As the clown was facing him he could see the surprise, the pain on the man's face. Booker looked directly at him as he aimed a second time and fired. There was no consideration of his career, of the legalities of his actions or even of his future as a free man. Carver simply fired again, intending to kill the man in front of him.

The second bullet caught him in the throat and blew a chunk from the back of his neck. Carver fired a third time and a fourth, striking his target each time. Holes blossomed from vines of blood and flesh, and John Booker twitched and shivered with each blow.

Carver unloaded his weapon into the man.

He wasn't alone. Tom Keegan stared at him for several heartbeats and then looked at the body of Captain Jenkins where he lay dead on the ground. The officer then slipped his registered firearm into his holster and reached for a revolver strapped to his ankle. Not every officer carried extra firearms. Not even half of them. Most of them also knew that fingerprints could trace any weapon fired back to them or by the television cameras aimed their way.

So not every police officer on the scene lost his temper. Not every single cop there committed murder that day, but most of them helped and the ones that didn't lied about it later.

The cast and crew heard about the madness, of course. It was on the news and it was spread all over the televisions, with graphic displays of the deaths that happened. It didn't matter that no one needed to see the deaths; they were played anyway, every fifteen minutes when the local news wasn't running and every five minutes when the news shows took over. The images didn't need to be blurred by digital enhancement. The heavy rains had already distorted the pictures that were filmed. Raindrops obscured details, but not enough to let anyone pretend they weren't seeing a massacre.

Tia watched it all with a growing sense of horror. She recognized the clown. She'd seen him on the stage here, watching her as she stretched. Him or someone who looked a lot like him, which meant someone who looked a lot like that creepy Booker guy they'd been after.

In any event, it looked like maybe the worst of that was over at least, but still, the poor family....

She'd be glad when they left Virginia and made it up to Philadelphia. Maybe then there would be less grief and everything could just get back to normal.

Her mother had called earlier, of course, as soon as she heard that there had been a killing. She didn't call every time someone was shot down, but when she'd heard there was a clown involved, she'd immediately assumed the Carnivale was involved somewhere along the way.

Talking the woman out of hysterics had been an interesting challenge. Her mother wanted Tia to come home, to be safe and secure in the arms of her parents. Tia wasn't having anything to do with that. She had bruises on her bruises and sore muscles that wouldn't give her a moment's peace. She'd earned every single bump and sore spot and had no intention of quitting now that she was positioned for her dreams. However, she was in no position to argue with her mother, so she instead lied and said the clown had no connection to the Carnivale.

That was a lie, too. She knew better. The family that had been murdered, the man Westingham, had been the head of acquisitions for the company. That was one of the things brought up at the meeting first thing when everyone got together. He was a member of the family as far as the Carnivale was concerned and they always made sure everyone knew when there was something to hear.

Funeral services weren't really being held for the people who'd been murdered by that Booker man, but the troupe had a brief service, just a time for people to talk about the three members of the cast and crew who had been done wrong.

There was a lot to say, too. Not so much about Elizabeth Montenegro—though there were some nice phrases, mostly people talked about her abilities and not about her as a person—but everyone had liked Gary Peck and Brad Lowman. Both had been hardworking men and both had always had time to shoot the shit or even buy an occasional round of drinks. Peck in particular had been a character, and there were endless anecdotes about him. She'd barely known him and had virtually no contact with the others; still, she felt the loss of the other people around her and that spread through her at the strangest times. Or maybe she was just more homesick than she realized.

Leslie came out of her dressing room with a frown on her face that aged her easily ten years.

"What's wrong?" Tia felt her skin tighten. Leslie was always in a good mood. Her frown was as unsettling as lightning strikes on a sunny day.

"The big wigs are supposed to be coming down to meet everyone."

"Is that bad?"

Leslie's pretty face seemed incapable of completely escaping a frown, but Tia thought maybe that just meant she was thinking very hard or was as puzzled by everything as Tia felt.

"Not really bad," she said. "Just different. I don't think they normally come down for the shows unless they have some business to take care of."

"Well, we've had some weird stuff going on."

"Don't remind me." Leslie's frown dissipated a bit. "I hear we're finally going to be able to move on at the end of the week. So, yeah, looks like they've got all the scheduling problems fixed at least."

"Well, good, because I'm pretty sure I have all this stuff down."

"Better hope you do."

"Yeah? What do you know that I don't?" It was the way that Leslie said it that had Tia nervous.

"The big bosses are going to want to see the show, so they're putting us on again tonight. An extra showing so we can entertain the big wigs and their special guests."

"What aren't you telling me?"

"It's gonna be all you, Tia. I'll be there to back you up, but they want to see you in action."

Tia felt her stomach fall through the floor at the thought. Her first show, and it was a command performance.

Life on the Road: Part Nine

I can't even say for sure exactly how long I'd wandered Serenity Falls before I found my benefactor, I just know that he looked at me and scowled as our paths crossed.

That was rather interesting, you see, because until that moment no one had been able to see me, or feel me, or hear me. No one. I tried; believe me, I tried. I did my best to get noticed and it was not meant to be.

The air was cold and winter had the town in its grip. I walked through the snow and felt no bite of the winter's chill, nor the caress of the wind against me. I just walked, looking for answers to questions I couldn't even ask.

The people of the town did not see me. Occasionally an animal would notice me, but most of them simply stared and then ran as fast as they could. When a person did get a sense that I was nearby, I could see them looking, searching for whatever caused them to sense something wrong and never seeing me, even if I was right next to them and waving my hands frantically. I did not exist for them in a conscious way, I was merely that odd breeze, that vaporous memory to come along and haunt them, I suspect.

I was a ghost, you see, truly and properly dead without a body or the limitations and advantages of the same. I wandered, yes, but I also explored. There were things to see, people to investigate.

I wandered through the farm where the Halston Carnival had been when I was murdered. There was no sign that we had ever been there.

I could feel the deaths of my friends, could sense the carnage that had fallen on the grounds not far from the main farmhouse.

I could see the farmer, the man who had shoved a shotgun against my face and asked to see his children. I saw him and I followed him for several days, infuriated by his mere existence, as if he was somehow the cause of all my suffering. Oh, I knew even then that it wasn't true, but he was a part of it, him and his miserable neighbors.

I suppose some part of being a ghost is being able to remember your life and death. Mostly your death. I stood where I had burned and felt the entire thing again and again, each moment of my pain easily accessed and relieved. I could step to my left and feel the loss of Carter. Experience the agonies he'd endured. A few paces in the opposite direction and I could feel the flames as they ran into Lou Crompton's lungs and cooked his heart. Back half a yard and I felt the burns that consumed Bert.

I lived the deaths of each and every one of my friends and myself again. I burned and they burned and then as I stepped past the confines of the trailer and walked further, I caught other deaths.

They murdered the Alexander Halston Carnival of the Fantastic. Make no mistake about that. It was murder, cold and calculated and very, very violent. Some people got burned, others got shot and still more of my friends and my second family were stabbed or beaten to death by the good people of Serenity Falls, New York. Remember that, because later you'll need to understand what I was thinking when I came back from the dead. Near as I can tell only two people got out of the show alive. The snake man and Doreen Miles. I don't begrudge either of them surviving. Oh, I know the details. They told the farmer exactly who was responsible for killing his kin. Exactly who. No mistakes. But that wasn't enough for Serenity Falls. The town demanded blood for blood, only they demanded it tenfold.

I counted the dead as I wandered around where the circus had been set up, and I lived each death no less than five times. I memorized them. I needed to, you see, because I needed to understand the reasons for their murders.

That's what they were. Murders. Someone came along and killed each and every member of the Alexander Halston Carnival of the Fantastic that they could get their hands on. The only ones spared as far as I could tell, were the animals. The people that got away? I think that was an accident, really, not a deliberate kindness.

I haunted that ground for a long time, day and night, for long enough to let the moon grow full and fade away to the merest sliver in the night sky again. The cold did not faze me, the ice did nothing to chill me and the sun was merely a brightness that was different than the moon.

I let the hatred grow and fester with each death I experienced again, and I fought against the pull of the ground. I felt the cold hands that pulled at me, tried to keep me away from the living and dead alike, but I refused to succumb. The forces that pulled at me were strong, but not fast enough to hold me.

Eventually I left the farm. I couldn't stay there, couldn't continue to lose myself in the memories of death without risking the loss of everything that made me who I am. So I left and wandered Serenity Falls again, moving from house to house and experiencing the murders that had occurred in each location where death was prevalent.

Murder was a common thing in Serenity Falls. Old or new hardly seemed to matter. Murder was something the town seemed good at. I wasn't surprised, merely disappointed.

The man who spotted me walked along the edge of the cemetery, his face set in deep concentration. He frowned as he stared at the cracked sidewalk surrounding the memorials to the dead and his eyes rose up and followed me.

I stopped walking, shocked to feel eyes on me for the first time since I had escaped my prison. I stared back just as intensely, half expecting the man was merely thinking and looking in my general direction, but no, he actually stared at me, our gazes locked.

Finally he pointed a finger at me. "You should not be here." His words were casual enough, but held a tone of accusation.

"You can see me?" I stared harder, unbelieving.

"I can see that you aren't where you belong...." He spoke then, to himself it seemed, muttered words that meant nothing to me and I felt the hands that had sought me before come back, eager to pull me into the depths.

I fought them, I tried to escape their grasp, but this time they were more determined than before. The cold fingers caught me, pulled at my essence and drew me down into the nothingness again.

And I escaped again, this time at a much faster rate. If I had to guess, only a few days passed before I met the stranger again.

He was an older man, pleasant enough in appearance, with short gray hair and a stocky body that was sliding comfortably into old age. He was as unassuming as anyone I had ever seen, right up until the time he saw me. For one moment only anger swept over him, a cold and dark thing that made him terrifying. Let me clarify this: I had relived my death and the deaths of literally hundreds of people while I wandered Serenity Falls, and despite all of that suffering, that anger and that pain, the man in front of me managed to scare me senseless.

Then the anger disappeared and was replaced by curiosity.

He waved his hand and cast me down again.

I got out of his trap faster than before, comfortable with my ability to escape the confines of the endless prison.

And this time when I escaped, he was waiting for me, his face set and calm as I slipped away from Hell and settled back in the land I was no longer a part of.

"You shouldn't be able to do that." His tone was conversational.

"Send me back again you sonofawhore and I'll do it again." I was angry and I was scared and I was ever-so-full of bluster. I had no desire to continue playing this game. It was inconvenient to say the least.

The man laughed. Not at me, exactly, but with great humor. When he looked at me again, he was still smiling.

"What's your name, boy?"

"Rufo the Clown." I wasn't willing to give him my real name. I had no desire to speak with him, or to deal with him any longer. I'd have not answered him at all, but anyone who could lock me in the nothingness was someone I wasn't overly fond of deliberately offending.

"Well, 'Rufo,' I think we might well become good friends."

"You sent me to Hell."

"Oh, not hardly, my boy. Not hardly. I just sent you to a holding station of sorts."

"I don't much care. You sent me there. Twice!"

"And you got back and Rufo, my lad, no one has ever gotten back from there on his own. Ever."

I could have bragged or preened or pointed out that I was an escape artist, but it didn't mean anything to me just then. I was scared. I did not want to go back to that place again.

"Calm down, lad. I won't be sending you there again. I just had to make sure I knew what I was dealing with."

I stared hard. I had no reason to trust him. He'd hardly proven himself worthy of anything but my hatred.

"Listen carefully, Rufo. You have certain needs, and I know you have a lot of questions. I have certain needs and a lot of answers. We should consider a little bargaining."

There at last was a concept that I could understand. Curiosity meant nothing when compared with a chance for real answers.

"Fine. What do you propose?"

The man looked at me for a few seconds, a smile playing at his lips, but not quite manifesting, and then he nodded his head. "Here's my deal. I answer your questions, you do me a few small favors."

The laughter that got past my lips was entirely accidental. "What can I do for you? I can't touch anything. I can't do anything."

"Well, now, that's not quite as true as you think it is. You just haven't learned how to do the things I want you to do."

You wouldn't think a middle-aged man sliding toward retirement would know much about ghosts, would you? It turns out my benefactor wasn't just a man speeding toward his golden years. His name was Albert Miles, and he was, well, he was something of a sorcerer.

We got along famously.

I could fill volumes about the things Miles taught me. I could fill more volumes about what he made me do in exchange for the knowledge. Instead, I'll hit the high notes.

He helped me manifest. Not the easiest thing for ghosts to do, but they can manage it. He helped me learn about being dead, and what it really means. In exchange, I did small favors. Sometimes I looked in on other places and checked on people he wanted to know more about. I became a spy, I suppose. I was very good at it as almost no one ever suspected I was around. Oh, sure, an occasional shiver down the spine but very few people actually saw me, and those that did, well, there are ways to take care of that sort of thing.

As time went on, I learned to do more. And I became more important to my benefactor.

It's rather difficult to fully explain and I really have no desire to go that far into details, but I became a harvester of sorts. Miles did things in different places all across the world, I suppose, but I worked exclusively in the United States. He set things in motion, you see, certain actions that, when they worked out the right way for him, garnered him power in one form or another, most often in the shape of human souls. I don't pretend to fully understand everything, and I never needed to. All I needed to do was collect for him. The dead are everywhere. Most of them move on to some other place. Some might even just dissolve. But the ones that were left, they belonged to no one or they belonged to Albert Miles. He made bargains and collected his debts; or rather he had me collect them. From time to time someone would renege on a deal and I was asked to handle the matter personally.

In exchange, I was granted favors. I started small. I learned about what I needed to know and I asked for his consideration for certain favors.

Though it hardly matters in the grand scheme of things, Albert Miles had certain designs on Serenity Falls. He had plans for the place that involved the destruction of almost every living being in the area. To that end, he had set certain actions in motion and those actions were in part responsible for what happened to my friends and me. Miles called it being caught in the crossfire and I suppose that was a good enough way to put it. What had happened would have probably happened anyway, and the trouble would have died, but there was a chance that his actions had caused the situation to become more volatile and had led to the deaths of the entire group instead of only a select few.

Because he was just possibly complicit in the deaths of my second family, Albert Miles and I came to an arrangement. I helped him and he in turn agreed to bring the dead back to life, because that was within his abilities.

Sort of.

It's complicated.

I was a ghost. I never expected to have a chance to bring my friends back to life, but that chance existed and I had every intention of making it happen if I could.

I would have done anything for that second chance, and I did, too. You see, Albert Miles was a very powerful individual, and he was also a madman.

I started as a collector. I soon became a hit man.

I came back from the dead on my own, and in the process I became a killer.

Life and death are just full of surprises....

Chapter Ten: Looking for Millie (Part Ten)

There's an old saying about looking for a needle in a haystack. That's pretty much all that comes to mind when it comes to searching for my grandniece. I tried to do things the right way. I know that some people will have trouble believing me, but I did. I wrote letters to her last known address, I wrote more letters to Meaghan care of the Carnivale, and I wrote letters to their corporate offices. I wrote more letters for the span of three months than I had in my entire life. And all I got for my troubles was a whole lot of nothing.

I am not always a patient soul, but for my last family member, I was willing to try.

The Carnivale never responded. I tried every name I could think of, every possible position within the company, and I got nothing at all by way of response. I would have probably been satisfied with a simple letter telling me that Meaghan was no longer with the troupe, but getting no response at all? Well, that was an insult, to be honest. Seems to me that people could at least pretend a connection to polite society better when I was young. These days they don't even try.

Meaghan never responded.

I waited in Florida for half a year—don't worry, I found plenty to keep me busy—but I got nothing. And then I decided it was time to move on to the next stage of the game.

I would be lying if I said I'd kept up with Albert Miles, but I had ways to get in contact with him and he in turn had ways of getting answers, so I hopped a train and made my way up to New England. The weather was cold and Salem, Massachusetts was beautiful. The man lived in an ancient house that was perfectly kept. He didn't even wait for me to knock. He opened the door as I was climbing the stairs to his home.

"Cecil! What a delight!" He always called me Cecil when he wanted to be on my good side and I always let him. I don't answer to the name all that often anymore, because there is a lot of baggage that goes with that name, including a very short career in Hollywood. That's a different story for a different time. The good news is, no one would look at me and make any association with the comedian who showed up and then disappeared less than three years later. They were good years. I enjoyed my second life. That's all I'll say about that.

"I need your help, Albert. I'm at a loss." I spoke after we'd settled into his living room with hearty mugs of hot cocoa. He made good hot chocolate.

"You're looking for your niece, aren't you?"

"Grandniece."

He nodded his head. "What can I do for you, Cecil?"

"Let's not play games. I know you can find her."

"Of course I can. But why should I bother?"

The rage came then. It was a white-hot blast of anger that would have had most people terrified if they had seen me. Albert Miles didn't so much as flinch.

"You lied to me, Albert! We had a deal and you lied to me!"

"I did no such thing. The Hunter got in the way and you didn't stop him. If you'd followed the plan there would have been no difficulties." At that moment I think I could have killed him. I had been afraid of Albert Miles since the first time we met, but I think I could have killed him and never so much as blinked. He held up a hand and stopped me from saying something foolish. "Calm down, Cecil. We have things to discuss. I certainly don't hold you accountable for the Hunter getting in the way. But a bargain is a bargain and I fulfilled my end to the best of my ability as you fulfilled your end."

I knew where we were going. "What do you want from me?"

"What have I ever wanted from you, Cecil? I want your help with certain matters."

"And in exchange?"

"In exchange, I find out all that I can about your grandniece's whereabouts. I'll even find out about where your niece is, if you'd like."

It was a small thing, really. A simple matter of a young man in Washington State who had discovered certain secrets Albert preferred remain secret. I agreed to handle the matter, and he in turn agreed to find out all he could. He arranged transportation for me and I had the boy dead in a matter of hours.

When I came back I brought him fresh apples and the boy's eyes. He wasn't expecting the apples, but he was delighted to get them.

We settled in for another cup of cocoa and a long talk.

Albert sounded genuinely sorry when he told me that Cecilia had died of a drug overdose and that Meaghan had been murdered. He couldn't tell me who, exactly, had murdered her, but he gave me a short list of names.

"Meaghan is dead, Cecil." Albert was direct, but not unkind. "She isn't at peace, but she's closer to it that you'll likely ever get."

"You want to explain that to me?" I didn't take offense. It was simple math, really. I was a ghost for a long time, and I was good enough at being a pissed off dead man that I managed what should have been impossible and escaped from a prison designed solely to hold the dead. Peace had nothing to do with my afterlife.

"I couldn't get all the details you'd like without involving serious necromancy. Not the sort where I merely talk to the dead, but where I have to bring them back to this realm to get the answers. If I did that to Meaghan, she would suffer the consequences." He looked at me hard to make sure I understood exactly what he meant. I did. In order to get answers, he'd have been forced to pull Meaghan away from whatever course her spirit was on in the afterlife. There would have been a chance that doing so would cause her to lose her way in the world that exists after this one. That meant wandering the earth as a ghost. Not really a pleasant experience and I say that as a man in the know.

"I got names for you. Those names should have answers to your questions. If the answers suit your fancy, all the better. If not, I'll bring Meaghan back and you can ask her yourself."

"Could you bring her all the way back?"

"Of course, but you wouldn't want to pay the price."

"Would it cost less if I brought her back and you provided...shelter?"

"Like what was supposed to happen in Serenity Falls?"

I stared hard. The rage was still there, the hatred. No matter how he explained it, Albert had betrayed a trust. I should have had my second family back and instead, there was some very interesting wild life in Serenity Falls.

After the silence had stretched to the point of being uncomfortable, Albert smiled and nodded. "It can be arranged if you decide to do it. But only this once, Cecil. I'm not in the business of resurrection. If I were, I'd have had a far less complicated life so far."

He told me the names and he even told me where they could be found. There were several. Not all of them had been involved in her death, but all of them knew something about it. That was enough for me.

I've never thought of myself as a detective, but I have been known to get information when I needed it.

I can be very, very persuasive when the situation rises.

The first name on the list was Elizabeth Montenegro. She was one of the other demon girls. I'd seen her perform when I went to see Meaghan. I couldn't have pointed out which one she was, but that hardly mattered. In the time I'd spent waiting, the show had closed down and opened again, only this time around, Elizabeth wasn't just a background dancer she was the star of the show.

According to Albert, the girl had connections in the show, people who wanted to help her with her career in exchange for her silence.

I intended to see exactly how good she was at keeping her tongue.

The footage was blurry. Too blurry to let anyone see exactly who the hell had shot John Booker dead. Only one living officer knew that Michael Carver was at the scene of the murder and that man was already being interrogated regarding his possible connection to the death of the clown-faced killer.

Tom Keegan had looked Carver up and down and then handed the detective the firearm he'd used to blow several large holes in the dead man they'd both helped execute. "Get out of here, Carver. I never saw you. You were stuck in traffic."

Carver took the extra weapon and shoved it in his pocket. He left the scene very quietly and drove exactly seven and one half miles before he stopped, wiped down both weapons, and then dropped them off a bridge that led toward D.C.

By the time he got back to the scene, the news crews were swarming and the bodies had been photographed from every possible direction. He had been standing in the rain for a full five minutes and watching everything before dispatch told him to get his ass down to the Medical Examiner's office in order to possibly ID Booker.

He left the scene and drove carefully, his heart pounding hard enough to make him wonder if his ribs could survive the sustained beating.

There was a very real chance that he'd just gotten away with murder. Only time would tell. There was news camera footage for the police to go over with a fine-toothed comb, and there would likely be a lot of eyewitness reports as well. In the meantime, his bags were still packed and he had a body to identify.

Michael had to wait for Booker's body to be delivered before he could attempt to identify it. While he waited, he listened to the stories that were already growing in fits and whispers. Jenkins had killed the clown, according to several eyewitnesses. It had been a shootout between the two of them, old west style, and in the end, it had been a draw. For all the world, that seemed to be the most prevalent rumor, and while the coroner's office would certainly make a lie of the situation in due time it was as good a tale as anyone was likely to hear and a lot more pleasant than the truth of the matter.

Warren Anderson was the Medical Examiner on duty when Michael was called back to make his identification. The step was merely a formality, as the fingers had likely already been printed and the set of prints was probably already working its way through AFIS to find a match.

Still, Michael felt a certain morbid sense of curiosity about the situation. He wanted to look at the man he'd murdered. He wanted to mark the face that had just bought the right to haunt his nightmares for the rest of his life. It seemed only proper to get the details right from the beginning.

Warren looked uncomfortable as he nodded his head and rolled out the body.

"Not a pretty one, Warren?"

"Mike, you have no idea."

He swallowed the guilt that tried to rear up and strike at that comment. "So enlighten me."

The white cover over the body was pulled back, and Carver got his first close look at the body of his murder victim.

John Booker, Marco Demillio, or whatever his name really was, was very obviously dead. His throat was mostly blown out, and Michael could see the stainless-steel table under the man through the holes in his overcoat and the body beneath.

His face was untouched, unmarked despite the numerous shots. Death had taken the look of surprise from the man's face, but the features were still obscured beneath the thick white makeup. Carver slipped a glove onto his hand and reached out, touching one closed eyelid. He opened the eye and stared at the cold, blue eye that looked back.

For a second he thought the pupil dilated and suppressed a shiver.

Then he ran his hand over the face and shivered again. "Jesus." The marks on the clown's face were indentations, deep cuts that had healed a long time ago by the feel of it. He could slide his fingertips a quarter of an inch into the grooves hacked into the otherwise smooth skin around the eyes and the mouth, forming the shapes that distinguished the clown from all the rest of his ilk.

"Jesus Christ."

Warren coughed into his hand. "Is that your man, Booker?"

"I think so, but these scars…"

"The sort of thing that would stick out, wouldn't you think?"

"Yeah, and I don't remember seeing them before."

Warren moved closer and ran his own fingers over the deep marks around the cadaver's mouth. "Don't be too surprised. These days you can hide almost anything with makeup."

"No shit?"

"Well, look at the man. Who would have known the skin you're looking at was his regular flesh tone."

"Excuse me?" Carver's skin tried to crawl away.

"These colors are permanent. Either John Booker was a very inventive albino or he deliberately had his skin bleached of all pigmentation."

"Is that even possible?"

"I guess it must be, we're looking at it."

Michael had seen enough. "Near as I can tell when you consider the disfigurements, that is, in fact, John Booker, also known as Marco DeMillio according to his fingerprints."

Warren looked at him for a long moment and nodded. "Thank you, detective. I'll have a full report done in a few hours, I expect."

Carver stared long and hard at the corpse and shook his head. "No rush. I don't think I'm in a hurry to know anything else about his guy."

If the medical examiner thought that answer was unusual, he didn't say anything.

Carver had only been gone a few moments when Warren's assistant, Taylor, came in. Taylor was young, good looking and for reasons no one really understood, morbidly curious about everything. Warren considered that a plus. The odds were good a few of the women who dated the kid probably thought otherwise.

Taylor looked the cadaver over for a few moments, his eyes fixed on the odd disfigurements and then, while Warren prepared for the autopsy itself, his assistant started removing clothing from the body.

"The color goes all the way down." Taylor's voice held an unsettling amount of excitement at the notion.

"We'll get to that. In the meantime, please make sure you check the contents of the clothes for any possible contraband or evidence."

Taylor looked like he wanted to make a comment about knowing how to do his job, but he wised up before he could get himself in any trouble. Curiosity was indeed a plus in the field of forensics but that didn't mean talking about your discoveries would win any bonus points.

When the man was done removing and cataloguing the personal effects, Warren looked down at the body. True enough, the white color ran the entire length of the body and all of the body hairs seemed to be the same dark blue. The wounds were made all the more startling by the difference in color between the flesh and the bloody insides.

Warren reached to turn on the recorder to document all of the pertinent information for later transcription. Neither he nor Taylor would have the time to finish the report until later in the day and both of them had atrocious handwriting.

His hand struck the "record" button at the same time that the white hand covered his fingers and pressed the "stop" button.

Warren turned toward Taylor, annoyed that the man would even consider pulling pranks.

Instead he looked into the face of the dead clown, who was smiling at him.

"No, Doc. No record of this, please. Things have already gotten messy enough." He spoke as he held Taylor off the ground. The clown was sitting up on the examination table, his wounds abundant and obvious, his hand clenched tightly around Taylor's throat. Warren's assistant had turned a deep shade of red that spoke of how little blood was flowing to his head. He stared desperately at the medical examiner, perhaps hoping that he could somehow make the nightmare go away.

Warren Anderson let out a very loud scream as the clown reached for him. The sound was cut short by the fingers that caught his throat and squeezed until something in his trachea collapsed.

"Shhhhh, Doc," Rufo whispered softly. "We don't want to have to kill everyone in the building, do we?"

The eyes that regarded him were a light, cold blue, but nowhere near as frigid as the smile that parted blood red lips and bared perfect teeth.

Warren got to see the teeth closely around the same time he realized he could no longer breathe. He was just starting to panic when the clown opened his mouth and lunged, biting through his cheek and lips and pulling back a thick wedge of flesh.

The meat and muscle he consumed worked quickly, repairing the deep trauma his body had sustained as he was shot again and again. He ate quickly, but not quickly enough for Warren Anderson, who had the misfortune of being alive for most of what was done to him.

When he was done with the man in charge, he moved on to the young assistant. By the time he started feasting he was mostly healed and feeling more himself.

He dropped the young man on the ground and stood up, reaching for his neatly folded clothes.

At his feet, Taylor whimpered, far too gone to even scream any longer.

"Do you know that bastard shot me?" The clown looked down at him. "And not just once; I mean, you saw the bullet holes. He shot me a lot. You'd think there were rules against cops just shooting a man. I'd dropped my weapons and everything."

The pants and shirt were too bloody to be saved, so he took Taylor's clothes from his twitching, ruined body. The shirt was once again too ruined, but the pants seemed to fit him well enough.

"I think his name is Carver. Gonna have to remember that. No way am I letting him just kill me like that without suffering the consequences…." He was mostly talking to himself, but he looked at Taylor as he spoke, just for the companionship. "Used to be there were certain rules for policemen, you know? I mean, I'm a monster, that's a given, but him? He's supposed to protect and serve."

The coat had several layers of cloth and they'd soaked up some of the worst blood trails, still, in the long run it was too far gone to keep. He sighed and headed for the door marked OFFICE and there he found another coat as well as a nice hat. Neither of the men he'd left behind would need them.

She was alive. Not just living, but alive in a way she had never imagined possible. The auditorium was filled to capacity and Tia danced, moving with ease through steps that had already become part of her being. She told a story with her body, lived the motions rather than merely making them, and in the process she finally understood the simple beauty of the story.

There was heroism and tragedy alike for the characters, but in the end there was a sad sort of redemption and a funeral beauty to the tale.

When she was done, Tia stood with the other players and looked out into the audience, surprised by the explosive applause that fairly shook the building around them.

Leslie's applause was the loudest. She stood in full costume, ready to step out on stage if she was needed, but never made a move toward the performance area. Instead she jumped up and down and clapped her hands together furiously, smiling as bright a smile as Tia had ever seen in her life. Seeing her did wonders for Tia's heart, but her nerves never became a problem. In the long run it was the dance that mattered, the performance. She never lost her place despite her fears, and it was a wonderful, magical feeling.

Front and center in the audience sat a gathering of people who almost gave off an aura of power. They were the people who came up with the concepts, who did the hiring and firing and, in the long run, who signed the checks that paid all of the bills. They were the Board, and they were all powerful in the world of the Carnivale de Fantastique.

And they were applauding as loudly as anyone else in the audience. Tia could have wept tears of joy for that simple fact.

She stepped off the stage after the curtain closed for the third time, and the people around her exchanged hugs and back clappings and she was included. Every one of them knew it was her first time on a live stage and every one of them seemed to congratulate her. It was a wonderful feeling, made even better because it seemed the first time some of them had been willing to make her welcome.

Leslie hugged her furiously and kissed her cheek and then fairly ran her to the dressing room. Before Tia could ask what was happening, Leslie started explaining.

"They loved the show, and they want to meet you. The Board. Not just you, of course, all of us, but you have to be ready, because this is the big-time stuff. If they like us enough, we get invited back for next year, so we want to make our good impressions now."

"What?"

"I'm babbling. Just get all prettied up. Come on, hurry, because if the Board likes your stuff enough, you don't even have to go through all the auditions again. That's what happened with Elizabeth

Montenegro. She never had to audition again, she just got the lead, so let's go impress us some big wigs."

Tia hugged her friend tightly, feeling the girl's heart beat next to her own and feeling, for just the briefest moment, like kissing her friend as deeply as she would a lover. It was more than physical, though that attraction was part of it. Leslie had gone so far beyond merely being a friend to her. The girl had guided her through every step of the entire process and been there again and again. Tia could hardly believe she'd have managed to get even as far as she had if the girl had set out to make her look like anything but a star. Leslie was her hero, pure and simple.

And when Leslie kissed her on the lips, she did not pull back. It was only the two of them in the dressing room, both of them still in their costumes, covered in Spandex and sequins and shiny foil capes that rustled and tinkled with every move they made and oh, how the sounds mingled as the kiss exploded into something more.

Tia's hands moved on their own, exploring the wonderful sleek curves and planes of Leslie's body and she felt her heart thud even faster in her chest as Leslie's hands slid over her stomach, up to her chest and then around her back. They kissed a second time with much more deliberate heat.

And the best night of Tia's life got more wonderful than she would have ever expected and a great deal more complicated as well.

The cast was a delight, just as the board members had expected. Of particular interest were the two new leads, both the initial replacement for Montenegro and the girl who was now working as the stand in. They were both late for the cast party, both looked a little shell-shocked and both also looked guilty as sin.

In their times each member of the board had been a performer. They could guess what was going on and most of them were right on the money. None of which mattered as long as the show continued on schedule without any added drama or negative news stories.

They'd come into town ostensibly to show their support for the recently dead, and that was as good a story as any. In truth, they had come to discuss certain matters with Todd Westingham, and that matter had now gotten out of hand in the extreme.

Todd Westingham was dead and most of the board couldn't decide whether or not that was a good thing. Adam Salinger had a firm opinion on the matter, but it was best to keep that opinion to himself until the rest of the board voiced their beliefs.

Adam stared at the carpet in front of him, trying to read his future in the patterns that had been woven into the fibers. There was no pattern to discern as far as he could tell and if things kept going poorly, there might not be a future worth noticing.

His phone rang as he was looking at the two girls who played Ramona.

"Hello?" the number was local, but not one he recognized.

"Helluva show you guys put on tonight." The voice was cheerful.

"Thanks, we do our best." He had no clue who he was talking to, but it didn't do to alienate strangers, especially if they were with the press.

"Fatima, though, the belly dancer? Not right for the part. Belly dancers should have a little meat on their bones." Adam couldn't have agreed less. He liked dancers: their bodies were pure muscle and every movement seemed enhanced when a dancer was moving over him. And he always preferred that the girls do the work.

"We'll take that into consideration. How can I help you Mister…?" He kept the edge out of his voice though it wasn't easy. The last thing he wanted or needed in his life was another backseat producer. They already had plenty of those in the form of investors.

"My name is Cecil Phelps. You can call me Rufo."

"Well, what can I do for you, 'Rufo'?"

"Here's the thing. My grandniece used to work for you. Last year I think it was. Her name was Meaghan Phelps. Does that name ring a bell?"

Did the name ring a bell? Of course it did. That was one of the reasons they were down here in the first place.

"No, I can't say that it does. But the Carnivale employs a great many people, Mr. Phelps, and I simply don't know all the names."

"Oh, I think you'd remember her. She was quite lovely, played one of the Infernal Dancers in the last show."

"No, sorry. I got nothing." Lies, lies, lies. He remembered her very well, both when she was alive and when they had to clean up the mess at the end of the show. She had been a beautiful girl, and an asset to the show. He still regretted what happened.

"Well, she disappeared after one of the shows last year and never turned up. Is she starting to ring any bells now?"

"Mister Phelps, any insurance claims you would like to make can be handled through the insurance companies that handle our benefits packages. Any attempts at a lawsuit should be handled by reaching our attorneys, who are on record and can be reached at their offices. Aside from that, what else can I do for you?" His annoyance was growing. There were people he wanted to get to know better, wanted to mingle with, and the imbecile on the phone was making that very, very challenging.

"Todd Westingham assured me that you were the man I wanted to speak to about where, exactly, my grandniece's body could be found."

He'd read the phrase "my blood ran cold" on several occasions, but it never seemed like a real possibility until that moment. His heart seemed to slow, his mouth tasted coppery, his vision faded for a moment and by God, his blood felt like it had suddenly frozen in his veins even as it pushed through his body.

"I have no idea what you're talking about." His lips felt numb, but he made them form the words anyway.

"Well, Todd was swearing on his son Hunter's life when he told me everything. I'm thinking he was probably telling me the truth." The tone hadn't changed at all: the man still sounded as cheerful as could be, happy to be alive and happier still to be talking on the phone.

Adam had seen the news. He'd watched the clown-faced man get blown to hell at least a dozen times before the carnage lost his interest. That man had been named John Booker according to police sources. Cecil Phelps was nobody. And he'd have remembered if he'd ever met somebody name "Rufo."

"I'm going to hang up now, Mr. Phelps. I recommend that you forget this number. If you don't, there might be legal consequences."

"Really?"

"We have excellent lawyers on retainer. Have a nice night, Mr. Phelps."

"Don't you hang up on me, rube." The words were hissed, filled with cold hatred.

Adam disconnected the call and powered down his phone. Let the man call. He could delete the messages later.

Around him the party progressed. The people were happy and having a good time, even the two girls who kept looking toward each other as if they might have made a horrible mistake.

Adam did his best to get back into the proper mood. It wouldn't do to have investors and reporters looking at the board members and wondering what they were hiding.

The girl who played Fatima, the devil girl and seductress of the story, walked past and delivered the sort of smile that caused men to get stupid. Adam smiled back and after a moment's hesitation, followed after her. It never hurt to get to know the cast a little better, after all.

Meaghan Phelps would have disagreed, but Adam had already put the dead girl out of his mind. The body was hidden very well, and no one would be finding her. Besides, the past was in the past and he preferred living for the now.

———

He stared at the cell phone and chuckled. It was not a pleasant sound. The man who had owned the phone in question had been yelling at a four-year-old boy and had called the child several names that Rufo felt children should not learn until they were much, much older.

The man was dead now, his body folded over itself and rammed deep into a trashcan. Rufo could have seen one foot if he wanted to look, but the dead man was no longer of any concern.

He had different things on his mind. The parking lot for the theater was only half as full as it had been on any of a dozen recent nights. The show was done and the reception was taking place. He walked slowly until he spotted Salinger's car. It took very little effort to sabotage the engine. True to Todd's word, the man was easily spotted and he believed in renting expensive vehicles. Rufo knew damned near nothing about cars, but he could tell a luxury vehicle from an economy model. The damage was nothing major, just the sort of thing that would cause a delay. Loosen a wire here, pull a plug there and the next thing you know, the cars are leaking all sorts of important things that help them run.

Rufo wanted the delays, but not too soon. He wanted everything to look just right when Salinger came to the meeting the board had scheduled for the next morning. He wanted to make sure Salinger got the message loud and clear.

Life on the Road: Part Ten

Being dead was not fun. Being a ghost had certain perks, but when you get right down to it, I wanted to be alive again, truly alive. I made a deal with Albert Miles. I served him and he helped me with my dilemma. I wanted to live again. I wanted the rest of my second family to live again, too.

To that end, I served the man faithfully. I won't lie and say we became close friends or anything of the sort, but we talked from time to time and we had certain similarities in what we sought from the world. We understood each other.

I got my second chance around the same time the curse Miles had put on Serenity Falls came due. He'd spent a very long time making sure that everything was just so, every possible contingency was covered, and then he told me to pick a few close friends and get back to the business of living.

Escaping death was an interesting challenge but rebirth? Whooo boy. That was a unique experience.

I needed a body, and he provided one. I'm trying to figure the best way to word this and I suppose I should just be direct. I had to claim the body as my own. It was already occupied by a no-account loser named Marco DeMillio. He made me look like a saint. Kid was already a murderer and a rapist when I took his form. I couldn't just climb on in, you know. I had to remake him in my image so to speak. I guess by that point I already knew certain things about myself, because the body was different when I was done with it. The least of the changes was the whole clown face thing.

Everything that happened in Serenity Falls is a story for another day, but I need to go ahead and get something off of my chest here. There's a thing out there that looks perfectly human, and it calls itself the Hunter. It's not human, and it has probably done a lot more damage to the world than I ever will.

The Hunter ruined everything. I was supposed to bring my friends back with me. They would have had new bodies, new lives, but they would have lived again. They'd have had a second chance to live their lives out, and they would have been comfortable. Jonathan Crowley, the Hunter, made sure that didn't happen.

I tried to kill him for that and I failed. He was in a big top tent that was under my control and I lit him on fire and the tent, too. And you want to know something? The fucker got away. I burned him, I know I did, and he managed to escape.

Albert warned me that he was hard to kill and I should have listened better. I made mistakes. I can admit to that. I screwed up.

But I made him suffer before it was done.

And then I ran like hell from Serenity Falls and I never once looked back. It might be a pretty town, but it's still Hell as far as I'm concerned and I don't much feel like chancing getting stuck in Miles's little prison again.

I got a new body out of the deal and it can do a lot of things that my old body couldn't do.

Want to hear a neat trick? I can heal from almost any wounds. I learned that after the Hunter and another man put big holes in my body. I should have been dead, but I lived through it. I also figured out—by instinct, I suppose—that I could fix the injuries as long as I had the right raw materials to work with. In plain English, I ate my way back to health. They'd blown away a part of my head and a part of my insides. I grabbed the closest available person and I ate the parts that got ruined. And just that fast, I was all better.

It was fatal for the man I chewed on, but I was better in no time. Yay me.

Seems like it works on almost any kind of wound, too.

That means I'm really, really hard to kill. Not that I like to test that theory too often.

Anyway, the thing is, everything that was supposed to happen to keep me alive and bring my friends back went wrong. The only one of us to get out of it alive was me. Serenity Falls fell down and it's still trying to get back up. I killed over seven hundred people with the circus tent fire. I also killed all but three members of the Pageant family, the good people who let us use their farm and then murdered me and mine. The other three? I'm not done with them yet. I'm just biding my time. I have all the time in the world these days, if you know what I mean. I'll get to them when the mood suits me.

In the meantime, I went off to see the sights and then to look for Millie. And, well, I'll be writing about that soon.

My life on the road? I think that's going to be a permanent thing. I think maybe I wasn't meant to settle down in any one place. Doreen Miles might still be out there somewhere, or the serpent man could be wandering. Maybe I'll find one of them in a traveling show and see if I can't hitch a ride.

Time will tell. And me? I have all the time I could ever need.

Chapter Eleven: Looking for Millie (Part Eleven)

My search for Millie or any other member of my family ended in disaster. That story is basically done. What I want to do now is explain a few things. See, at first I thought I was looking for my sister just to see her and as I look back on this entire mess, I realize that there was more to it than that. I've been searching for Millie or Meaghan and I've also been searching for a way to keep Cecil Phelps.

Let me explain. Cecil died in a fire in Serenity Falls.

Cecil stayed dead. Cecil was a dreamer. He wanted to make his family proud and gain fame and fortune.

I don't want those things. I don't need those things and I don't even aspire to them. They hold no special appeal for me. Not like they did for Cecil.

I think if I'd found Millie and had a real chance to say goodbye that maybe Cecil could have come back to stay instead of just visiting, but there's nothing for him in this world. It's too far removed from what he knew in the past. The circus isn't the life it used to be and the only people he loved are gone.

I don't need a family. I don't even need friends. I have my values and I have the kids. Oh, I know, you can look at the things I've done and wonder how I could say a thing like that. But there are exceptions to every rule.

I do love children, and that's the truth. I love to hear them laugh and to watch their eyes light up when they see a good magic trick. I love to see them smile and to watch them when they are happy.

And now and then I even like their parents. Only sometimes daddy says bad things and does worse, so I have to punish him. Now and then mommy thinks a drink of scotch is the bee's knees and that her little ones can do just fine without her, so I test that theory. Occasionally, little Johnny decides to be a brat and so I have to punish him, or that nice Mr. Jones down the street does something to little Suzie that he shouldn't and so I have to fix that, too.

There's always a reason for what I do. Just don't expect me to explain them all.

I'm a clown, and I like to make people smile.

And if I can't make them smile, then I have to do other things to keep myself amused.

Cecil Phelps is dead.

My name is Rufo the Clown, and I believe in fixing the world one little step at a time.

Cecil mourned his sister and his parents and even his grandniece whom he never met.

Rufo doesn't mourn anyone.

But now and then, Rufo gets even instead of getting angry.

The Carnivale de Fantastique caught my attention.

Killing my last kin caught my ire.

Payback, folks. I learned all about payback when I traveled with the Alexander Halston Carnival of the Fantastic. Only I have to say, in hindsight, I think Alex was a little kinder than me.

Michael stared at the special agents and shook his head. "You're kidding me, right? This is a joke."

Cantrell shook her head. "Nope. Completely serious."

He looked from one undercover agent to the other again and again, waiting for one of them to crack a smile and give it up, but they were not smiling.

"Somebody killed two people and took Booker's body?"

"That's the way it looks." King's voice sounded dubious.

"What aren't you telling me?"

"If this was TV, I'd be calling on Scully and Mulder and this would be an X-File." Cantrell crossed her arms over her chest and shook her head. "Nothing adds up."

King came to the rescue before Carver was forced to ask for clarification. "Both bodies were badly mauled. Very badly. There are pieces missing."

"Jesus."

"There are also footprints leading away from the examination table. Bare, bloody footprints, complete with a toe tag."

"Oh, bull shit!"

"Completely sincere, my man." King held up a hand to God. "Got no reason to lie to you."

"So this is still considered an open investigation?"

"Yep. And that means we still want you going to Philadelphia with us."

"Yeah, well, I never unpacked, so that works for me."

"Excellent." Cantrell smiled as she stood up. "The troupe is already on their way, and we can meet up with them before the next show starts." She fished in her pants pocket until she found her keys. "I'll drive."

"I need to get my stuff."

"We'll stop on the way."

King chuckled and Cantrell shot him a murderous glare.

The man held up his arms in surrender and Carver watched them with no idea of exactly what was going on between the two of them. He'd figure it out as they went. In the meantime, he had other places to be.

The breakfast spread was elaborate. There were pastries, urns of coffee, chafing dishes with scrambled eggs, sausage and bacon as well as biscuits and gravy. Enough food to feed easily thirty people and all of it set out for the members of the board and a small army of lawyers. Twelve people in all.

Almost everyone was there. Adam Salinger was having engine troubles, exactly as the clown had planned it.

Everyone else was eating, sitting down at the tables provided by the hotel in the private office that they had rented for the occasion. Absolutely no one was to disturb them for at least three hours, not even the hotel staff, because the nature of their discussions was sensitive to say the least.

Rufo the Clown stepped into the room with grease painted smile firmly in place, and an ax slung comfortably over his shoulder.

Eloise Fischer was the first to notice him. She stared for several seconds, her mind refusing to accept what she was staring at as surely as if a purple bear had tap danced into the place. The man was dressed in casual clothes, but his garish face, his blue hair and the ax certainly slid him away from the mundane category.

"Howdy, folks!" His voice was good-natured.

Eloise stood up, her mouthful of bacon forgotten and pointed at him. "You aren't supposed to be here."

"Nonsense," he said. "I was invited."

"By who?" Her tone brooked no argument.

"Meaghan Phelps." With that answer he swung the ax off his shoulder and drove it into the meaty neck of Richard Emery, the private investigator they'd hired to learn more about John Booker and anyone else who might be connected to the unexpected deaths.

Emery never even had a chance to scream before his life ended.

Eloise tried to scream, but as she drew in a deep breath for that exact purpose she sucked half-chewed bacon into her airway and started choking. The clown smiled in her direction and winked. "You wait right there. I'll get to you, too."

He hauled the ax out of Emery's dead body and whipped it around with almost casual ease, a thick stream of crimson spraying the wall as he changed directions. Neil Porter had just stood up and was trying to get away from the madman when the ax drove into his upper back and the point of it burst through the front of his neatly pressed white shirt.

Paul Hammet, one of the sleaziest lawyers Eloise had ever met, tried for the door and the clown caught him, long elegant fingers hooking into the fatty jowls on the lawyer's face and bringing him to a very abrupt halt.

Hammet tried to scream, but the sound was muffled. The clown shoved him backward and sent him crashing into the buffet table, spilling coffee, food and Sterno containers in the process. They got lucky: none of the jellied fuel cans caught the room on fire.

Hammet did not rise from where he had landed.

Chaos was the only word that came to mind as the rest of the people in the room tried to find a way out of the area as fast as humanly possible.

Eloise charged at the door with a lowered head, still coughing violently in an effort to clear her airway. The clown whipped a hand at her and a second after that she felt the throwing knife slam through the side of her neck. The blow was brutal, harsh enough to split her vertebrae and sever the spinal column. Eloise fell hard, slamming her face into the ground. The pain was a scintillating blast that flared and then vanished a moment later.

And after that, she lay still despite her best efforts to move.

The sounds continued for several more seconds, and more than once she saw a body fall at the edge of her vision. When silence reigned for a full minute she began to think that either she had gone deaf or the lunatic had departed the area. Neither proved to be the case.

The man in the clown face lifted her easily and moved her over to the table. He set her down and the table creaked threateningly under her weight.

"Now, see, I thought for sure you would be dead by now." He smiled as he looked her over. "That's okay, not much longer." He moved and her head rolled to the side of its own volition. She wanted to move, but could not. That meant she got to see what he did to her long-time friend Andy Finch, despite her prayers to the contrary.

The clown found his ax where he had left it buried in Porter, and hauled it free with a grunt. It took three swings to sever the head from the rest of the body.

When he was done and the stump was still bleeding freely, the clown grabbed a knife and started carving away at Andy's face. Eloise cried, her mouth working, but very little sound coming from her throat. She was having trouble breathing, but couldn't think of that as a bad thing as the clown-man turned Andy's face toward her and showed her his workmanship.

"You know, when I was a kid we did this thing with potatoes, called potato stamping. I've kind of wondered if this would work." He stared at her as he spoke, his mouth no longer smiling behind the blood red slash of makeup that made him grin just the same.

The clown looked at the wall that was currently covered with the charts Eloise had put up before the breakfast started and then dipped the freshly carved face into the pool of blood that flowed from the stump where the head had previously been attached.

Eloise tried to scream as he slammed the bloodied face into the chart and rolled the ruined head against the paper until he had left a bloody imprint. Potato stamp, indeed. She couldn't gather up the breath to scream, nor could she force her lungs to work at breathing in or out.

When the print was done, the clown dropped Andy's head and chuckled to himself. "Oh yes, I think I like it!"

He reached for Eloise and turned her head harshly to the left. Her mouth opened as the pain exploded in her neck. She was looking right at him when the knife came down and drove into her left eye socket, quickly, brutally cutting the organ free from her flesh. Oh, how she wanted to scream. Oh, how she wanted to die.

He finished cutting away the meat and viscera that were in his way in her left eye and commenced with the rest of the cutting. The man laughed and laughed again before he took the ax and ended her agonies.

And after that, Rufo the Clown worked on each of the heads available to him and used them exactly once. Then he settled back to wait.

Because he was hungry, he took a Danish from the tray that hadn't fallen over and began to eat. And as he paused to chew, he contemplated what note to leave for his new special friend, Adam.

He crowed when the right message came to mind and then he wrote it in block letters across the wall, above the facial imprints.

Then he settled back to wait.

He couldn't wait to see the expression on his buddy's face.

Adam paid the cabbie and made sure to get a receipt. Taxes were a necessary evil and tax breaks were a force for good in his universe.

The car not starting had been a pain in the ass, but not the end of the world. He'd have been in much poorer spirits if he hadn't spent the night getting to know Mary a lot better. She played a demonic seductress very well on stage and she fucked like an animal in real life. He'd already decided she would have a larger part next season, and that he would get an encore or two out of her before he told her she could have a larger part.

The performers had all left first thing in the morning and he'd stayed in her room long enough for one more quickie and then a shower. He wasn't staying at the same hotel, but he'd planned on just driving back when he was finished. The rental car refused to start and he'd already called to bitch about the situation. They'd fix the matter in the next few hours and in the meantime he had a meeting to attend to.

He took his time riding up the elevator and swinging by his room before the meeting, because it wouldn't do to come into the meeting in the suit from the night before, especially since it now smelled very heavily of the rather exotic perfume that Mary overindulged in.

And then it was down to the meeting room, pleasantly relaxed and as ready for business as he ever would be.

Somebody had a very twisted sense of humor.

The words came into view one letter at a time but he processed the line quickly enough: GRAY SKIES ARE GONNA CLEAR UP....

And under those wet, red words, were a dozen wet, red smiley faces, each one with a happy grin and round, ragged eyes. Someone had been busy and had even painted teeth in some of the mouths. The details were lost in fuzz half the time, but they were there. He looked at the graffiti for several seconds, frowning and puzzled, before he noticed the first body.

He couldn't see a head, just a body. There was blood all over the place, and the raw stump where the head should have been was a jagged, ragged mess.

"Oh God." His stomach lurched hard to the left and Adam staggered forward, his traitorous eyes taking in the sights that would last with him for as long as he lived.

He found most of the heads in a pile. They'd been stacked together on a silver platter that was already holding a spread of pastries. Each face had been mutilated; the eyes cut away, the lips sliced off to make the smiling mouths on the faces he'd seen stamped on the walls. In every case the nose on the heads had been brutally mashed flat. The teeth he'd seen vaguely painted in place were real. That information alone made his ears ring with a high-pitched note. A severed lip hung on the edge of the table, bloodied and limp, a white slug with a trail of red.

"You get it?" The voice was the same one from the phone the night before. "'Put on a happy face,' get it? Isn't that a hoot?" The man laughed as he walked forward, his hands holding the last head, the features too mutilated to let Adam even guess who it might have been. His face was hidden under clown makeup, only Adam could clearly see the mutilations along the too-thin face. He looked almost as dead as the head he was casually tossing from hand to hand with a series of wet, meaty noises.

He tossed the head into the air, his hands soaked bloody red and the sleeves of his shirt washed in shades of crimson.

"I asked you a question last night, rube, and then I told you not to hang up on me." All the cheer vanished from his voice as he spoke.

Adam started to run and saw the man throw his prize with a savage swing from the corner of his eye. He felt the head slam into his leg and knew before it happened that he was going down. Adam let out a shriek and crashed into the ground, his hands failing to catch him before he was sliding through coffee, pastries, eggs and blood.

His mind wanted to go completely blank, and his gag reflex kicked him in the guts and sent a dry heave through his entire body.

"Oh, oh dear Jesus." He coughed and felt a cold saliva drool from his mouth as he looked down into the bloody froth he was laying in.

"What did I tell you? What did I say to you just last night, Adam? I told you to let me know where you hid my niece's body! If you'd just opened your mouth and told me what I wanted, you could have avoided all of this!" The venom in the words was enough to make him shiver, even if the rest of the madness around him hadn't been there.

Salinger opened his mouth and instead of words, gagged on the miasma that was still inches from his face.

"Get up!" The hand that lifted him from the ground was far too strong to be human. "Play time is done, Adam! I want to know where you buried Meaghan Phelps, and either you tell me now, or I swear what I do to you will make you scream for days and days and days!"

He looked at the clown, horrified to see that the thing looked even less alive than it had a moment before. The eyes were still blue, but buried deep in fleshless sockets and the gums had receded from the open mouth, the lips had withered and peeled back. There was a faint smell of old death on the thing that mingled with the coffee and blood and fresh murder to make a sickening scent.

Adam tried to answer, but when he opened his mouth to speak he vomited a thin stream of bile past his lips.

The clown monster hurled him across the room, smashing him into the stack of heads and then into at least two of the bodies tossed around like so much garbage.

"What the hell kind of man are you, Adam?" The voice was a dark rasp, a dry, lifeless thing. It mirrored the clown-corpse that stalked toward him, grinning twice over.

The hand that caught him was dry and leathery and oh, so hot. The face that loomed above him stared hard and then like magic a large blade blossomed from the other skeletal hand the thing held up.

"I'll start with the toes, Adam. I'll take them one at a time, peel the meat from the bones, do you understand me? One at a time until I have to work my way up your legs and then I'll cut off your balls and keep going!"

"Nooooo! Please! Please!" Oh, how he cried. His tears came fast and hard and hot, furious, desperate pleas to save his life and his body from the bad thing leering down over him. He wet himself and wouldn't have been shocked to shit himself, too.

The knife came down fast and slammed deep into the edge of the broken table that he'd landed on.

"Where…is…her…body?"

Adam spoke quickly, giving very detailed instructions on exactly where the body was buried, and how far the nightmare clown would have to dig. He cried throughout the entire process, having no doubt in his mind that he would die a horrible death as soon as he was done confessing.

Instead the clown stood up and calmly straightened out its clothes.

"I'm going to find her, Adam. If she's not where you say she is, I'll be back before the sun sets to kill you." The face looked fleshier now, more alive. The twisted rage that had marked the features was faded as well, leaving a smile within a smile and cold glittering eyes that shone with amusement. "And Adam? Even if I DO find her body, that's no guarantee that we're done. You understand me? Do you get my meaning here?"

The man nodded silently and did his best not to cry anymore.

The clown moved, walking slowly away from him, not once bothering to look back.

Adam sat where he was for a long, long time, too weak and frightened to move. His heart hammered away inside his chest and adrenaline left him shaking.

When he finally stood up, the screams came out of him of their own volition. He couldn't have stopped them if his life depended on it.

He was still screaming when management showed up, and when the police showed up not much later. He only stopped screaming when the sedatives were injected into his arm.

Chapter Twelve

The clouds had built up again and took away all hopes that the day would be pleasant. The air was heavy and motionless and Carver headed for the crime scene with a deep, deep dread filling his stomach.

There were already enough cops around to potentially compromise the crime scene but the good news was none of them seemed overly interested in going past the yellow crime scene tape and checking out the scene. Several reporters hovered around the edges. But none of them were allowed past, and judging by the looks on a few faces, it was obvious that they had tried their luck already and failed. The ones that were hanging around were the dregs, the paparazzi and similar ilk who sought the sensational for a quick profit. He scowled as he saw them.

King and Cantrell walked with him, both of them in suits that made them look like real agents and not like kids dressed for the part.

King coughed into his hand and Carver looked toward him as they reached the tape barrier.

"What's up?" Carver's voice was no nonsense, which was exactly how he was feeling.

"You want to do me a favor? Get your guys to lose the photographers?"

Michael smiled at that. He hadn't thought about the fact that the two were here at a crime scene and still ready to go undercover in the very near future.

One quick gesture brought Caras and Jansen running. "Want to get the camera jockeys out of here? And if they look like they want to take a picture of anyone or anything, you take the cameras from them.

Caras cleared his throat. "What about their rights?"

Carver grinned. "They don't have any. This is a crime scene and the feds will back us on that decision."

That put a smile on the slender cop's face. "Cool."

The two headed toward the photographers and gestured for a few more to join them. While the shutterbugs were busy, the trio slipped past the yellow tape.

And stared at the carnage.

Heads, bodies, blood and viscera.

Carver felt proud of himself, he wasn't the first one to run past the tape to vomit.

That had been three hours earlier and they were still on the scene but now the coroner had come through and most of the bodies and their shredded parts had been bagged and removed.

King and Cantrell were in charge and that suited Carver just fine. He sat back and let them handle all of the details while he recovered himself.

Cantrell walked over to where he was leaning against the wall and joined him, her face as pale as he suspected his was.

"This guy...he's not normal."

"Yeah, I'm getting that."

"The survivor, Adam Salinger...he swears it was a guy dressed as a clown."

Michael managed not to jump completely out of his skin.

Cantrell studied him for several silent seconds, her face carefully neutral.

"I heard a story about a few cops cutting loose all over a clown faced guy involved in the kidnapping. I also hear the body of the killer went missing."

Carver looked at her for several seconds, his face just as carefully neutral and finally she nodded her head.

"So where do we go from here?" His voice was calm. His heart felt like it would never slow down again.

She shrugged her shoulders and forced a very small smile. "Philadelphia."

"You still want me along?"

"Of course." There was no subtext that he could decipher.

Finally he nodded his head. "So do we know why Booker or whoever is after these people?"

"No clue. All we know is these were most of the higher ups inside the Carnivale's corporate offices."

"So he's got a hard on for the show?"

"Yeah. Big time."

Carver stared at the floor. The blood was drying quickly, turning everything a dark, rusty color.

"The guy give you anything else? Does he have a clue?"

"No," she frowned. "Well, yes, I think he does, but he isn't talking much. He's too freaked out."

Carver nodded. There was nothing to say to that. Everyone who'd come into the room had been horrified and none of them could have called the dead people acquaintances or business partners.

The two of them stayed next to each other in comfortable silence for several minutes until King came over, shaking his head and frowning.

"This," said King "is getting messy."

"Not much messier than whoever did this."

"You think it was Booker?"

Carver shook his head. "I saw the dead body. His face was still intact but that was about all that was still intact. Seriously, he got all kinds of hell blown out of him." There was a surprising lack of guilt as he spoke. He'd expected to feel something, some sort of dread at having taken a life, but all he could see whenever he thought about the situation was the casual way in which the clown had thrown that poor baby boy into the air and let him fall.

"Well then, maybe he has an accomplice." King scowled and crossed his arms.

"That's not a fun thought."

"Beats all hell out of Booker coming back from the dead." Cantrell was trying for a joke, but Michael couldn't make himself laugh. The idea was just too damned creepy, especially when he considered what had happened to the people preparing to autopsy the body.

"I just want this done." His tone was dark. "Whoever this is, whatever he wants or they want, I want this shit done with."

Cantrell's hand patted his. It could have been a patronizing gesture, but her fingers felt good and gave him comfort. Maybe it was just any human contact after so much bloodshed. He hadn't let himself bother with people in a long time. The job made it too easy to shut yourself off from the world and even knowing that, he seldom did anything to stop it.

"So let's finish this if we can. The show has gone to Philadelphia and we're going after them." King's tone was calm, secure. "Next show is in two days and I won't be surprised to find our man out there somewhere."

Carver nodded, but his stomach twisted into a nervous knot at the notion. He wasn't completely sure that they were dealing with a human being anymore and that thought scared the hell out of him.

The shovel cut through the hard soil, and with each scoop of dirt he got closer to finding his last relative.

Above him the concrete floor of the warehouse had been shattered and pushed aside. The skin growing over his ruined hands hadn't finished mending him yet, but he would take care of that as soon as he was done digging. The one security guard had only provided enough flesh to heal him once and breaking the concrete had been traumatic to his hands and arms.

The warehouse was silent, save for the sounds of his digging, and that suited the clown just dandy. He wanted time to think and he had all the time he needed as he dug the hole. The structure had been built in Virginia for two reasons. First, the price was right and second, it was convenient to where the body of Meaghan Phelps had been stored for several weeks.

You know the right people, you can hide anything. Good ol' Adam knew lots of people and the ones he didn't know were handled by Todd Westingham. Todd wouldn't be helping anymore. Being dead slowed him down more than it did Rufo. Well, so far at least. He hadn't been the only one to ever climb out of the grave and he knew that.

The blade bit into hard dirt again, and struck something with a harsh, ringing note. He set the shovel to the side and crouched lower, brushing at the object. It only took him a moment to identify the limb he'd hit. It was a leg, mostly meatless now, but a leg.

Five minutes of frantic digging and he had the cadaver freed from the dirt. What was left of Meaghan Phelps was wrapped in a canvas sack. He stared at the package for several minutes after climbing free of the hole he'd dug.

The bundle was so tiny, so fragile, and it unsettled him. This had been a life, a living being. He unveiled her corpse with more reverence than he'd expected to feel, and looked up the ruination of his family line.

Dead and rotted, lost to the world and lost to him. Here lay the girl he'd wanted to meet, wanted to see dancing and smiling and happy. He'd have left her in peace if he'd known she died happily, but that wasn't the case, was it? Someone had done her wrong. He knew the name now, but still had not seen the face.

Long fingers brushed dirt away from the face of a dead woman. He could see the trauma that had been done to her skull and even see the lines that the rope had made around her neck as it was pulled tight. Similar ligature marks covered her wrists and her ankles.

"How long did it take you to die, Meaghan? How long before he let you go?" Rufo barely even recognized his own voice as he spoke. Odd, to ask a question that he had never once asked of his victims over the years, especially since he had killed so many….

She did not answer him. There was nothing but flesh here. No spirit, no life, just rotted meat, and a husk that was as useless as the canvas that had surrounded the body.

"Well, let's finish this, shall we?" His voice was more cheerful again, but it was a false cheer. "Let's get this done once and for all. So we can put paid to the Phelps name."

He wrapped her back in her canvas and then pulled plastic from the closest pallet of supplies. The thick plastic sheet worked beautifully to wrap canvas and corpse alike. When he was done, Rufo carried the bundle over his shoulder like a sack full of toys made just for old Saint Nick.

He chuckled at that thought. He hadn't even considered Christmas in years.

But, oh, he would be thinking about it when he finished his tasks. There were a few more things that had to be done, a few more accounts to be settled and then he could move on with his new life.

Sometimes accounts have to be paid. Sometimes they have to be paid in blood and pain.

And sometimes they have to be paid with a great deal of interest. Rufo the clown knew all about that sort of thing. He'd been paying for years.

Tia unpacked her meager belongings and then started sorting through the rest of the packages that comprised her costumes for the show. There were enough bundles to be unsettling.

Her stomach was a knot of frayed nerves, but she didn't much mind. The trip up had been uneventful and even though neither of them had spoken about the situation she knew that Leslie was as unsettled as she was.

She'd never even looked at girls that way before.

Tia pushed the thought aside. She couldn't be a lesbian; her dad would have a coronary.

It wasn't something she could handle, so she settled for thinking about other things.

The show was still two days away. That night there would be more interviews, more cameras and another party to attend. They would work better than most things to distract her from her thoughts of Leslie.

A quick sigh. The memory of Leslie's touch left her feeling flustered and wanting to feel that soft, beautiful caress again. She'd been raised with the firm understanding that her parents wanted lots of grandkids. The two were not supposed to work together.

Justin Burton, one of the assistant choreographers, knocked on her door and called out, "Staff meeting in fifteen minutes, Tia. Make sure you aren't late!"

"Okay, Jus…. Thanks!"

Justin's feet were already in motion, scrambling off toward Leslie's dressing room.

Thinking of Leslie brought her back to the same thoughts again, where her mind stayed until she heard the sounds of everyone leaving for the main stage and the meeting.

She left her room at the same time that Leslie did. It was a coincidence, but one that left her with the same edgy excitement twisting through her stomach.

Leslie looked at her with an expression that Tia had seen in her own mirror a thousand times since they'd kissed. Then Tia made herself smile and was rewarded by Leslie's beautiful smile cast back at her.

Leslie moved to her and before she could leave her dressing room's threshold the girl urged her back into the room and closed the door.

"I—we're gonna be late to the meeting." Tia was at a loss for what to say. Feeling Leslie's body heat so close to her was already making her flustery all over again.

"Hush." Leslie's finger pressed against Tia's lips, urging her to silence. "Listen, I didn't expect it and you didn't. I know that. I just…I wanted you to know, I don't regret it. Okay? We can talk later. We need to talk later, but I wanted you to know, I'm *glad* it happened, no matter what."

Tia felt her eyes mist and her body relax. She'd been so afraid that Leslie would blame her, maybe even hate her.

Before she could do more than nod her head, Leslie was kissing her. Not a deep, passionate affair, but a quick peck on the lips before she pulled back. "Let's go listen to the bosses talk."

Tia nodded her head, made breathless by the words, the actions of the girl she stood with.

Did she know what was going to happen in the future? No. But maybe now she could get through the day without wanting to cry and that was something. That was a big something.

They walked toward the meeting and Tia felt like she was floating. She was barely even aware of moving at all, but she felt the fingers wrapped into hers and loved the way those fingers felt.

The auditorium was huge, bigger by far than the one where they'd been performing, and most of the sets were not fully assembled, but were getting there. She looked at the ice palace again, as she did almost every time she walked along the stage, and smiled. It was a beautiful prop and she loved the way it made her feel.

Almost everyone was already there, and most of the performers had chosen to sit Indian style on the floor of the stage. Leslie and Tia did the same, relaxing among the people who were almost like a second family. There were several new people in place as well, most of them looking a little nervous. She recognized one of them as the Alexandria cop who had interviewed her after the first bodies were found. Carter, or something like that. He was a good-looking man and sort of scary with how intense he could be, but she was glad to see him, because from what she'd watched before he was determined to stop anyone else getting hurt.

Justin was the one who spoke. Most of the big wigs weren't there to be seen and she figured that meant they were dealing with the regular problems of handling the press and everything else.

"Okay, people. Let's keep this short and sweet because I know we all want to get unpacked and get back to having lives." Justin's hands waved like hummingbirds as he spoke. "Some of you might remember Detective Carver, he's with the police. He's come along to work with the local police and to make sure that everyone stays nice and safe. I better not hear about anyone giving him any shit, because first, he's cute and I want to seduce him...." Justin rolled his eyes playfully as he spoke. The detective turned a deep shade of red that had most everyone chuckling. "And second, he's here to protect us. So don't disappoint me here, make him want to stay around for as long as he has to."

If anyone expected Carver to say anything, they were disappointed. He waved politely and then went back to crossing his arms and looking at everyone like a potential suspect.

Justin kept talking and introduced a dozen new people. Most of them were new hires to take care of everything behind the scenes. Four of them were dancers and performers. Not surprisingly, a few people had decided not to keep on with the show.

None of it mattered. Tia wanted to get unpacked and then she wanted to act like a high school girl and crush all over Leslie for a while. It was nice to be young and to have someone who liked her back. The rest of it could wait for now.

The new dancers looked around with a puzzled expression and Leslie nudged her. "Let's meet the new kids." Tia nodded and smiled. Leslie could have suggested that they go shopping for chainsaws and barbed wire to wear as their new outfits and she would have nodded and smiled.

The hotel room was nothing spectacular. It was, in fact, a dive. The bed had a cover that had probably last been washed a few months earlier and he would have doubted the sanitary condition of the sheets if he hadn't been setting a rotted body on top of them.

Meaghan's corpse seemed smaller in the room, which was saying a lot as she wasn't very large to begin with. He sat next to the corpse and moved the bones delicately, positioning them so that she looked more at peace, at least to his eyes.

One long finger ran along the face, touching the moldering flesh. He didn't need to be a forensic specialist to know that the skin over the bones had once been lovely. He had memories of her, fleeting though they were and diluted by technology that had let him see her in the first place.

"Were you ever happy, Meaghan?" The question was conversational, but he wasn't expecting an answer.

He opened the cell phone he'd stolen an hour earlier and dialed the number he'd memorized a long time ago. The voice at the other end was comforting, familiar and a little scary.

"This is Albert, how can I help you?"

"Albert, it's Rufo."

"How are you, my boy? I was wondering when you would get back to me." His tone was confident and assured. He knew the score. The clown needed his help for almost anything he wanted to do at this point.

"I've found her body, Albert. I have Meaghan."

"Well, come along then. Do you want her brought back or not?" That tone of almost boredom was a barb aimed at him and he knew it. He was also wise enough not to let the man's attitude get in the way of accomplishing what he wanted.

"Ask her, Albert. Ask her. I'll be at your house in Salem soon and I'll bring the body with me."

Miles disconnected the call and Rufo carefully set about rewrapping the remains of his last flesh and blood kin.

"We're going to get this all taken care of, Meaghan. Just you wait and see."

News gets around. It was inevitable that most people would find out about the murders involving the Carnivale. They did their best to suppress the information and they did a good job, but by the day after the murders had occurred the media was examining every possible angle for the connections between the board of directors and the bodies left behind by the man who called himself John Booker.

To make matters worse, there were people who wanted to know exactly how it was that he had survived being shot repeatedly by police at the scene of his showdown.

The speculations were epic and completely wrong. A bit actor from two seasons earlier had attempted to sue the Carnivale and failed. That would have been the end of the situation, but he bore a passing resemblance to the killer and for the next two days his life was examined by the best investigators the media could afford. Instead of focusing on where he had been during the crimes, they focused on what he had done in the past and Andy Nuell, a dancer who had tried to sue for sexual harassment and had all but been laughed out of court—became the center of several farfetched speculations. He was accused of nearly every crime by some of the more zealous reporters and denounced by most as the worst sort of sleaze.

The lawsuits are still pending in most of the cases. His chances are slightly better this time around. In the meantime, the celebrity has increased his marketability and led to several offers of bit parts on soap operas and even a walk on role in a forthcoming movie.

Despite the negative press, or maybe because of it, tickets for the Philadelphia shows became extremely prized among scalpers. A few sold for as much as a thousand dollars over the original asking price.

The demand was so much, in fact, that four additional shows were added. They'd have probably added more, but New York was after Philadelphia and they had already committed to Radio City Music Hall.

In the city of Philadelphia, the people were ready to go to the circus, to celebrate the mystery of how the Alexander Halston Carnival of the Fantastic had vanished from the face of the earth. The papers held interviews with the performers and carried bios of the more famous members of the troupe. One reporter from the Examiner actually took the time to track down a few documented sightings of the carnival and discovered that it had come through Philadelphia no less than four times before it disappeared.

That reporter, Lacey Champlain, managed something that no one else had managed to date: she found and posted a picture of the troupe, a grainy black and white thing that had been taken over fifty years earlier.

The clown that stood in the background looked quite a bit different from the man who'd terrorized Virginia. The markings on his face were similar, but beyond that they had almost nothing in common. The clown in the picture was wearing a tuxedo and had a top hat in his hand. The killer in Virginia had been wearing less flashy attire. The man in the picture had eyes that could be said to know of kindness and hope. A certain detective who was visiting Philadelphia—and who had seen the photograph and slipped it into his wallet more on a whim than anything else—would have been the first to say there was nothing remotely like compassion in the eyes of the madman who killed a family of three and then fired on the police as well. He knew, because for the last five nights he's dreamed of that psychotic bastard and shivered in his sleep.

Philadelphia was ready for the show. They were excited by the notion.

So was Rufo the Clown, but he had one last matter to attend to before the time came for him to visit the circus.

That matter he attended to in Massachusetts.

Chapter Thirteen

Albert Miles held the door open for him as he carried in the remains of his grandniece. The old man did not smile, but neither did he frown. He simply moved into the room and quickly pulled the rug away from the hardwood floor in his living room. He had already moved the furniture aside in preparation for the tasks ahead of him.

"Cecil, my boy, you are not the easiest person I've ever dealt with. You know that, don't you?" His voice was conversational.

The clown looked at him without speaking for several moments. The patterns of color on his face made all but the most blatant expressions impossible to read.

Miles chuckled.

"Fair enough. You're not in the mood for jests. Let's see what we can do for you then, shall we?"

He waved the clown aside and unrolled the canvas package himself, brushing dirt and flecks of rotted flesh aside with his hands.

"She must have been lovely in life."

"She was. I've seen pictures." Rufo's voice was a low hiss.

"Calm down, my boy. In the long run, nothing that has been done is permanent unless you and she decide it is."

"Albert, do you think I'm a bad person?"

The old man stared at him for a long, long while, a smile playing at his lips but never quite surfacing. "My boy, I am absolutely the last person in the world to ask about good and evil, or right and wrong."

The clown nodded his head and allowed himself a genuine chuckle. "Good point."

"Now is not the time for philosophical debates in any event. I have things to do and so do you. Let's get on with this."

Rufo nodded and then squatted next to the corpse.

The man on the other side of the body placed a hand on the forehead of the skull and another over the place where her heart should have been.

"This will not be pleasant for her. It will cause her pain. Are you absolutely sure you want to do this?"

The clown nodded his head and pressed his lips together tightly. "Do it, but make it fast."

The scream that came from the dead body sent shivers through Rufo's body. Until that moment he thought he was beyond chills.

———

Michael Carver smiled at the pizza in front of him like it was a long-lost friend. He'd spent the last two days with the troupe, getting to know them and asking questions until his head felt thick with answers and trivial responses. He made sure that everyone saw him and made it clear that he was accessible if they needed anything, because officially that was why he was along for the ride, as extra security.

Unfortunately, that meant he'd managed to miss a few meals, like all of them, and the pizza that the cute waitress placed in front of him looked large enough to make amends to his stomach, which growled in delight the moment he walked into the pizza place two blocks from the show, close enough that he could get back in a hurry if he needed to. The place was busy, crowded with college kids and a few families despite the fact that it was rather late for dinner.

He smiled at the waitress. She was a pretty little thing, short with curly brown hair and a zillion freckles hidden under too much makeup, but pretty despite that.

"Can I get you anything else?" her accent was pure Philly and so was her attitude. He liked it. "Yeah, can I get another Coke?"

"You got it." She was off in a flash and detoured to another table to take their order before getting his refill.

His cell phone rang and Carver sighed. The number was local, maybe from the hotel, so he answered it. "Carver."

"You shot me, Detective. I ask you, was that really the best way to handle the situation?" His skin tried to crawl off his body and hide away. He recognized Booker's voice instantly.

"How the fuck are you alive?"

"Who said I am?"

Carver looked around, trying to spot anyone who might be watching him, who might want to pull a prank on him because, despite everything, he was still sure the clown was dead and someone else had come along to play games. Now, hearing the voice of the man again, he had doubts.

"Listen, whatever you think you're playing at, this isn't funny. You need to turn yourself in."

The man laughed. "Seriously? That's the best you can come up with as motivation? Why would I turn myself in when this is just starting to get fun?"

He made himself stay calm. There were people around him, families, and they didn't need to hear this conversation or what he wanted to say. "Booker, if that's you, people have died—"

"Boy, howdy, don't I know it! Killed most of them myself."

Carver's teeth clenched down hard enough to make his jaw creak. "You listen to me. This stops now."

"Nope. I'm not finished, Detective Carver, but I will be soon."

"Turn yourself in, or I'll make you regret it."

The door to the pizzeria opened and Michael turned toward it as the bell above it jangled shrilly. Three girls were coming in, each of them with a backpack instead of a purse and dressed in jeans, sweaters and enough bling to blind anyone if the sun should catch them. One of the girls was nearly braying laughter, her face filled with the simple joy of being alive and hearing a good joke.

Carver didn't care. He barely noticed the girls at all. It was the man behind them that caught his attention. John Booker stood in the semidarkness, the last light of the day playing across his painted features as he looked directly at Carver and waved his fingers.

"Come get me, rube. Come on. Come get me right here and now."

The man pushed into the restaurant, his face set in a broad, mad smile, his wild, curly hair jouncing with each step, the cell phone held to his ear. He was dressed in jeans, a t-shirt for the Carnivale de

Fantastique and a warm trench coat that flowed like a cape in the wind from outside.

The three girls who'd just entered looked back as he stepped into the building and close enough to them to enter their personal spaces, more amused than anything else. It wasn't every day a clown came storming into a restaurant like gangbusters.

"Excuse me, ladies." He flashed them a dazzling smile and executed a flawless bow as he slipped past them. The cell phone was folded and slipped into a coat pocket with one smooth motion of his right hand. At the same time his left hand rose up and three roses seemed to blossom from between his fingers. The girls looked at him and smiled and each of them grinned all the brighter as he handed them the blooms. "Come see me at the show."

He moved past them and one of the girls looked at the rose, looked at him as he walked toward Carver and let out a shriek of joy and surprise. "Holy shit, thank you, mister!"

She held up the rose, and Carver stared. It looked like a ticket from Ticketmaster had been attached to the stem. If he'd had to hazard a guess, he would have bet money on the ticket being for the Carnivale.

"Well, you're welcome my dear." He smiled brightly for her, turning to face her even as he continued toward Carver, walking backward now, fully exposed. One hand went to his face, cupping near his mouth in a parody of someone whispering. "But watch that pretty mouth of yours, there are little ones present." The admonishment had a cheerful enough note and the girl—who was possibly as old as twenty, but the detective would have been surprised if she'd graduated high school—blushed and nodded her head, duly chastised.

Carver stood up fast, knocking his small table over and spilling the meal he'd been looking forward to in the process. Most of him understood the need to get to his weapon, but his stomach was rather unforgiving.

The clown spun fast and smiled at him, white teeth showing past red lips. His eyes flashed with good humor even as Carver started to take aim with the pistol he'd drawn.

All around them the people sitting down to eat were turning, noticing the drawn weapon, those that had not already noticed the man with the clown face.

Carver's hand shook. Not because he was scared of Booker, but because he was afraid of what the man might do and even more frightened of what he might do to the clown. There were witnesses this time and he wasn't nearly as angry as he had been before.

The clown stepped toward him, not even flinching from the pistol pointed at his face.

The blue eyes that regarded him had laugh lines and glistened with merriment or insanity, or both. "I'm right here, Carver." His voice was a soft, low purr. "You gonna kill me again? Right in front of all these lovely people?"

His hands shook and he hated that. He wanted so much to pull the trigger and damn any possible consequences, but there were people all around them, innocents who could get hurt.

"You stay right where you are, Booker." His voice shook as much as his hands, adrenaline kicking through his system like lightning, flashing through his limbs and racing his heart.

"Please, no reason for formalities. Call me Rufo." Damned if the clown's smile didn't grow wider. "Come on, you know you want to. I can almost taste how much you want to pull the trigger." He leaned in until his forehead was almost touching the barrel of the .44. "Go on, do it. Do it. Make it happen…." His voice was still soft, his eyes unflinching, and the smile so broad and eager and feral. "Pull the trigger. Be a hero."

"What the hell are you doing, mister?" The voice was loud, almost thunderous, and Carver looked toward the speaker, a heavyset man rising from a table, his eyes scared but also determined. He had a family, Carver had seen them laughing and chatting as he settled into his seat. The man did not look like he wanted to be there, but he also didn't look like he was willing to back down.

"This is police business! Please sit down, sir." His voice was louder than he wanted, but at least it no longer shook.

The clown's smile did not change. His eyes kept staring and if they'd been lasers they'd have surely incinerated him by now.

"Well, I need to see a badge and you need to put that gun down."

He frowned. Civilians did not, as a rule, make demands like that. He was afraid to look over. If he looked in that direction he had to take his eyes off the madman with the double grin.

"And who are you?" He spoke without taking the risk.

The clown answered for the man, his voice as calm and cheery as before. "He's the man who's now pointing a gun at you, Detective Carver." He kept his voice soft enough to be intimate.

"My name is Tom Sneigoski. I'm a cop, and currently I've drawn my weapon and have it aimed in your direction. Do not make this go down the wrong way." He wished he could have taken some satisfaction from the man sounding just as nervous as he felt, but it did nothing to help him stay calm.

Booker stepped back, his smile still in place, his eyes still locked on Michael's own. "I'm guessing we've had a misunderstanding, Officer Sneigoski. I'm just here to pass out a few free tickets to the Carnivale de Fantastique." His voice carried now, louder, but no less confident. "I think this man has mistaken me for someone else."

The officer stepped closer to the two of them, his eyes hard. "You take your free hand and show me your badge, or we're going to have a serious problem. You understand me?" There was a lot of shuffling in the background, but Carver was still afraid to look. He didn't trust the clown for a second, not an instant, really, and he couldn't risk anything but his peripheral vision. Several people at different tables were on the move and that was just fine. The less people around the better off he'd be. Booker couldn't kill them if they weren't here for whatever happened next.

The clown shook his head. "I can't believe you shot me six times." His voice was a whisper again.

"You need to stay right where you are." Carver's voice was steady again. He reached for his wallet and his badge.

"Carefully, carefully...." Sneigoski's voice held warning, which under the circumstances made perfect sense.

His hand slid across his jeans, reaching for the billfold and the badge and ran across nothing instead. Carver's stomach sank fast and hard.

"What?" They were gone, his identity, his proof that he was a cop. And there was no reason to believe for an instant that the policeman behind him, the one who actually had jurisdiction in Philadelphia as opposed to Virginia, would take him on his word.

And there it was: the knowing look on the clown's face. His eyes held their merriment, his lips twitched, wanting to smile even broader than before. He didn't need to speak; he knew exactly how fucked Carver was.

"I—I can't find my wallet. My name is Michael Carver, I'm a detective with the Alexandria Police Department, out of Virginia...."

"Put down the gun, mister. Nice and slow."

"The man in front of me is wanted for murder in Georgia and in Virginia."

"Then I'll make sure he doesn't go anywhere. In the meantime, put down your firearm. Now."

Michael nodded. In the long run there were no options. He'd be free and clear in half an hour, tops, but until then he needed to make sure he did nothing that would result in getting his fool head blown off.

He lowered the weapon carefully, switching on the safety before he let it touch the ground. As he crouched to set the pistol on the scuffed tile floor, Booker stepped back even further, taking away that edge of danger that had kept him ready to pull the trigger.

He looked around. The room was almost completely empty, and he could see the crowd of people who had been inside a few minutes ago gathered outside, in the chilled weather. The man he'd seen earlier was standing in a proper firing stance, his eyes looking strictly at Michael.

The cop came up behind him and spoke calmly. "You need to assume the position. Now, please." He used his foot to push Michael's pistol away from easy range and kept his weapon trained on Carver as he crouched and picked the piece off the ground.

Michael nodded and moved his hands to the back of his head, interlacing the fingers. He'd certainly made enough perps stand that way in the past to know every action by heart.

The hands that patted him down were fast and confident. In front of him, Booker stood perfectly still, his eyes glittering, his mouth skewed into a malignant grin.

Carver waited as his hands were moved down into the small of his back, his wrists locked together by cuffs. The clown waited with him, patient to the point of being annoying.

Carver stood still in return as Booker was frisked. The most dangerous things taken from the man were twenty tickets for the show. Carver had no idea how the man had gotten them, or how he had paid for them, but he had no doubt that they were legitimate.

"Can you tell me your name, sir?" Sneigoski spoke to the clown with more deference than Carver liked. He also understood why he was so careful. Aside from a comment from a man without any identification, there was nothing at all to indicate that the man in makeup was anything but a circus performer.

"Cecil Phelps." The man's mouth twitched into a pleasant smile. He gave an address and claimed he lived there. It was local, not far from where they were standing, he suspected. The sort of address a cunning perpetrator might have memorized for himself if he was trying to come up with a good alibi for being in the wrong neighborhood.

"Mister Phelps...do you have any identification on you?"

"You know, I'd swear I took it with me this morning, but I can't for the life of me find it...." The sincere look on his painted face was almost enough to convince Carver, and he knew better. The son of a bitch was good.

"I'm going to have to ask you to stay here, while I call and confirm everything. Is that all right with you?" Sneigoski was polite, but his voice held an edge to it that made clear he was being polite, not making a request.

"Of course. You do whatever you have to do. Nothing to worry about." Booker nodded his head and stood still as the officer reached for his radio and then reached for his phone instead. Doubtless the radio was with his uniform, in his car or at home.

The man dialed, his eyes staying on Carver.

Booker smiled at Michael and spoke softly as the officer began explaining his situation to whoever was on the other end of the phone line. "You know what the best part of this is, Detective?"

"No, but I'm sure you'll tell me."

"The best part is, I could kill you and no one would be able to stop me."

"Keep threatening me. Soon as they confirm who I am, we'll get this all taken care of."

"I'm trying to do you a favor. I know you don't believe me, but it's true."

"Really?" He didn't try to hide the sarcasm in his voice.

"Absolutely. See, despite the bullets and all of that nonsense, I think you're an okay guy. I think you should maybe get away from what's going to happen at the Carnivale."

"Oh? And what's that?"

"Revelations, my good man. Epiphanies and dramatic moments. Oh, and bloodshed." His voice rose as he spoke, loud enough that Sneigoski looked in his direction.

"You need to turn yourself in." Carver shook his head. "Better yet, you wait ten minutes and I'll take care of it."

Booker leaned in closer, just out of reach, and whispered again. "Ever see a baby try to fly? That kid bounced a good five feet when he hit the pavement."

The words were completely unexpected. That was the only justification he had for losing his temper and trying to head butt the man in front of him.

Booker danced back two steps and let out a cackle.

Before Carver could try again, a hand grabbed his shoulder and spun him around. "Knock it off! You try anything else like that and I'll cuff you to the men's room wall!" Sneigoski's threat wasn't overly serious, but his tone was.

He nodded his head, too outraged to actually speak. The clown stared at him, amused, not the least bit intimidated. He was a nutcase. He had to be. It didn't matter who you were, no one in their right mind deliberately taunted a cop. Of course, he'd already proven that he was insane on several occasions.

When Sneigoski was distracted by his phone call, Booker leaned in again, his voice low and dangerous. "Betcha a dollar I can kill him before he can draw his gun."

"Shut your fucking face."

"Give me a reason, Carver. Give me a reason. You so much as flinch and I'll cut your new friend's face off." The facial expression stayed the same, taunting and feral.

He bared his teeth. The worst part was he believed the bastard. "Why are you doing this?"

"It's personal."

"You killed a baby." His breaths were harsh, but he kept his voice down.

"Kid wouldn't stop fidgeting. He was getting on my nerves." Booker shrugged. "Besides, I did him a favor. Poor brat was an orphan."

Carver's blood pressure soared to all new heights and he took one step forward.

And Booker winked. The bastard winked at him. "Come on...you can take me."

"You're fucking crazy." He stopped himself from reacting. Maybe the man couldn't do what he claimed and maybe he could. Either way, Michael didn't want to give him any excuses. He could deal with the prick after everything was resolved with the locals.

"Detective Carver, I need your badge number, please." Sneigoski listened while he called out the numbers and spoke them into his phone in a soft voice.

Carver looked around the restaurant, surprised to see that there were still people in the room. He'd lost track of almost everything but John Booker for the last few minutes.

The officer stepped behind him and a moment later a key was unlocking the handcuffs that had held him.

"I'm sorry for the trouble, Detective Carver. No one bothered to let us know about your visit."

"Strictly in an unofficial capacity, Officer Sneigoski." It was a lie, but there was no way in hell he was going to tell Booker that he was here with the FBI.

Booker kept smiling, a knowing, patient smile that fairly glowed, even past the makeup and the red lips.

Carver looked toward the clown and smiled back. Everything had changed now. He was in control.

Booker stood perfectly still while Sneigoski frisked him a second time and then used the same cuffs he'd had on Michael to put the man under arrest.

Carver stepped back and watched while the Philadelphia Police showed up and took control of the situation. Throughout the process, he kept looking at Booker, half expecting the man to disappear on him.

And in return, Booker kept staring back at him, smiling that enigmatic smile of his, a promise that he was in control of everything around him.

And damned if the detective didn't half believe him.

———

Billy Ray Hopper sat in the back of the police wagon and stared at the clown-faced man they led into the vehicle and locked in place. As soon as they were done and the cops had left the back of the van, the clown stared at him for several long seconds, until Billy Ray bristled.

"The fuck are you looking at, freak?" It was best to let the nut cases know who was in charge early on. That way, when you got stuck sharing a cell with them—and you almost always got stuck in holding with the nut jobs—they were properly scared of you and didn't try any crazy shit.

The clown looked at him with blue eyes that were so light they almost looked white and shook his head. "Not much."

"You lucky I don't just fuckin' kill you."

The clown laughed at him. Laughed! Like Billy Ray wasn't bigger than him and didn't have seventy pounds or more on him.

"What's so fuckin' funny?" He could feel his blood pressure rising. You didn't get into the street gangs of Philly without having balls, and you surely didn't stay in them without having the skills and attitude to back up the balls.

The clown leaned in closer as the van started moving. His mouth opened in a broad, predatory smile that made Billy Ray's stomach flutter. Clowns had always freaked him out, ever since he saw that Batman movie with the Joker. This guy, he was sort of like that, different makeup, but just as twisted looking.

"See, you're making threats. That's funny." The man shook his head and chuckled. "Funnier than you know."

"What's so funny about it, bitch?"

The clown held up his hands and stretched them out on either side of his body. Billy Ray felt his stomach do a slow roll to the right. The man shouldn't have been able to stretch his hands out like that. They were supposed to be cuffed closely together. They *had* been cuffed a few minutes earlier. He'd watched the cops securing the man and had seen them double check the restraints, because cops didn't much like surprises.

"See, the way I figure it, the guy who can't move his hands to defend himself shouldn't try to threaten the guy with the knives." Clown-boy was smiling as he talked, and he leaned down until his hands lowered to his ankles and almost instantly his fingers pulled back, holding the manacles that should have been wrapped snugly in place.

"Knives?" He had trouble making his mouth work.

The clown man stood up, easily compensating for the motion of the van. He winked, and the smile on his face twisted into a deeply ugly leer as he moved his hand up and tossed a long-bladed shiv into the air.

"Knives. Always loved 'em. They're more…I dunno…more elegant than guns." His voice was cheerful, conversational, and positively chilling.

Billy Ray screamed. "Hey! Hey guards! This guy is breaking loose!"

The clown laughed, a wild, cackling noise that made the local gangster think of hyenas. "Better get to it, boys. I might have to cut up the big bad hoodlum!" He laughed again, as jovial as if he'd just heard a great joke.

"The both of you better shut your mouths, before I have to come back there." The voice was thick with threat. The man standing in front of him chuckled softly and stepped forward, driving the knife through the meat of Billy Ray's shoulder and slamming him back into the plywood wall behind him.

Billy yowled, the pain a hot wave that washed through his body with unexpected fury. Worse was the shock: there had been no warning other than the threat, and threats were constant on the street, and most of them were bluff and bluster. The psycho yanked his blade back out and stepped back while Billy Ray tried to get the hell away from him.

"Guards! God damn it, Guards!" He sobbed the words, the blood flowing freely from his shoulder as the madman sat back down and shook his head.

"The thing about it is, I wanted the guards back here anyway. So, really, you're just making my life a little easier. Makes me feel a little bad for the fact that I'm going to kill you."

"You get the fuck away from me!" He stared hard enough to damn near burn a hole through the man, but the clown ignored him completely, focusing instead on the rear door of the paddy wagon as it slowed down and then stopped.

The clown shook his head. "Seriously, how stupid can you be? You just told them there was a problem back here and now they're going to open the door and make everything even easier for me."

"Guards! He's got a knife! He fucking stabbed me!" Billy had been arrested more times than he could easily count, he'd been in and out of trouble since he was thirteen and the last eight years hadn't gotten any easier. He had no love of the police, but in this one case he was ready to help them all he could.

The back door of the wagon opened and one of the cops looked inside while the other one covered him.

The one with the drawn weapon let out a gasp as the knife punctured his eye and drove deep into his brain. He fell back and crashed into the ground, dead before his knees could buckle.

Before the other cop could do more than connect the dots, the clown was on him, reaching out with his hands and catching the man's head, then twisting violently. Bones cracked, snapped and gave way and the cop flopped to the road in one violent motion.

Billy Ray let out another scream, more surprised by the sudden violence than scared. He'd been banking on the cops to keep him alive.

The clown didn't bother with him. Instead he climbed from the back of the van and moved out of sight.

Less than two minutes later, the man came back and tossed the bodies into the back of the van. He closed the doors and left Billy Ray alone with the dead men. He thanked God that neither of the corpses was facing him. He didn't think he could take seeing the men looking at him with their dead, drying eyes. Another minute and the van was in motion and rocking hard enough to knock him from his seat.

The van shuddered to a stop and a moment later the rear door opened again. Billy had a brief moment when he allowed himself to think that the cops had surely stopped the lunatic.

Then the clown opened the door and smiled at him, police cap firmly planted on his head.

"I forgot. I promised to kill you."

"No! No please!"

"Sorry sport. I'm a man of my word." With that the man lifted the pistol he'd taken from one of the officers and aimed at Billy Ray's face. There was just enough time to notice the flash of light from the muzzle before his world went black.

———

Fifteen minutes and he could feel the headache building in his skull. It ran in perfect sync with the grinding of his teeth and echoed his pulse. He knew the first signs of a migraine when one was coming for him.

Sneigoski talked to a detective who looked Carver's way several times before he came over. "Detective Carver. Sorry for the confusion earlier." He looked over at Sneigoski and then back at Michael. "I've got the details from Tom, but we're going to need a statement, of course."

"You know what? You got Booker in custody and that's worth the inconvenience."

"If he's the man you think he is, we're glad to have him. How many people did he kill in Virginia?"

"At least seventeen."

"Jesus."

Sometimes the universe seemed to have a great sense of humor. The call came over the radio a moment later announcing that the police wagon had been hijacked. The reports mentioned the white face makeup on the driver.

The police were suddenly very busy and he'd been released, so Carver did the only thing that made sense to him and headed back for the Carnivale.

Every action that Booker had made was connected to the show and there was no reason for him to believe that was going to change. The man was responsible for deaths and chaos in two states and now he was in a third.

He called Agent King as he walked as fast as he could. The man answered on the third ring. "Yeah?"

"King?"

"Yeah." His voice was overly casual and he could hear voices in the background. A lot of voices. "We're having a meeting, Mom. I'll have to call you back."

Shit. That's fucking perfect.

"Booker is in town. He might be headed for you. I'll be there as fast as I can." He cut the call off and walked faster. The problem with the undercover part was the people he was trusting as his back up probably wouldn't be armed all the time.

And that meant he had to get there before Booker could do anything else to the people he was supposed to be protecting.

Carver ran faster, sparing just enough energy to curse God on his way.

Chapter Fourteen

The radio crackled and a voice demanded that the man who was driving the stolen paddy wagon stop immediately and surrender himself.

Rufo looked in the rearview mirror and laughed. There were a dozen squad cars behind him, most of them with flashers going and sirens wailing.

He didn't bother to answer, but just for fun veered across three lanes of traffic and watched while the cars behind him shifted and followed.

One of the cars roared forward and came closer to his rear bumper. He'd watched enough episodes of Cops to get what the plan was. He slammed on his brakes and swerved so that the cruiser rammed into the center of the rear bumper instead of the side. There was less chance of them stealing control that way. The impact rocked the entire wagon and he smiled again, felt his pulse increase and gripped the steering wheel with all of his strength. It bucked and tried to escape him, but he was too strong and the wagon too heavy.

The car behind him slowed and limped off to the side, making room for the other cars that were still going at a higher speed.

The bridge was coming up, but there was a truck between him and the signs on the side of the road. He couldn't tell if the bridge was over a river or over another road.

In the long run it didn't matter. He'd managed to work out a distraction and that was all he'd been looking for in the first place.

Rufo jerked the wheel to the right and slammed into the squad car that had been trying to creep in closer. Car and wagon collided with a loud metallic crunch and he fought to keep control again as the impact continued. The van wanted to go left and he fought until the squad car rammed into the side of the bridge, shooting sparks and debris until it broke through the concrete.

The cops inside the car screamed and while the driver fought to maintain some semblance of control the passenger waved his hands as if they might somehow erase the inevitable.

Rufo howled laughter and wrenched the wheel to the right again, pushing the wagon into the wall until metal and cement both shattered under the impact.

His forward momentum flipped him over the steering wheel and through the windshield. He was still laughing as he fell free of the ruined van and soared toward the river below.

He got lucky. The waters were deep. The car and the van and the clown all hit near each other, but neither of the vehicles caught him in their drag or took him to the bottom of the river. He didn't bother to check if either of the police officers survived. They were of no consequence. Nothing mattered beyond the distraction.

Misdirection has always been the best friend of magicians. The police in Philadelphia were about to be very, very busy taking care of the resulting traffic jam and the search for his body.

The river sang to him, the same song he'd heard for years, ever since the fire had burned his flesh and freed him from the burden of life. The waters surrounded him, held him in their cold embrace, and offered him the solace of oblivion if he would simply accept their gift.

There was a part of him that was tempted. He'd have been lying to himself if he said otherwise. Still, there were things he had to take care of yet. There were people who still hadn't paid for what they'd done to Meagan.

He turned in the water and watched the bubbles as they drifted upward. He followed them a moment later, when he was sure they weren't merely moving around him. His lungs burned, but he wasn't foolish enough to think the waters would soothe that particular flame.

Swimming, swimming and swimming until he felt the air touch his face and gasped at the shock. Rufo bobbed in the current and let it carry him for a moment, regaining his sense of place. The bridge was to his left and he could see the flashing lights that covered it as well as the red strobes from the van and the taillights of the squad car.

He spit the river from his lips and smiled.

The shore wasn't that far away. He kicked the shoes from his feet and wrestled his way out of his jacket, his shirt, and his pants.

When he was free of the burdensome clothing, the clown dove toward the distant shore, as far from the bridge as he could get. Searchlights were cutting through the gathering darkness, looking for any possible survivors, or maybe just for the ones in uniforms. You always took care of your own first. It was human nature. It didn't matter if you were dealing with family or comrades in arms; you looked for your own to save before you dealt with others.

At least he hoped that was true. It would make hiding easier.

Three minutes found him on the shore and dressed in only sodden boxers.

He climbed up from the shoreline and walked into the rough grass and weeds along the side, moving up a slope until he found an access road. There were houses nearby, but they didn't matter. He didn't need to worry about clothes. They came with the skin these days.

As he walked, the shoes formed on his feet and the fabric of his tuxedo glistened along his flesh.

"Almost time, kiddies." He laughed softly, speaking only to himself, for himself. "Almost time to finish this. There's a special audience tonight and a special show."

Rufo walked quickly, faster than a normal human being could easily have managed. He checked his coat and made sure he had all the supplies he needed for the night ahead. The plans were ready, the preparations had to be just so or the performance would fail.

And that would not be allowed. Not this time.

Carver looked around the stage area and sighed. The cast was where they belonged. The crew was setting up the props. The business of running the show was going the way it was supposed to, and that was exactly what he wanted to see.

Booker was out on the streets and being chased by half of the Philly PD. That was all he could hope for.

The dancers were all ready, including King and Cantrell. They came over to his side while everyone was getting over their last-minute jitters.

"We're all ready to dance." Cantrell flashed him a playful smile. He nodded back. He didn't feel too much like grinning.

"We should probably not have a problem. The damn fool hijacked a paddy wagon."

"Seriously?" King looked shocked. He hadn't dealt with Booker. He could understand the confusion.

"He's a mental case. Seriously. He proved it to me again tonight. No regard for his own safety or anyone else's."

Cantrell did a stretch against the wall that let him see exactly how flexible she was.

"Any news on the people he killed in Virginia?" He asked the question to stop himself from staring at the agent as she worked out.

"They were the board of directors for Fantastique Carnivale Entertainment. Just like we thought."

"So this whole show is going to be cancelled?"

King snorted. "Hell no. There's a new board being formed and the financial backers will take over. This is corporate America and damned big business. The show will go on as long as it makes money."

He shook his head. Some things never changed and when it came to money you could bet there would always be a way to make up for the unexpected.

"So what's the plan here?"

"We wait. You guys do your dancing and I check around and keep up with the police chase. I have a guy who told me he'd call me if he finds out what happened with Booker."

Cantrell finished her stretches and looked toward the stage. "Showtime."

King nodded. "We're going to do our part. Try to let us know."

"No problem. I hear anything and you'll hear it, too."

The agents walked away and he settled in on the sidelines. The clown couldn't easily get to anyone from the front, so he'd have to come from the back of the place. That was just the way it worked.

He walked toward the dressing rooms, sliding down the permanently twilight hallway with an eye toward checking the fire escapes. Alarms were always a good thing when you were looking to keep someone out.

The sound was small, but he was still wired and Carver turned fast when something scuffed the ground behind him.

He didn't expect the clown. He got the man anyway.

Rufo's gloved fist crashed down on his chin and sent him reeling backward. Before he had a chance to recover, the man slid forward and struck him again.

There were stars in his head and they were exploding, stealing away his ability to think, to react. He tried to shake them from his skull, but long before that could happen the murderous bastard hit him again.

Michael Carver hit the dusty floor and stayed there. His vision was as blurry as his brain, but his ears were working just fine.

Strong hands hauled him off the ground and slapped something over his mouth to stop him from screaming. After that he struggled and cursed as his arms were bound across his chest and wrapped around to his back. He smelled the musty canvas and leather and tried to fight again, but it was too late.

"I was trying to let you out of this, but some people can't take a hint, can they?" The man's voice was still cheerful.

Carver shook his head again and was rewarded with a little clearing of his senses. He could see the clown again as the man grabbed his feet and started pulling.

He was wearing a sequined tuxedo done all in red, and dragging Michael toward the area where he'd been talking with the FBI agents. "Seriously, do you have a death wish? Because I could accommodate you. I don't really want to, but I could."

Carver struggled, pulled at his arms and felt the pressure shift as he fought. Somehow the man had bound him in seconds when it should have taken several minutes. He'd never seen one from the inside, but he knew a straitjacket when he saw one just the same. Bright satin ribbons in a rainbow of bright colors had been added to the jacket; a lunatic's restraint decorated by the man who should have been wearing it.

There was a doorway at the very edge of the curtain, hidden from the auditorium, but remarkably close by. The clown opened the door despite the EMPLOYEES ONLY sign set at eye level and dragged Carver up the steps. He struggled to avoid having each stair smack into the back of his skull and took the blows across his shoulders and back instead.

The stairwell led to a walkway over the stage itself. There were pulleys and levers above him, the hidden machinations of the stage. Booker set him down and licked his lips, smiling again. His eyes shone with amusement and the madness seemed to seep out of him like heat from a blast furnace.

"You and me, we can have our showdown when I'm finished here, okay? I'm sorry to put you off like this, but I have unfinished business. So, relax. Enjoy the show. Then, if you really need to, you can go ahead and try to kill me again."

He mumbled into the duct tape. It was industrial stuff, used to tape down power cords and keep the world safe from loose wires. The damned stuff did a wonderful job of gluing his mouth shut.

"Not to worry. I'll make sure you have a good view before I begin." He patted Carver's face with his left hand and a moment later hoisted him back to his feet. Before Carver could even regain his balance the man pushed him halfway over the railing toward the stage far below. His stomach and hips hit the metal rail and the impact sent a shock of pain through his lower abdomen. A grunt was the best he could manage noise wise, but he tried hard for a scream as he was flipped forward until his weight was balanced weakly on the same rail. The clown's hand on his jeans was the only thing that stopped him from falling to his death. The ground was almost forty feet below him. It looked more like four hundred.

With one hand on his back and the other in motion near his legs, the clown leered up into Carver's view. "Here's the deal. I'm tying your legs together, and then I'm tying the rope to the railing. If you struggle too much, you're probably going to fall. You might hit the ground, you might not, but I wouldn't recommend moving too much. Got me?"

Carver looked away from the blue eyes and nodded his head. There hadn't been a time in his entire adult life where he felt as helpless, but there was nothing else he could do that didn't risk getting him killed all that much faster.

"Good man. Stay here. We'll talk later."

The clown walked away, never bothering to look back.

Carver listened to the sounds of the man's footsteps on the metal stairs and closed his eyes, praying he was hearing properly. He couldn't afford to screw up.

After a few seconds, he started working his arms with methodical patience. It had been a very long time since he'd tried to escape from being bound, and he'd never actually used a straitjacket back then. There had been too many restrictions in the high school talent show and his magic tricks had been more limited to pulling a bunny from a hat.

Sweat trickled down from his scalp and ran into his eyes, but he did his best to ignore the sudden stinging pain. Deep breaths, slow and steady, and maybe he would get out of this madness.

Tia's heartbeat was hammering in her chest. This was it. She was the one they'd all be watching this time around. Well, the guys would be watching Mary, too. The girl who played the seductive belly dancer was off to the side and practicing. She had circles under her eyes, but they were barely noticeable past the makeup. There were rumors she'd been seeing one of the bigwigs, one of the dead bigwigs. If so, she hid it well.

The music started and a man she'd never seen before walked past her in a dark red get up. The crimson tuxedo flashed, covered in sequins, and the top hat the man sported was just as flashy.

Tia stared, shocked, because the man shouldn't have been there. He wasn't a part of the show that she knew of. The red and blue and white makeup on his face stood out. He was a clown, but the design wasn't the same as the stylized makeup for the Carnival. The clown looked her way as he passed and winked. There was something about him that seemed familiar, but it was nothing she could easily place.

He was in the palace, frozen in the ice castle….

She shook her head and made herself smile back. Maybe he was a local celebrity announcing them. They did that now and then, didn't they?

He slipped past the curtain and began speaking.

"Layydieees and Gennnntlemeennnah, Girls and Boys! If I could have your attention please! Welcome one and all to the Alexander Halston Carnivale of the Fantastic!"

"The what?" Mary laughed softly as she spoke and Tia couldn't help giggling herself. How embarrassing for the man.

"My name is Rufo the Clown, and I'm your Master of Ceremonies tonight. You are, I promise you, in for one hell of a show!"

She started toward her place on the stage, near the wagon set that advertised Ramona the Gypsy Mystic, but stopped when the dizziness staggered her. Her vision grayed out and an involuntary moan escaped her mouth.

The clown man walked toward her as the curtains started to rise. As her legs began to buckle he was there, his hands on her arms, supporting her.

"Careful now, we can't afford to have you falling down. You've got the most important role of all." She nodded her head despite the way the simple motion made the world rock unsteadily. As she regained her feet, he let go of her, his fingers hooking the cloth of her gypsy blouse.

He yanked and the fabric pulled from her body with a ripping purr. Tia let out a gasp and staggered again, her balance ruined and now her clothes torn away.

But when she looked down, her body was not bared, merely wearing the wrong clothing. An outfit almost as red as the tuxedo on the clown flashed in the stage lights, covering her body like a second skin. She recognized the design. She'd seen the same outfits in dozens of pictures from the previous show put on by the Carnivale. The costume had been worn last season by the demon-women of the Infernal Chorus.

She opened her mouth to speak, fully intending to ask the man what he had done and how he had managed it.

Instead, her mouth formed different words; spoke them with an accent that was pure Midwest and in a voice that was not hers....

The clown smiled at her, leaned in close and whispered, "This is going to be fun. Just relax and go with it."

What are you doing to me? She tried again and instead heard the words: "It's nice to meet you, Mr. Winkler. I didn't expect a private meeting."

Billy Handler, the man who was playing Samson the Strong Man, looked toward her and responded, as if the lines were natural and part of the show. He walked toward her with a smile on his face and a definite strut that had nothing to do with the way Billy normally acted when he was playing his part. "Well, Meagan, from what I've seen so far, you're an amazing talent. I wanted to talk to you about next season. We're looking at who should be the leading female dancer and I'm interviewing several different girls from inside the show before we consider calling for open tryouts."

This was madness! She could see the confusion in Billy's eyes. His face made all the right moves, his body the proper gestures to go along with his words, but they were still all wrong.

She stepped toward him, her hands moving of their own volition, her mouth forming words that were not her own and as much as she fought to resist, her body refused to listen. Panic caught fire in her stomach and spread madly, but her face and her body showed no signs of her distress.

Off to the side, the clown stood and watched, his eyes glittered, his face was like stone and his body trembled as if he were straining in a monumental effort.

"Well, I'm flattered, of course, but I'm not the best dancer in the troupe. This is my first time on stage, I mean, what about Liz Montenegro? She's just about the best dancer I've ever seen."

Michael listened to the words and stopped struggling for a moment. Liz Montenegro. Elizabeth Montenegro. Not a coincidence and not the dialogue that was supposed to take place in the show. Hell, there wasn't any dialogue in the show except for narration at the beginning and two of the performers below him were talking loud and clear.

"Well, Liz is also being considered, but we believe you have a lot more potential than you've had a chance to show so far." He looked down at the actors. They weren't even dressed the right way. The woman was wearing an outlandish red costume that had nothing to do with the show. He knew, because he'd seen parts of it several times.

"Well, thank you. I appreciate the opportunity." Her voice was pleasant, but neutral. Guarded. There was no denying the undercurrent.

The man stepped closer to her and smiled. "We want to give everyone a chance to shine at the Carnivale, Meagan."

The girl stepped back, trying to stay just out of easy reach, but the guy wasn't taking the hint. He stepped closer again and as she tried to avoid him he reached out and caught her shoulders.

"There are a lot of girls vying for the lead role, obviously, but I think we can almost guarantee that you get the part, with a little personal practice and coaching."

She looked around, caught and worried, and shook her head. "I— Listen, I'm very flattered but I don't—"

The tension was high, the acting nearly flawless. Despite his situation Carver was drawn in watching what happened below.

"Try not to be too hasty, Meagan."

"It's not hasty, sir. You're old enough to be my father, and I don't need any job where I have to sell myself—"

He cut her off, his hands squeezing hard enough that the girl gasped in sudden pain. "Old enough to be your father? What? You want to call me daddy?" His tone and attitude changed, growing more menacing.

"Stop it! I mean it!" She fought to get away from him, but he shook her violently, a rag doll in the hands of a temperamental toddler.

"Who the hell do you think you are, girl? You think you're something special? You're nothing! Another little dancer with delusions."

She broke his grip for the moment and slapped him across his face with a resounding noise.

His fist drove into her midriff and the girl gasped.

Below him the stage faded to near black and the figures below struggled as little more than silhouettes.

In the darkness, the girl screamed and the man first growled and then laughed as her cries became whimpers and then sobs. The effect was more chilling than he would have expected.

———

The rape didn't happen. For a moment Tia thought Billy meant to tear her clothes off and force himself on her, and the sounds that came out of her were closer to real than she wanted to think about, but as the lights faded and he pushed her to the stage she understood that it was for the show, whatever insane show they were being forced to act out.

Moans and cries came from her mouth as Billy loomed over her, going through motions that, happily, were only pantomimed. She felt him pressed to her. He had no erection; he took no pleasure from the acts. Even if she hadn't seen his eyes or known that Billy was homosexual, his lack of arousal would have offered some small comfort.

While the stage was lost in darkness she heard people moving around, feet shuffling, boards creaking. Tia looked out into the audience and saw the people there watching, lost in the show that was not what they had come to see.

The faces in the front row were close enough that she could see their individual expressions. Some seemed to enjoy the show; others looked disgusted by the intimations of rape. All of them were affected, though it was impossible to say if they were enjoying the show or merely too shocked to react.

Off to the side, the clown watched on, his face heavily shadowed by the hat on his head. Only his mouth could easily be seen and the red smile hid whatever he might have been thinking.

Tia closed her eyes, her body once again refusing to answer her commands. She wanted to see what was happening, especially when Billy climbed off of her and stepped away.

Past the closed lids she saw the lights brighten and knew the next act had begun.

———

The figures below had multiplied while the darkness hid almost everything, and Carver shrugged his shoulder free of the ropes that held him secured. The blood surged back into his arm that had been deprived for several minutes and pins and needles of heat pricked the limb.

"What the hell did you do, Mitch?" The man who spoke to him looked down at the girl on the stage who now lay motionless, her eyes closed and her body twisted into an awkward shape.

"I—It was an accident! We were just, it got rough and the next thing I know she's not breathing. You have to help me here, Adam. I can't handle this alone!"

The man playing Adam paced, his features twisted into conflict. "This can't keep happening! I helped you the last time, and I've heard from others, Mitch. Other people who helped you hide this sort of thing. Bad enough when you—when you get rough, but Jesus, you killed her!"

"Just this one last time, Adam." The big man whined, pleading, his hands clasped in front of his chest in a gesture not unlike a prayer. "Never again, I swear, and I'll make it worth your while."

"'Make it worth my while?'" Adam laughed nervously. "What the hell could you possibly do to make it worth my while to hide a murder?"

"I could step down as the head of the Carnivale. You, you could take my seat. The salary is outrageous."

Adam spun to look toward the audience, his troubled brow slowly calming, his frown briefly becoming a smile before fading into a calmer expression to neutrality.

"Okay, Mitch. This one last time. But never again, I mean it."

Mitch moved toward him, relief changing the lines of his face. "Thank you, Adam. Thank you so much. I'll be better, I promise I will."

"You have to, Mitch."

"It's a sickness, but I'll get help. I'll make it right."

The men fell silent and moved. Two more men joined them on the stage and quickly wrapped the girl's body in a heavy drape of fabric. Carver saw her chest move as she inhaled and exhaled, but otherwise there was no sign that she was alive.

He looked away from the show and saw Booker standing off to the side, watching the performance. The man looked up at him, his face expressionless. A smile broke through as he stared at the detective.

Then he stepped onto the stage and looked out at the audience, clapping his hands savagely.

The audience joined in, reluctantly at first but then with more enthusiasm.

The clown stood facing the applause and bowed sharply, his hat held out formally as he accepted the accolades.

"And so we come to intermission, my friends. A moment or so before the final act begins!" He stood and once again donned his hat. "The story you have just seen is truth, though no one will find record of the murder of Meagan Phelps." He paced, his hands moving animatedly, waving and carrying on as if they had a life of their own. "Look it up if you doubt me. Officially she's been reported missing."

A few people in the audience started speaking and he stopped moving, looking at one of the speakers until the silence was once more complete.

"It took a little looking, and in places most people would never consider, but I found out all about our Mitchell Winkler. He came up with the idea of the Carnivale. According to what he told a few close friends, he actually saw the circus it's based on when he was a kid and loved the show so much it stuck with him. Isn't that amazing? He saw the show and liked it so much he had to come up with new ways to show how it might have ended."

Rufo stopped his pacing and stood tall, facing the audience and taking his time, looking from person to person as everyone stared back.

Far behind him the players for the Carnivale stepped onto the stage. All of them moved slowly to the last person they stared out at the audience, expressionless.

"These fine folks have entertained audience after audience with tales of what might have been. I'm not going to ruin their work. I know the truth, but I'll not share it with you. Let them speculate and entertain you. I've revealed the one secret I needed to show."

He pointed out into the audience and a spotlight cut through the twilight of the auditorium, lighting up a single empty seat.

"Mr. Mitchell Winkler is not here tonight. That seat was reserved for him, but he failed to show. That's all right. I'll meet him soon and we'll take care of his final curtain call. In the meantime, I have a message I'd like to have passed on by anyone who sees him."

The clown stepped toward the audience and lowered his hat until it was held in both gloved hands. His actions were slow and solemn.

"Should you happen to run across the man, any of you, feel free to tell him that Meagan's Uncle Rufo is looking to settle the score."

Another pause, and this time he tilted his head as he looked out into the masses and his grin spread wider until his teeth flashed.

"Of course, there's always the chance that I've missed my chance with Mitch. I think he might already be dead, because I haven't found any sign of where he might be hiding."

The clown did a fast stride that covered the length of the stage. "But enough about me! What we need here is a showstopper! How about a magic trick?"

He waved his hands high in the air, his fingers wiggling frantically and they descended. "Abracadabra!"

Several gasps became a wave of noise from the audience and Carver looked out toward them. The people were looking around, in some cases covering their heads and in others studying the water that fell from above.

Mist reached the edge of the stage and Rufo stepped back a bit. More people in the audience were looking around and the voices rose from murmurs to shouts.

"Oh, calm down. It's not really rain, just water from the sprinkler system." The clown laughed and the sound was carried over the speakers despite the water and the flickering lights. "Still, I had you there for a second."

Rufo shrugged and laughed again. "It's just water! If I were you, I'd be worried about the electricity!"

Carver had no idea how the clown managed it, but he saw the end result. The lights above the audience flashed and shattered, raining down glass shards and fragments of superheated metal.

Most of the people ducked down and let out surprised noises, a few tried to run from the shower of sparks and slivers.

Rufo raised his arms above his head and lifted his hands toward the heavens. He drew his fingers in until he'd clenched them into hard fists.

When he brought his hands down abruptly, the lightning followed a second later. Arcs of electricity flashed through the air, leaping from the light sockets and stroking the audience with fiery fingers. People screamed, they danced and died as they burned and bled and through it all, the clown looked out at them with a broad, savage smile twisting his features.

The lucky ones died. A surprising number of individuals in the audience survived the electrical burns and the deep cuts from falling fragments, but if Carver had been given a chance to look around right then and there, he'd have placed money on the survivors wishing to join the dead rather than suffer the agonies of living through the unexpected storm.

The clown laughed, threw his head back and roared his merriment to the heavens until he seemed incapable of doing anything else and all around him the performers, King and Cantrell among them, stared toward the ruined audience with no expression on their faces.

When he'd finished his laughing jag Rufo the Clown waved an arm at the performers and gave an order. "Take a bow, folks. These people are here to see you." And they listened. As one the entire troupe bowed formally. The dead in the audience did not applaud. The living were in too much pain to notice.

Booker looked up again and winked at Carver as he removed his hat. Without another word he walked away from the stage and Michael followed his progress for as long as he could, too shocked to do much more than observe.

Chapter Fifteen

The rage came on him a few moments later as he tried to slither the rest of the way from his bonds and finally slipped one arm completely free. Carver let out a groan and shook, his blood pressure surging dangerously, his pulse a rapid-fire staccato that would have terrified any sensible cardiologist.

He fought against the straitjacket and forced it lower down his body, pushing past the leather and canvas and buckles, barely even aware of the garish bows and ribbons that had been woven into the thing.

His feet slipped and Carver sucked in a breath, freezing himself instantly as he balanced on the edge of the railing. One wrong move and he was dead. He had no doubt the fall would kill him or worse, leave him shattered on the stage below.

He must have made a sound, though he couldn't recall hearing one. The girl who'd been in the unexpected performance looked up at him and screamed, pointing in his direction.

Her voice worked like a slap on the people around her, waking them from whatever odd slumber they'd been experiencing. King stared at the girl and Cantrell looked up, spotting him. Her hand swatted at King and before he could protest she was pointing.

The two of them ran for the stairs, and Carver whimpered as he sent a silent prayer toward Heaven. Despite the horrors down below he wanted to live through this.

If only so he could kill the fucking clown once and for all.

Tia collapsed on the stage, her breaths jagged and cold, her skin feeling as wintry as the sets behind the curtains.

She held herself and rocked back and forth, staring out at the audience and seeing only the dead and dying. She had lived a sheltered life and knew it. She had seldom dealt with death, and never on this scale. She wasn't alone. Several of the performers joined her. Some cried, others merely stared and a few staggered off to get sick as the stench wafted toward them from the auditorium.

She was aware of the people around her, but they didn't seem to matter. Nothing seemed to matter except the deaths and the strange voice that whispered in the back of her head. Just to escape from the horrid sight in front of her, she tried to make sense of the whispers, but no matter how hard she strained she could not hear words, only the sibilance.

Leslie's warm, wonderful hand touched her shoulder, and Tia looked over and up at her friend and felt the world slide back onto its axis. Everything was shaky, but with Leslie there, at least she felt there was a chance reality could make sense again.

Somehow Leslie wound up next to her on the ground and they hugged each other with desperate strength and need.

For a while that was all that mattered. For a while it was enough.

King held his legs while Cantrell pulled him back from the brink. Had he been completely free to do so he would have hugged them both. Instead, he fought the straitjacket away from his body and then caught the railing with his hands as he recovered his equilibrium.

"Oh, fuck. Oh, fuck me…."

"It's all right. You're safe." Cantrell's voice was meant to reassure, but Carver shook his head.

"We need to go after him."

"He's gone."

"Then we find him!" He could see in their eyes that they were still recovering from whatever the hell the clown had done. He would have loved to take the time to examine their state of mind and understand what had occurred, but there wasn't time.

220 / James A. Moore

Booker was getting away, and he needed to kill the man once and for all.

"Get your guns and help me find this fucker."

"What about them?" King's voice sounded a little clearer than it had when he came up the stairs calling for Carver to stand still. Whatever had happened was wearing off. That was good. That helped a lot. The man's hand waved toward the dead and dying in the auditorium, as if there were any doubt what he might be referring to.

"Call for ambulances, lots of them. Do whatever you have to. I'm going after Booker."

The bastard couldn't be allowed to live. He'd shot the clown before, or he'd shot someone who looked like him in the rain. It didn't matter. He'd kill him right this time. That was all there was to the matter.

Cantrell said something else, but he didn't listen. Instead, Carver pulled the pistol from the small of his back and stormed down the stairs. Performers were wandering around, lost inside their own heads and he left them to find their own ways. The clown had gone toward the back of the place, toward the exit where he'd caught Carver flatfooted earlier.

This time around, the detective took the time to pay attention and kept his weapon drawn, but lowered toward the ground in front of him.

"Booker! Show yourself! You told me we could finish this, don't you fucking start lying to me!"

The door to the alley behind the theatre opened with a squeal and he saw the shape of the man as he slid outside.

He resisted the urge to shoot. He wasn't in the mood to fire at shadows when he could save every bullet for when he needed them. Was he losing his calm? Yes, but he hadn't gone completely crazy, not yet.

Carver followed the clown through the threshold and looked around, carefully, cautiously, trying to spot his prey.

The clown stood fifteen feet away, staring at him again, a half-smile showing past the red grin painted on his face. His eyes were hidden in shadow, his face made nearly alien by the same darkness, and yellow sodium lights of the alley sent a thousand flashes from his sequined outfit.

"Come to kill me again?" Booker's voice was calm, mocking.

Carver took careful aim. "Don't you fucking move."

The clown promptly broke into a soft shoe and darted toward the left.

Carver fired once and blew the hat off his head.

"I said don't you move!"

The man laughed, his eyes wide with the shock of the unexpected gunshot, but his expression one of pure amusement otherwise. "Oh, I heard you." Booker's voice didn't change at all, no sign of nerves or worry carried past the smile on his face.

Michael moved toward him and sighted on the spot between his eyes, the area where the blue triangles tried to converge. "Don't think I won't kill you."

"You already did that once. What makes you think it'll work better this time?"

"I don't know or care how you lived the last time, you fuck." He stepped closer still and the clown stayed where he was, letting him move in. "I'll burn your body to ashes if I have to."

"Would you like your shield back, Detective?" Conversational, casual, like a gun wasn't aimed to cause maximum damage.

"I'll get it when I'm done with you."

"You're just not very swift, are you?"

His vision went red. Every word the bastard spoke was just another reason to kill him.

"Fuck yourself."

Rufo's hand blurred as it snatched the pistol from his hand. Carver's grip was as solid as could be, but the clown almost broke his fingers with the force he used. He wrenched the detective's wrist to the point where it felt like ligaments got torn. Carver screamed in surprise and shook his wrist.

The clown flipped the pistol in the air and caught it an instant later, the grip now held properly in his hand. "Also, you're rude. Your mother should be ashamed."

"Leave my mother out of this." His voice was shaking plenty.

The clown stepped forward and shoved the gun against the side of his neck with enough force to leave an angry red scrape. "Like that feeling do you? Want to know what a bullet feels like when it goes through your head?"

Being mostly of sound mind, Carver kept his mouth shut and did his best not to panic. The barrel of his pistol traced roughly down his neck to his chest and he held his breath unconsciously, expecting to die.

"Too easy." The clown stepped back ten paces and let the pistol hit the ground.

"The police will be here soon."

"They're still looking for my body in the river a few miles from here."

"You just murdered three hundred people! Trust me, they'll be here."

Booker shook his head and turned his back on Carver, reaching down for his ruined top hat. "It doesn't matter. I'm done in this town, except for you, of course."

"What is this all about? What the hell are you?"

"I showed you what it's about. It's all about my grandniece." The smile dropped from his face, replaced by a murderous rage. "They killed my family. I'm not a very forgiving person."

"You've murdered hundreds to get revenge for one?" His stomach fell away at the thought.

"See, you're a detective. You know how to get answers. I had to work it out on my own." He looked over the top hat and threw it to the side. Even from fifteen paces away Carver could see the bullet hole that blew through the thing.

"What?" He shook his head. "Are you fucking serious? You ever think to call the cops?"

The clown ignored the questions and shrugged his shoulders. "No one wanted to answer my questions, so I beat it out of them." Carver stepped forward two paces and kept his eye on the pistol. Back at home there would have been a backup piece. Before he threw it in the river.

"That still doesn't justify murdering all of the people in that auditorium!"

"Oh please." The clown waved a hand in dismissal. "They're rubes. They don't count."

That was it. Carver lunged for the pistol, scraping his fingertips and knuckles as he lifted the weapon. The pain flared like a struck match, but he ignored it, taking aim at the man who'd driven him to murder, not once but twice.

"Put your hands up!" he roared the command as he sighted, and then stopped. The man was gone, vanished from where he'd been. Carver looked around, making sure of himself. "What the hell?"

"You're getting a little obsessed, aren't you?" The voice came from behind him and he spun hard, aiming at the sound. The clown was there again.

He should have waited. In his defense, he wasn't thinking clearly. Carver pulled the trigger and watched the bullet smash a hole in the wall to the right of the clown. He aimed again and fired as the man moved toward him. Booker was too fast. No one could move at that speed. But he wasn't fast enough to stop the bullet. It pounded his arm and sent him staggering.

"Yes! Come on! Do it!" The man's voice broke as he came closer. His hands reached out and grabbed Michael. Carver pushed the pistol in closer, until he could feel the pressure of the muzzle against the fabric of the tuxedo, and then he fired again and again until the trigger did nothing more but make clicking noises.

The clown jumped with each shot. Meat and blood flew in streamers and the smell of cooked flesh and burnt gunpowder overwhelmed the alley.

Booker crumbled, his hands slipped down Carver's chest as he fell, and left lines running from his shoulders to his stomach. Michael stood still and watched. He made himself watch. If you're going to murder someone, you need to make sure. He'd learned that lesson at last.

His hands twitched. His mouth was dry; his eyes ached from the adrenaline and blood pressure surges. He kept staring down at his victim, wishing he could feel something inside. There was nothing. A man wasn't supposed to feel nothing.

The clown took care of that for him. Just as soon as Rufo stood back up, Carver felt again. He felt absolute terror. It was one thing to think that someone had come back from the dead and quite another to see it.

The man didn't rise slowly. He fairly jumped to his feet, his eyes looked around insanely for a moment, trying to find Carver perhaps, or merely to understand where he was and what was happening.

Then he looked at Michael and his smile came back, a sadistic madman's grin. Michael pulled the trigger again, the reaction purely instinct or panic, and got an empty click for his trouble.

Rufo slapped the pistol aside with a wild swing. Carver felt the bones and tendons in his wrist break and separate, the pain larger than anything he'd ever experienced before, enough to make his eyes swim. He opened his mouth to scream and the clown covered his lips, pressed them into his teeth hard enough to mash them flat and leave them bleeding.

Impossible strength from an impossible dead clown, and the alley shifted as Carver was lifted from the ground and smashed into the wall violently. Before he could recover he was rammed into the wall a second time.

The clown held him there; the hands on his arms trembled, but did not lose their strength.

"Do you have any idea how much that hurts? Have you ever been shot, you bastard?"

"Fuck you." His voice trembled. The pain in his arm had calmed down enough to leave him merely nauseous, but his head rang from the impacts with the brick wall.

The clown held him to the wall with one hand, pinned like a butterfly, his arms waving just as uselessly as the wings on one of the insects. The knife came from nowhere and slashed quickly, stroking fire on either side of his face. Carver let out a small scream as the blood began to flow.

Rufo stared for several heartbeats and then nodded his satisfaction and stepped back, letting Michael stand on his own. "We're done now, Detective. I let you ask your questions, and even gave you a chance to punish me." The voice was weak, made frail by the holes in the clown's chest and lungs.

"Why don't you just fucking die already?" He shook his head to clear it and was rewarded with a case of the bed spins. His legs buckled and he fell in a nearly perfect imitation of the path Booker had taken moments before.

"I'm already dead, rube. Been dead for fifty years now." The man laughed, but it was soft and the sounds gurgled.

He wanted to ask so many questions, but he couldn't make them form in his mind. "Why?" It was the best he could manage.

Another chuckle and the clown looked down at him. "Why? Why am I still standing? I don't want to fall down." He shrugged.

Carver shook his head. "Why am I alive?"

The man shook his head. "Because I need you."

Carver shook his head and fought against the gray that wanted to swallow him. Nausea haunted him, threatened to steal his control and force him to his knees again even as he managed to crawl up the wall and regain his feet.

Rufo watched, his cold blue eyes amused by the struggle.

"Why do you need me?"

"Every performance needs an audience, Detective Carver. You chased me. You volunteered to be my audience for this show."

"You can't get away with this."

"Really? I already did. It's done. I'm leaving." To make his point clear, the clown started walking, heading down the alleyway toward the road that was only a few yards off and a thousand miles distant. Carver tried to follow and promptly fell on his face in the dirty back area.

"No. Come back here." He whimpered the words, frustrated by the pain that kept trying to steal him away.

"Have a wonderful life, Detective." He paused for a moment. "Man, I haven't seen that movie in years...." And then he was gone, around the corner and out of the detective's sight.

Carver tried to stand again and gave up when the gray came and swallowed him whole.

Looking for Millie: The Last Curtain Call

I stared at Millie's headstone. It was simple and elegant and a solitary angel carved from the same granite looked up toward Heaven and held onto the cross at the side of her name. The expression on that stone face was perfect for expressing grief and that made me happy. These days the smile on my face gets in the way of expressing much of anything aside from happiness and that wasn't quite fitting for visiting my sister.

I'd like to say I cried, but I think I'm past that stage now. Instead, I just listened to the wind and set down the flowers I'd picked up.

I waited for a while and then I made myself presentable. Growing flesh feels strange and it always makes my face tingle. I'd rather go without, but the men who were coming to bury Meaghan wouldn't have understood.

I made sure they found her body and I paid for the burial and the headstone with cash. Best not to ask where I got the money. Let's just say the good detective left me needing to heal myself again and there was a wallet left behind by my organ donor.

I watched them when they put her into the ground. I never said a word. The priest that gave the sermon spoke a lot, but the only audience to listen to him was me and I barely even noticed. I was lost in thought again, remembering my little sister and the life she had.

In the end, I think I hate myself most for never getting her that damned pony. I know she would have loved to have one and I would have given my soul to see her smile again.

Tia sat in the darkness with her eyes wide open and stared at Leslie where she lay sleeping. The other girl never had trouble drifting easily into slumber and she envied her that.

The Carnivale had closed shop, but only for a short time. The plans were already in place for next season and both of them had been invited back. She should have been thrilled. She was, really, except that she couldn't get the clown out of her head.

It wasn't all the time, just now and then, but when she closed her eyes, she saw him smiling at her and felt her heart thump in her chest like a bass drum. He didn't invade her dreams, but rather stopped her from meeting up with them. She didn't know which was worse.

When she did manage to sleep her rest was always fine. She had dreams of her family or dreams that she was dancing on the stage and the audience was cheering.

Tonight was one of those nights, however, when actual sleep refused to come.

The clown stared at her; his eyes glittered.

Leslie rolled over and let out a tiny sigh. She smiled at the sound. That at least was going well. She hadn't been prepared for any of this, for falling in love with another girl, but at least the feeling was returned. She hadn't told her parents. They wouldn't understand.

Leslie hadn't told her parents, either. That was something neither of them wanted to discuss much, but they knew they'd have to before the holidays came around. In due time. For now they were just happy to be happy.

She closed her eyes, rolled toward her lover and watched her sleep. In the back of her mind she heard a distant song, a lullaby that meant nothing to her, sung in a voice that was unfamiliar. It was old-fashioned and oddly comforting.

When sleep finally came, she dreamed that she was a different woman, a dancer, who lived alone and often spoke with her grandmother.

Carver looked at the mirror in the hospital bathroom and grimaced. His skin was too pale, his face too thin. He stared at the lines of stitches on either side of his mouth and contemplated whether or not to try shaving his face.

"Fuck it. Let it grow." He reached for his toothbrush instead and took care of cleaning his chompers, but he did it carefully. The cuts were mending, but every time he opened his mouth too far he risked ripping the stitches or starting the bleeding again.

Booker had cut his face into a smile before he left. The scars didn't quite match up with the paint on the clown's face, but they came close enough. Plastic surgery had already been scheduled for the start of next month. The doctors claimed he was luckier than he knew, that the injuries would be almost unnoticeable when they were finished. He hoped so. He didn't want to remember anything about the last month.

King and Cantrell were the ones who found him on the ground, beaten down with a few concussions and a green stick fracture of his right wrist. The wrist had been fixed up and put in a cast. If he was careful he could even move it a little without wanting to cry like a baby.

The two agents dropped by the day after everything went down. Both of them looked like they'd been anally raped with barbed wire covered posts. Verbally speaking, of course. Their bodies were fine, but their posture and expression spoke of their epic reaming from the powers that be.

You stand around on the stage and let a few hundred people get electrocuted and things tend to go poorly for you. It was possible that they would eventually recover from the shit-storm their careers had become, but he wasn't holding his breath. He told them both that he could work out gigs for them with his boss and he meant it. He wouldn't be too surprised if he heard from them in the future.

When he was done scrubbing his gums to the point of bleeding he spit out the toothpaste and rinsed. That was as much of a morning constitutional as he felt like dealing with.

Back in the main hospital room—he had to share, because the insurance wasn't going to foot the bill for a private room—his roommate was snoring noisily enough to make him consider murder again. He decided against it. So far his attempts at ending lives were going poorly, with a score of 0 and 2 working against him. He had just flopped down on his bed and cranked the volume on his TV as high at it would go—not enough to silence the snores, but at least they'd been beaten down to tolerable levels—when Cantrell came into the room. The woman smiled brightly and set down a vase of flowers next to the ones that had been left by the department the day before.

"You look like shit." She smiled as she said it.

"Thanks. I feel like shit, too. Nice when the body and mind work together, don't you think?"

"Absolutely." She fidgeted and so did he. There wasn't a case to talk about anymore and neither of them really wanted to discuss it much.

"So, looks like there really is a Mitchell Winkler."

He had to think about that for a moment. "Yeah? Any luck finding him?"

"Oh yes. He died of a massive coronary about nine months ago."

"Really?"

She nodded. "He'd just picked up an escort for the night. Died in her arms so to speak."

Carver looked at the agent and did his best not to smile, but eventually the grin broke through. She snorted laughter in a very unpleasant way. Still, she was cute enough to forgive having a bad laugh.

"So Rufo the Clown failed to get his man then?" He felt a savage flash of satisfaction that was completely inappropriate.

"Well, the grave was robbed yesterday. King is looking into it to see if there might be a connection."

He nodded his head and scowled just a bit. He'd rather find out that Booker had nothing to do with it. In a perfect world the clown would have been roasting in Hell.

"How's things on the home front?"

"Looking up a bit. Every member of the troupe verified the same story we gave. No one remembers much of anything. It was like coming out of a deep sleep."

He held up a hand and crossed the middle and index fingers for her to see. She smiled a quick thanks.

"When are they letting you out?"

"Later today. I'm just waiting for the official dismissal papers. I get to come back later for the facial work."

Cantrell gave him the strangest look, but kept her comments to herself.

"What?"

"Nothing. It's stupid." Her voice was defensive.

"Tell me anyway."

"I've just been wondering if he'll show up again."

"He will."

"What makes you so sure?"

"This isn't the first time he's killed and I don't think it'll be the last. I don't think he has the self-control to stay away from killing."

"But what makes you so sure?"

"He told me he likes to have an audience. He'll do it again when he wants attention."

"That's some scary shit." She hugged herself for warmth.

"So, wanna give me a ride home?" He really didn't want to take a cab.

"Yeah. I've been wondering what sort of place you have."

"Oh, really?"

She nodded, a grin playing at her lips. He refused to play into it. She was too young for him and he didn't much like getting his hopes up. The last time he got optimistic it ended in a divorce.

"Yeah. I mean, from the outside it looks like a house, but inside, I figure you've got a collection of survival magazines and about a thousand guns in an arsenal."

"How did you come to that conclusion?"

"Anyone that goes after the bad guy without back up is bound to be a weapon freak." She was teasing and he made himself remember that. She was the one who found his pistol and gave it back to him when no one was looking. King was the one who managed to collect the casings and the both of them lied about him shooting Booker repeatedly. Mass murderer or not, most of the brass frowned on trying to kill unarmed suspects.

"Yeah, well, I guess you'll just have to come inside and find out."

She stood up walked over to the next bed, shaking the man's leg until he grunted and rolled over. The lack of snoring was an unexpected bliss.

"I guess I will." Cantrell sat down again and waited with him. Suddenly going home didn't seem like such a scary notion and he thought maybe he could avoid dreaming of clowns again. The dreams had been coming too often already and it had only been a few days.

Life on the Road

So that's it, really. That's my story. Not much else to say for now.

I found Mitch and took him with me. Albert Miles can make a person suffer even after they've died and I want Mitch to scream for a long time. I want to hear it, know he's in agony and then record the sounds so I can make them my own little lullaby.

What? You thought I'd be forgiving? Not a chance.

Albert and I came to an arrangement. He gave me the power to make my last show something memorable and in exchange I decided to forgive him for screwing over my troupe back in Serenity Falls.

He asked me to go to work for him again and I suppose I will for a while. I have nothing else planned and I don't see myself settling down to life on the farm if you catch my meaning.

First though, I have a little unfinished business in Serenity Falls. According to Albert, there's a boy back there who's a little upset that I killed his entire family and he'd like to settle the score.

Seems only fair to let him try. Besides, I only carved up one side of Davey's face. I think I kind of like the idea of matching scars.

There's a great big world out there, and it's populated by rubes. I want to meet them. I want to get to know them and make some kids smile and if it suits me, I might even teach a few people to laugh now and then.

I like laughter.

It really is the best medicine to get you past a bad case of the blues.

About the Author

JAMES A. MOORE authored more than forty novels. The first decades of his career focused on his love for horror, as seen in many novels including the critically acclaimed *Fireworks*, *Under the Overtree*, *Blood Red*, and the Serenity Falls trilogy. Later, Jim earned a reputation as the "prince of grimdark fantasy" with his hugely popular Seven Forges series as well as the Tides of War trilogy. The author loved collaborating with other writers, most frequently with Christopher Golden on the Bloodstained Worlds trilogy and with Charles R. Rutledge on the Griffin & Price series, among others. Nominated for the Bram Stoker Award twice, Moore won the Shirley Jackson Award for co-editing *The Twisted Book of Shadows*. He first came to prominence as one of the principal world-builders involved in the World of Darkness from White Wolf Games, most famously Vampire: The Masquerade and Werewolf: The Apocalypse. At the time of his passing, Moore left behind one completed solo fantasy novel, as well as completed collaborations with Charles R. Rutledge and Mary SanGiovanni. Plans are afoot to bring those to readers soon.

Bibliography

NOVELS

The Black Stone Bay Series
Blood Red (with "Blood Tide")
Blood Harvest
Bloodlines

The Bloodstained Series (w/Christopher Golden)
Bloodstained Oz
Bloodstained Wonderland
Bloodstained Neverland

The Tides of War Series
The Last Sacrifice
Fallen Gods
Gates of the Dead

Standalone Novels
Deeper
Fireworks
Harvest Moon
The Haunted Forest Tour (w/ Jeff Strand)

NOVELLAS
Dear Diary: Run Like Hell
Homestead
The Wild Hunt

SHORT STORY COLLECTIONS
Slices
This is Halloween

Curious about other Crossroad Press books? Stop by our website:
http://crossroadpress.com
We offer quality writing
in digital, audio, and print formats.

Subscribe to our newsletter on the website homepage and receive a
free eBook.

www.ingramcontent.com/pod-product-compliance
Lightning Source LLC
Chambersburg PA
CBHW031133210626
46816CB00014B/696